WHEN KINK AND REALITY COLLIDE, COMPROMISE AND LOVE KEEP EVERYONE SATISFIED.

Living a BDSM lifestyle, Polly is devastated when her husband and Dom of ten years dies. Although she is capable of supporting her daughters and maintaining her home, she aches for the companionship of a partner and the dominance of a sexual master.

A decade has passed since David lost Polly to his best friend. For ten years she had been the one who got away and his desire to be with her never faded. With the death of Polly's husband bringing them back together, their attraction is instantly rekindled.

Settling into the role of surrogate father and dominating partner, David knows the family needs time to heal. But will the questions people ask about their lifestyle and betrayal within their BDSM group be challenges too great to overcome?

DAVID'S ANGEL

By

Stephanie Beck

Shannon –

Enjoy!

Stephanie Beck

Lyrical Press, Inc.
New York

Lyrical Press, Incorporated

David's Angel

13 SBN: 9781616502515

Edited by Pamela Tyner

Book design by Renee Rocco

Cover Art by Valerie Tibbs

Lyrical Press, Incorporated

337 Katan Avenue

Staten Island, New York 10308

http://www.lyricalpress.com

Published in the United States of America by Lyrical Press, Incorporated

First Lyrical Press, Inc electronic publication: October 2010

First Lyrical Press, Inc print publication: March 2011

Dedication

For my sweet husband who shook his head as I spent hours researching details for David's Angel. I love you, my honey.

Acknowledgements

Thanks to Scott for all his insight and honest answers to bizarre questions. And also to Jo for critting outside her comfort zone and helping me to make *David's Angel* a better story.

CHAPTER 1

"Can't I just have a few more minutes, Mommy?"

"No, Faith. Bedtime means bedtime so get your little bottom to your room."

Polly watched her youngest pout. Five-years-old was so tough, she thought indulgently. Used to getting her way since Nana and Papa fell for her charms, her baby had become a professional pouter. Polly appreciated her parents, especially when they'd helped the girls get through their birthdays while still grieving for their daddy. Now though, since she and the girls were home and they had to get into their routine it was time to replace excess with moderation.

"But Mommy—"

"No more. Up to bed. Hope is already waiting for you."

"Are you coming to tuck us in and say prayers?" the blond-haired angel asked.

"Have I ever missed a night?"

"Sometimes when we were with Nana and Papa you forgot," she said solemnly.

Sometimes, Polly thought guiltily, she'd accepted the medication the doctor gave her to help when the pain and grief were more than she could handle. Being drugged unconscious wasn't her finest moment as a mother, but Polly knew she'd needed the time to heal and her babies had been safe with her parents.

"I know, and I'm sorry, sweetie. Now that we're home it'll be me every night. We'll pray, have our story and tuck in, but first you have to get in bed."

Polly watched as her daughter finally headed up the stairs. There were sure to be more battles, with kids her age some days were nothing except drama, but with her eldest she'd had a partner on the roughest days. Mark might have been her Dom but to their kids he'd been the ultimate pushover. Yet, he'd had a way of being pushed that always made things right in a roundabout way.

She didn't have his magic touch with them, but she could handle them easily. As she turned off a lamp she caught sight of herself in a mirror. She looked tired. Her blond hair was back in a ponytail again, and without makeup her eyes looked tiny and shadowed under her black-rimmed glasses. It wasn't a new look. She'd been a stay-at-home mom for six years, she knew tired. Usually it didn't last so long though. One day she'd have to put her jeans and blouses back on. But not today.

Tonight she would focus on being a good mom, like she had since the day Hope was conceived. After the girls were in bed she would concentrate on writing. Once the words were dried up for the night she'd try to sleep. Exhaustion was what she needed, but she knew in her soul she wouldn't rest.

It had been four months since she'd slept more than an hour at a time. For two months Mark had been sick and needed her often, and then after he died…sleep just didn't come.

"Mommy, we're ready!"

She silently thanked God for the interruption. If she'd kept on the road her mind was leading her down, she'd be bawling and that was one of the things she had to ease back on in order to be the good mom she needed herself to be. It was okay to be sad. Her children could see her cry, but they didn't need it all the time. For all the sorrow, there was still so much love and beauty in her life.

When she stepped into the pink and white bedroom she had to smile because 'love' and 'beauty' were tucked together in their double bed, arms already around each other with a story book between them. Her girls. They looked just like her, blond and brown eyed and so fair Mark bought stock in Coppertone after she'd gone through five bottles one summer.

Mark was gone. He was dead and she would always miss him, but he'd left her the very best gift any woman could ask for. She knew he'd loved her every minute he'd been alive, and he'd left her the proof in pigtails.

She lay in the girls' bed long after stories and kisses were done. It was hard to walk away even when they were sound asleep and completely okay. Between needing meds and crying jags she'd slept every night in Des Moines with them. The habit was one she was trying to break, because she had to stand on her own feet and the girls needed to rely on her, not the other way around.

Eventually she forced herself downstairs, taking the stairs slowly and running her hand lovingly down the banister she'd sanded herself. They'd bought the house after Faith was conceived. Before, they'd been in a townhouse. Having a home and yard of their own had been Mark's dream, and she'd wanted it too. The fixer-upper took almost all nine months of her pregnancy to fix but Hope had been a trooper, painting her areas with water and sharing their bedroom while the plaster was repaired in the room the girls now shared.

She loved her home and thanks to Mark's foresight, she could have it as long as she wanted. He'd had more life insurance than she thought. The second policy was one offered through his job. He'd paid out-of-pocket for it, and the money was enough to pay off their cars and start college funds for both girls. The other policy covered the house, with enough left to pay the bills for the next five years.

It made complete sense that he would try to take care of them even after death, especially because no one in his family was left to help. It was what he did. There hadn't been a day in her life after she met him that she didn't have complete faith in his abilities. Maybe it was sacrilegious to put so much on a single human, but it was true. Even when things had been hard, and there had been many difficult times throughout their ten-year marriage, she'd never doubted that his perseverance would make things okay. The situation wasn't over until it was okay, he would say.

She shored herself up as she sat in front of the computer. Mark hadn't let her give up on writing even after she'd gotten ten rejection letters and a recommendation to have at least a PhD before she tried to submit a non-fiction book again. Her tea was cold, but she sipped it anyway as she looked through the notes she'd forgotten after watching her husband's last breath.

No more thinking about Mark, she scolded herself. She had a deadline. Her publisher had extended it indefinitely in light of her personal tragedy, but Polly wanted the book done.

If she was moving forward, then she wasn't in jeopardy of falling back into the madness that consumed her while her father and mother tended the girls. She felt bad she'd let her children down for a week, disappearing into her own misery. She couldn't change the way she'd reacted, but she would be better now.

After a few hours of losing herself in birds, she poured another cup of hot water and thought about making cookies. Baking and cleaning and other busy work helped the time pass. Hope's first day back to school was coming up and bringing a treat might make the transition a little smoother.

Her cell vibrated and rang. She left her teabag to steep and went to the phone, figuring it was another call from her mother. They'd always been close, and she'd been an anchor the last few months. She'd called half a dozen times since they'd left the day before, but that was okay. Polly needed the support, and her mother was not only her mom, she was also a preacher's wife and licensed family therapist. She understood, gave Polly space and loved her. That's what she needed.

The number on the screen was unfamiliar, but that wasn't surprising. Since she'd sent out the notices about Mark's death, stating his request for not hosting a funeral, people had been calling to share their support.

"Hello?"

"Polly?"

"This is she." The voice was familiar, but she couldn't quite place it.

"It's David."

"Oh, my goodness." She sat down because she had to. David wasn't like the other well-wishers. He was as close to Mark as a brother, and somehow she'd forgotten about him in the last few months. "Hi. It's good to hear from you."

"Yeah, you too. I know you were with your parents, so I didn't call. How are the girls?"

"They're good. Sleeping. Hope goes back to school on Monday, and I got a call from the school with a late opening, so Faith will start preschool a few days a week. They're sad, but okay," she said, falling into the same comfortable pattern she always did with him.

He was her husband's best friend even if he never came around. He still called and emailed regularly, but never made attempts to visit. She understood why. She was the reason. When she'd chosen Mark, David had backed off completely. It was a good thing because contrary to the rapid timing, her decision to marry Mark hadn't been an easy one. Part of her had always held affection for the other man, even if it was Mark who'd eventually stolen her heart.

"How's Arizona?" she asked, wanting to know how he felt about Mark's death but it was too soon for that question, especially over the phone.

"I'm actually in Green Bay." She nearly dropped the phone when she saw headlights pull into the driveway. "That's me. May I come in?"

"Um, of course. I'll unlock the front door. Just a minute."

Why was he here? She set aside her phone and looked down at her clothes. It had been nearly a decade since she'd seen David and things had changed. The last time he'd seen her she'd been a size four in a white wedding dress, manicured and buffed. Children had turned that four to a ten, time had done away with her desire for manicures and grief took away any polish she had left.

After the wedding, she'd missed him. For a summer they'd been best friends. Mark claimed David liked her too much and that was why he stayed away. He'd never lied to her, so she believed him. They were both such strong, dominant men that it wouldn't have been good to be between them.

She took a deep breath and walked to the door. No matter how much time had passed, and whatever the challenges that might exist, she still considered David a friend and she needed one.

She flipped the four locks on the door. She'd had two more put in while she was away. The Master of the BDSM group she and Mark belonged to was a construction contractor, and he and his wife had taken care of things while they'd been away. When she said she wanted to feel safer, Max added double window locks and put in deadbolts on each door. She undid the last lock and turned the knob.

"David."

"Hi, Polly."

He looked the same. Older for sure, more filled out than he had when he was a young, twentysomething, but his hair was still blond with a touch of curl. The clean-shaven face she remembered was dusted with prickly whiskers, he probably hadn't shaved since early morning. There were a few deep wrinkles along his eyes and forehead, and the depth of concern in his blue eyes was enough to bring back the tears that she'd been so diligently fighting.

"Hell."

She heard his curse and was grateful he didn't wait for an invitation, just stepped in and took her in his arms. She felt no shame in clinging to him. He was big and warm despite the early October chill, and he was holding her. Over her sobbing he was saying something, but she didn't listen. The vibration of his voice helped soothe her, and the heat from his chest on her cheek helped her center again.

"Oh, rats. I'm sorry, David. This is the first time I've seen you in ten years, and I start by crying all over you."

"No problem, Polly. I'm… Damn I had this whole first meeting planned, but I should have known that no plan would make this easier." The intimacy of a decade earlier came back as he gently brushed a tear from her cheek. He'd done it a few times the summer they met. "Mark called me a few weeks before he died. I should have figured he'd have refused a funeral. If I'd been thinking I'd have gotten up here right after his first call."

"It was better we did it how he wanted." She relocked the door and led him to the kitchen where the kettle whistled from its red glowing burner she'd accidentally left on. "My dad picked us up and drove us to Iowa after, we um…after we put Mark to rest. It was good to be with my parents, especially for the girls. It's nice to be home, though. How did you know we were home, by the way?"

"Your dad and I have stayed in contact over the last few years. He called."

She poured a second cup of hot water and steeped peppermint sprigs along with the tea leaves. It was how Mark liked his tea. Every time she made some for herself she made him a cup, whether he'd asked for it or not. That way she didn't forget to offer. When she realized what she was doing, she stopped.

She didn't know how long she stood there, staring at the cups. Mark's cup. It was blue. His favorite color. The same shade as the stones on the collar she no longer wore because he'd wanted it cremated with him.

"It's okay." David's hand wrapped around hers on the kettle and set it down on a potholder. He led her to the table and helped her sit when she couldn't focus enough to control her muscles. "Polly, look at me."

"You remind me of him," she whispered without following his command. "The way you stand. The way you look at me…it's all so much like Mark. You've been here ten minutes, David. How can this be happening in ten minutes?"

"I know. We are a lot alike," he said and paused as if he heard the mistake in his words. They both did and she finally looked at him. "Were. We were a lot alike. Ten years and distance didn't make a difference. It's why we were such good friends, and why we couldn't both be around you. Confusion and jealousy would have crept in, and neither of us wanted that for you. What caught you over there, just now?"

She nodded, his explanation making sense. Many of the Doms in the group she and Mark kept company with had the same sort of presence, though David was different for a glaring reason. With him, she had history, one she cherished.

"The mugs. I was thinking that I was making you tea like I did for Mark. It was part of the rules. We had a cup of peppermint tea together every night. Except when I was pregnant because then I liked chamomile. I would stop buying peppermint and he would give me these looks, but he never said a word because it wasn't the tea that mattered. The important thing was that I was thinking of him, you know?"

"He's only been gone since August. That's two months. You can't expect not to think of those things. That's a good memory."

"Yeah," she agreed and sniffed hard at the tears that wanted to fall again. "So, why are you here? Like you said, it's a little late for final goodbyes. He's scattered around Green Bay by now, fertilizing the fish."

"I am here..." When he paused her curiosity mounted and killed the rest of her tears. "Polly, I'm here, first and foremost, because I care about you and have always cared about you. I hated that Mark got you. He poached and I never forgave him, but I wanted you both to be happy."

"Okay," she said slowly. "He told me about that. It doesn't explain why you're here. And just so you know, I've missed you these past years, David. You were my friend too."

"I've missed you, too. So, you asked, why I am here. There are a couple reasons. First, I have this for you." He pulled a paper from his jacket pocket and slid an envelope across the table.

"What is it?"

"A letter Mark sent me to give to you. I didn't read it, because it wasn't for me. He called when he knew he was dying and told me if I thought being with you was where I wanted to be, even ten years after I'd lost you, that I should come."

"That's, that's really blunt," she said, startled away from the letter for a moment.

"You are a smart woman. I haven't seen you in a decade but I know it. That doesn't mean you're immune to bad decision making when your senses are foggy with grief. Mark took care of a lot of things, which he wrote to me about. Without his parents around, there was no one else he trusted to help you. I can teach you what you need to do with your finances, lawn mowing, water heater or..."

"Or?" she asked when he continued to let the sentence die. This discussion was not what she'd expected when she opened the door, but she should have known Mark would do something like this. He was always in charge, always taking care of his end of their agreement even after death.

"Or you and I can talk and come to terms for a contract between us," he finally said. His blue eyes were earnest, but she recognized desire and hope even if he was very good at hiding his emotions. "I won't promise it will be easy to start, but I know what I'm doing in the BDSM and Dom world. I would take care of you. We could discuss details eventually, when you're ready."

"I'm not ready for this. I don't know how long it's going to take me to even think about having another man in my life. It's not just the Dom part. I'd need a husband, someone to raise my kids with, not just a—a… I don't know. I'm just not ready."

"I know." He wrapped his hand around hers across the table. "Which is why I said 'eventually.' There's a lot we would have to discuss and a lot you would have to learn about me. So much has changed in ten years but I'm willing, hell, eager to relearn every damn thing about you and your family."

"You would do this for Mark?"

"No." He looked at her, and she felt inner peace for the first time since Mark's diagnosis. David's eyes, even more than his expression, showed he had no hesitance in his convictions, something she desired greatly from her mate. "I would do this because I want you. I've always wanted you, Polly. Mark was my brother in the ways that mattered, but you are everything I've ever dreamed of having."

"I'm not the girl you remember."

"You're the woman I knew you would be," he corrected. "And you won't put yourself down. You're a beautiful woman, just like you were a beautiful girl, and nothing would make me happier than being with you."

She had to look away from him. She wanted to sit on his lap and have him tell her everything would be okay. Her desires didn't run to needing someone to control her life, but she thrived on structure and loved being loved by a man who proved his worthiness every day.

"I'll think about it." She pushed to her feet, unsure of what was next. "Are you staying in town?"

"I was going to check into one of the hotels on the main drag down by Shawno," he answered and stood.

"That's silly. You can stay here. I just made up the beds."

"Thank you. This place is nice. You guys did a great job putting it together," he said and followed her out of the room.

"If you'll get your suitcase, I'll get your room ready."

Five minutes later she had her room prepared for him with fresh towels in the bathroom and a glass of water beside the bed. It was impossible for her to sleep in her bed alone with her memories. The futon in the office was small, so it made more sense for David to sleep in the master bedroom. Master.

Mark had never been one for Master-slave titles, and they'd never had that extreme of a relationship. He preferred Mister in his title. For eight out of ten years she'd called her husband Mr. Angelin and had felt a little thrill every time.

"I'm not taking your bed, sweetheart."

She looked up from the bedside table where she'd been about to grab her toiletries. David had taken off his leather coat and was in a black t-shirt and jeans. He looked strong. The years of working construction had added layers of sinew and muscle on his arms and chest.

"Sure you are," she said brightly, placing her almond-scented lotion in the crook of her elbow. "I'm more comfortable sleeping downstairs or with the girls. Someone should enjoy the bed. It's nice, and the room has its own bathroom right through there. Take a shower, get some sleep and you can meet Hope and Faith in the morning."

She tried to walk past him but he tucked his hand around her arm. She saw the motion and could have moved away, but chose not to. It had been years but she knew David wouldn't hurt her. Mark wouldn't have sent him to her if he thought his friend would cause her harm.

"Could you stay up here with me? Nothing physical. Just sleep."

His hand was warm through the thin material of her thermal shirt. It felt amazing to have a man's hands on her. It had been several months since she'd felt masculine contact. The last month of her husband's life had been consumed by too many migraines to enjoy the sexual life they'd thrived on. He'd been affectionate, loving just like always, but he'd required lots of rest. The time he'd been awake she'd pushed for them to do things as a family, needing their daughters to have their moments more than she needed hers.

"I would like to," she whispered. "But not yet. I can't yet. Forgive me."

"There's nothing to forgive." He pressed a kiss to her hair, not pressuring or invasive, just another piece of sweet contact. "It's an open invite. Wherever I sleep you're welcome, whether it's here, at a hotel, on the couch or on the floor. You have complete permission to touch me, speak to me and look at me whenever you need to. I'll let you know if that changes."

"Thanks." Her throat was too tight for much more; his words and instructions the balm her heart needed. "I'll be in the den."

"And I'll be here. I'll be here for you, Polly. Always."

CHAPTER 2

"Who is it? Is it Daddy?"

"Of course it's not Daddy. He's dead, remember?"

"But there's a boy in Mommy's bed, and that's always been Daddy."

David was surprised the little girls had been able to sneak up on him. He kept his eyes closed as he listened to their continued whispers. Usually he woke at the slightest sound but little feet were apparently quiet feet. It was something he'd have to remember in the future. Not knowing when the girls would be up, he'd slept in a t-shirt and boxers in case they came in early looking for their mom. He was grateful he'd remained mostly dressed when the voices started.

"You look, Hope. You're bigger."

"We should get Mom."

"Wow," he said, opening his eyes in time to see the little girls freeze at the sound of his voice. "You two are even prettier than your pictures. It hasn't been that long since your mom sent them but you've both grown so much."

"Hey, you sound like Uncle David. But we only talk to him on the phone," the little one, Faith, said suspiciously.

"Hmm, maybe the reason I sound like him is because I am your Uncle David." He didn't try to hide his amusement. The sisters dressed in matching mint green footie pajamas could have been twins if the ages weren't different, and they looked just like Polly. Nothing at all of their father showed in either and he was looking hard.

"Why are you in Mom's bed?" Faith asked.

"Because this is where she wanted me to sleep. She's downstairs in the office. How about we let her sleep for a while longer and make her some breakfast?"

"Daddy only made breakfast on Wednesday," Hope informed him.

"Sweetie, I'm not your daddy." Maybe it wasn't the nicest thing to say but the therapist he'd spoken with before coming told him to be honest right from the start. "But I love your mom, and I loved your dad. And I know for a fact my pancakes taste better on Saturdays than Wednesdays."

Faith giggled like he anticipated, but Hope looked skeptical. Maybe there was more of Mark in her than met the eye. They scooted out to get dressed but promised to stay quiet so their mother could sleep. With them gone he threw on his clothes. The parenting classes he took were clear that a closed door meant very little to a child when they were curious.

If a situation was not suitable for children, it was best to keep it under permanent lock and key or out of the house completely. He saw the drop lock at the top of the bedroom door but didn't think throwing on jeans and a fresh shirt required that level of privacy.

He paused, the silence of the room disturbing when he expected to hear the girls' voices. A grin pulled at his lips when he realized the room was soundproof. There was an intercom jack on the wall and when he flicked the switch, giggles erupted. It didn't surprise him that

Mark had thought ahead. Family life had to be carefully maintained in a BDSM lifestyle relationship, and apparently they had it covered.

Hope and Faith waited for him on the staircase landing when he opened the door. They were dressed alike again in jeans and pink thermal shirts much like Polly had worn the night before. Each had a fuzzy white vest too, in deference to the Green Bay chill that seeped into the house despite the central heating.

The smell of baking and sausage greeted them, and his brilliant plan for surprising Polly with breakfast was canceled when he found her in the kitchen. She wore a pink apron over her clothes. Her hair was damp from a shower, and like the night before she wore no makeup. If she'd slept much it didn't show. When the girls ran to her though she smiled happily and pulled them close, gushing over the dreams they quickly shared and their morning discovery.

"Why's he here, Mommy?" Hope asked as she helped set the table with the plates Polly had on the counter.

"He's here because he loves us," she answered firmly. David recognized the tone and apparently the little girl did too, because she backed off with the questions and did her work. Polly might be a submissive in her romantic relationship but in her kitchen with her girls she was their mother and that was excellent.

He'd seen some subs, male and female, totally lose their sense of self when their Dom died. Granted, it had been three months since Mark's passing, but Polly, he could see, maintained a healthy balance. She was able to function, because even though he was sure she'd given Mark her very best, she'd been able to compartmentalize and keep herself and her role as a mother in the equation. It was such a fine line to walk. Her flexibility made him want her all the more.

He watched her move around the kitchen. She was confident, smart and efficient. He'd met her mother, so he knew she came by it through her upbringing. The pastor and his wife had an old-school relationship. He couldn't venture a guess whether they used leather and chains in the bedroom, but they practiced a very respectful relationship in public. She called him 'Pastor'. He called her 'Mother'. She always brought his coffee and deferred to his judgment in social situations. He held doors open and always helped her out of the car.

Polly's parents might not understand it all, but they personified what it meant to be in a relationship based on discipline and respect. It wasn't all sex. A good portion of it was, but it was the respect and deference that drew him into the BDSM lifestyle. The baser part of him needed to be in control and needed to provide and care for those who were important enough to be in his life. But he needed that to be appreciated and reciprocated. Was it a personality flaw? Maybe, but he had control over himself as well. He demanded that control and didn't regret the way he chose to live.

"David?"

He realized the girls were staring at him, and Polly was looking at him with a compassion-filled gaze. He wondered how long he'd been spaced in his thoughts, but the smell of cinnamon and sugar distracted any in-depth pondering.

"This smells amazing, and I don't even know what it is."

"It's Mommy's soaked French toast," Hope answered when her sister nudged her, the little girl's cheeks puffed out with food. "None of my friends' moms know how to make it, and Uncle Max comes over a lot because even Aunt Mary doesn't make it right and she's really good at cooking."

"It's baked French toast with nuts and raisins," Polly explained. "The milk sauce is caramel infused, then there's caramel on top."

"Damn," he muttered in appreciation.

"Uh-oh."

"Uh-oh."

He looked over to find four wide eyes on him and wondered what he'd done. He looked to Polly whose eyes gleamed wickedly. He hoped whatever he'd done he could repeat very soon.

"What did I do?"

"Swore," she told him smartly while Faith ran and presented him with a red piggy bank with little devil horns glued on its head. "Pay the good piggy, sir."

"How much?" He reached for his wallet.

"Ten bucks."

"Seriously?" He looked to Polly who shrugged.

"They set the price. To be fair, I have to pay a price if I curse too. But I have my own punishment for it."

"Don't worry, Uncle David," Hope added as he folded a twenty and shoved it in the slit in the pig's back. "Daddy never got his mouth washed out or a time-out or anything like that. Mommy gets spanked though."

He choked on the sip of coffee at the announcement stated so innocently. The little ones giggled at his reaction, and Polly rolled her eyes.

"I burned my hand on the stove and after Mark cleaned it and put cream on it he swatted me with the spatula," she explained. "For cussing. My big punishment. The girls thought it was hilarious."

"'Cause it was," Faith said, and they dissolved into giggles.

"Eat, you monkeys. Uncle Max is coming over with Felix in an hour and we still have some unpacking to do."

David knew Uncle Max was actually Maksim Dorkov, the head of the local BDSM group. He didn't make partner decisions, but he did help broker agreements and contracts and if someone went too far, he was the third party that helped remove the injured one from a relationship.

He and his wife were also Mark and Polly's best friends. David had checked with the community online for the reputations of the people Mark had mentioned in his letters over the years, and Max was beyond reproach. He was an expert caner, wicked with whips and willing to teach, though his willingness to swap slaves and partners was something David personally avoided.

He wanted to believe he was open to anything and willing to give each their own with sexual practices, but he was honest with himself. Some things went further than he was comfortable with. He hoped he and Polly could come to a happy medium that allowed them to grow and press their boundaries without pressing the moral standards he demanded of himself.

He didn't know what her sex life entailed. Mark had left those details out of their communication, and it was probably for the best. He wasn't Mark, couldn't be him, and Polly wouldn't be the same with him as she'd been with her spouse of ten years.

"Uncle David, are you going to help Mommy with the dishes?" Hope asked after breakfast was through.

"I sure can," he said, surprised at the question. "Did your dad help a lot?"

"Only at breakfast 'cause Mommy usually has to get us ready for school," she explained as Polly put the sticky dishes into the waiting suds bath. "I help sometimes too, but I'm not real good at getting all the bubbles off."

"I see. What do you do on the days you don't have school?" he asked, gathering the rest of the dishes.

"We go make our beds and play dolls while Mom does the dishes. Daddy always came and got us when they were done."

He could see when the new reality hit Hope. Tears welled in her eyes, and Faith must have noticed because the smaller girl glued herself to her sister's side. It was crap that they didn't have their father to love them anymore. David knew how much Mark had adored his daughters. On the girls' birthdays David had always gotten phone calls from his friend. Those were the days Mark remembered how blessed he was.

"How about you go up and play?" Polly asked gently. "Uncle David will come up in a few minutes and you can show him your dollhouse."

Hope nodded tightly, and Polly handed her a few tissues. The little girl shoved them in her pocket before turning away, Faith still tucked to her side. He watched them walk away with renewed determination to make something work between him and Polly. The thought of anyone else in their life, even if the guy was genuinely great, left a bad taste in his mouth.

"I can do the dishes if you want to go up with them," he offered, moving beside her at the double sink.

"Sometimes Hope just needs a minute." She plunged her hands into the suds and began scrubbing. "She's a lot like her daddy in emotional things. It takes a lot for her to break down and really need extra love, and I know she's trying to control herself more so I'm trying to give her the space she needs."

"That must be difficult for you." He picked up the fresh white towel on the counter and began drying.

"Oh, yeah. Those tears in her eyes break my heart every time I see them, but I know my daughter. We don't hide things from each other, and she knows my arms are always open. When Hope needs me she comes to me, which is plenty often. If it wasn't I would worry. Having you here is probably helping and hurting the situation, but she'll be okay. She starts school again on Monday and is preparing herself for that. And Felix too. She doesn't cry in front of Felix."

"Why?"

She laughed. "Well, if you haven't noticed, my eldest has a lot of her father's dominating personality. Felix has his mother's more submissive, eager to please attitude. He's softhearted and very sweet. They have the most interesting relationship. Hope is the one who comforts and protects while Felix is the one who makes her feel better and stronger. It's good that he's coming over."

"That is the craziest thing I've ever heard."

"I thought so too, but if you look at children's friendships, it happens all the time. Most grow into themselves sooner or later and roles change, so I'm not concerned. It's too early for anything to be set in stone and above all, they are innocent friends who love each other. She needs that now."

"Is it what you need too?" he asked, and she looked confused. "I mean, do you need an innocent friend whose only concern is making you feel better?"

"I have plenty of those kinds of people in my life. I know eventually I will want more, David. I know myself enough to make that declaration. I thought about what you said last night. I'm not proud of it, but I'm afraid I could fall into a bad relationship because I miss Mark and the lifestyle. I would hope I'd be better than that because of the girls, and I know I wouldn't go into an outright abusive one because of them, but now that it's been pointed out I'm terrified I would miss the subtle things."

"You've got other fail-safes in place. Max wouldn't steer you into something you couldn't handle."

"I agree, but there are people in the club who Max thinks are fine that Mark didn't like. Boundaries, you know? On my own, I would defer to Max and I think that's why Mark called you. You two used to scene together, didn't you?"

"Ah, yeah. We did."

They'd spent a lot of time in BDSM dungeons in the time between their eighteenth birthdays and Mark's wedding. "Mark never went into personal details about your sex life, but we did discuss things in the general sense."

"Right, so he knows—knew. Dang it." She had to stop, and he realized that though she tried to maintain distance and speak of things with a clear head, it wasn't happening. "He knew me better than I knew myself sometimes. He knew my hopes and fears and what would drive me away and what would make me stay. If he sent you, then he thought you could press the boundaries without breaking me, because David, I won't break. I will gladly be a submissive, but I refuse to be a slave."

"That's fine."

"It had better be." The fire in her eyes confirmed there was a reason she felt that way.

"You also have permission to ask me to leave without repercussion at any time. You can also ask me back."

"Those are basic rules," she pointed out.

"And now you know I follow the basics," he replied calmly. "Things change when families get involved with play. I understand that. Some people are able to do the full Master-slave thing. I don't expect it and wouldn't ask. I want you to know when you do have a request list compiled I will be willing to defer to your judgments on your body and your family. You managed the lifestyle and a family before, I don't see any reason why we can't make it work together."

* * * *

A hard knock came at the door, and Polly was more grateful than she'd probably been in her entire life. The situation was becoming more intense than she was ready for, yet it was also what she wanted. Mark had spoiled her in the love and affection department. Her body craved it now; her soul ached for the peace and guidance she felt when she had the love and attention of a man who made her want to be her very best.

She broke eye contact with David and hurried to the door. No matter what was happening, it was progressing too quickly. She cared about David, trusted him and knew he was coming from a good place, but she needed time to think. Opening the door, she pasted on a smile.

"Max. Felix."

"Hello, Aunt Polly. Where's Hope?"

"She's upstairs with Faith," she said. The boy was already running up the stairs.

"Son." One world from Max had Felix stopping in his tracks. Just that quickly Felix launched into her arms, giving her a huge hug.

"I missed you," he said, and she blinked back tears. "I'm glad you're feeling better, and if you need someone to rake the leaves, me and Peter, he's my cousin, we'll do it for you."

"That is the best offer I've ever heard," she said, hugging him back. "I missed you too, Felix, and I know the girls did. If it's okay with your dad, I'm sure they'd love to play."

"Is it okay, Daddy?"

"Of course, son. Good job remembering your manners."

Felix ran up the stairs, and the look on Max's face held the light annoyance of any parent who was working on a behavior with their child. Felix's challenge was remembering to not run indoors, something he usually did quite well but in his excitement forgot.

"Welcome home."

When Max opened his arms her first instinct was to accept the comfort offered there. He was like an uncle or older brother, and Mark had always respected that relationship. Mary also didn't begrudge the mild affection between them as she'd shared the same with Mark. For some reason though, Polly looked back to David first. He was watching, and when he gave a small nod she flung herself into Max's waiting arms.

"Thanks for everything," she said. "I don't know what we'd have done without you and Mary."

"You would have done fine," he assured her gruffly. He was in his mid-fifties, and though he'd stopped smoking when Mary was pregnant with Felix, he still had the gruff voice of the long-term smoker he'd been. "But it's good that you are home and back to work. Mary asked to come. She'll be by next week after she's over her cold."

"I'll be happy to see her."

The Dorkovs had a more intense relationship than she'd ever had with Mark, partly because Max was from a different generation of Doms and from Russia. His family had been under an extremely dominant father. His mother had walked naked in their home every day of his childhood. He didn't do that with Mary, as far as Polly knew, but it wasn't unheard of during play sessions. Mary was a model slave, one Polly would never be, but out of deference to their young son who'd come to them later in life, they'd toned down their lifestyle.

The lifestyle they chose also meant Max controlled everything his wife did, and he preferred to make plans only with a relationship's dominant member. It was tedious, but it was their life, and Polly accepted that. Mary and Max hadn't judged Mark for being a 'fluffy'

Dom as some called their relationship, and they had never judged the other couple for being more extreme.

"Max, this is David Lowe, an old, dear friend of Mark's." He'd entered the room and waited silently at the side while they'd embraced. His expression was calm and accepting, but she knew it was better to put some distance between herself and Max.

"It's nice to meet a friend of Mark's." Max's accent was muted from his thirty years in the States but still lightly colored his voice. "I'm Maksim Dorkov."

"Pleasure," David said, shaking his hand formally. "I've heard many good things about you, Mr. Dorkov."

"Nice, nice. You're familiar with the community?" Max asked.

She wished the issue wouldn't come up so soon, but it seemed impossible to avoid. Once a person was part of the BDSM following it touched all parts of their life.

"I am very familiar with the lifestyle, most recently in Arizona. I attended a few of your workshops in the early nineties," he replied, and Polly had to fight herself not to look to David for permission to get coffee. He turned to her and smiled. "Is there any coffee made?"

Relief surged through her at his question. "Yes, there is."

"Mr. Dorkov, would you join us?"

"Yes, thank you."

She hurried off to fix the coffee. It was an easy task, one that required little thought, but it was normal, and her world seemed less and less normal every minute. Two spoons of sugar for Max, she thought, carefully stirring. And David…she couldn't remember how he liked his coffee. Unexpected devastation hit her. She didn't know how to best take care of him.

That was what drew her to the lifestyle. She loved to please. She loved to nurture, and without another outlet for it she would probably smother her children or work herself into an early grave. Mark saw that in her and had helped her focus on pleasing him and doing it without going overboard into the slave route. It allowed her to be herself, remain true to her faith, and enjoy life.

Now she didn't know how to please David, and she really wanted to. She couldn't show preference to Max by knowing his. A part of her knew she was being ridiculous. Two days in her life, less than that, wasn't enough time for her to learn everything again. It wasn't even feasible that she would know the best way to make him happy.

"David?"

She bit her lip after she called. Now she was interrupting for something stupid. Coffee. It was unimportant, but she was taking him away from his discussion for it. What kind of undisciplined, crazy woman was he going to think she was? It shouldn't be so hard to find a new groove and be patient with herself. The freezing and indecision weren't parts of her makeup. She could make decisions and think on her feet. She wasn't helpless or unorganized. There was no reason she was suddenly unable to do anything.

"Baby, relax."

She heard him before she felt him, but when she did come to herself again his body was pressed against her back. He was taller than her, and when his arms moved around her, drawing her away from the counter and deeper into his arms, she sighed. Peace was back, the calm that without Mark had come only after many hours of prayer and reflection surged through her soul. In regards to the kids she seemed to stay focused and in charge but in the face of anything relationship-oriented she was a disaster, a mess David was calmly putting back together.

"I like my coffee black," he said, a forearm across her chest and his other hand palming her hip in a very restrictive pose. "And very hot."

"So." She cleared her throat. "I should put away the milk and sugar and warm this up in the microwave."

"That would please me." The timbre and tone, as well as the words, helped calm her more.

"Okay. I can do that. Thank you."

"You're doing fine, Polly. I promise things will get easier as we get reacquainted. It's been ten years since we've spent time together. I don't expect anything right now. Nothing but a chance, and even that isn't an expectation so much as a hope."

"Everything all right in there?"

"He's nosey," David said. She heard his annoyance and smiled at the normal reaction many dominant men experienced around Max.

"He's the dungeon Master and the top guy in northern Wisconsin. He takes the job very seriously, especially when new tops come into the equation," she explained, making no attempt to move away from his proprietary grasp.

"That's good, I guess," he admitted reluctantly. "Do you need help getting the coffee together?"

"No, I'm all right now."

"Good." He let her go, and she immediately wished him back. This time she was able to bite back her cry as he left the room.

Coffee, she chided again as she caught herself watching him walk away. He wanted coffee, and because he had shown at every turn how much he wanted to take care of her and help her, she wanted him to have it exactly how he wanted it.

CHAPTER 3

The house was too quiet. Polly knew she should be grateful for the alone time while the girls were at school. She and Mark researched and discussed kindergarten options for weeks. While she wanted a smaller program to ease Hope into her school career, Mark had insisted on the all-day, every-day option and Hope did very well with the challenge. He'd seen that Hope could handle it while Polly had been occupied with thoughts of her baby growing too fast. The program was the best option. If Hope hadn't thrived Mark would have been willing to drop her down to two days, but he'd been right.

He never made Polly feel bad for being wrong, just like she didn't remind him of his shortfalls. It was not a system all Dom-sub couples followed. Some liked humiliation, lots of it, and both agreed to the practice. She was a positive reinforcement kind of girl. That didn't mean she wasn't punished or spanked on occasion, but usually that was more for the enjoyment they both received from the act.

Their relationship worked because neither she nor Mark pushed for perfection. He wanted her happy and to be the best she could be. As she sat on the sofa with a book in her hand, she thought the life situation she'd chosen wasn't the most easily explainable thing and was grateful she didn't have to do it often.

The book made her smile sadly because she'd neglected it lately. She was halfway through. She ran her hand over the smooth paperback cover. It was one Mark had given her. Every month she had an assignment. She had to make the time to read at least one book for pleasure. When she didn't make the time his paddle came out. He'd bought this book while working at the police station because one of the other detectives recommended it. After finding out it had a bird and romance theme he'd brought it home for her next assignment.

The following week he'd been put on leave for the migraines. The one after, he'd been double-checking all their directives and planning for the inevitable.

Tears filled her eyes as she realized it had been five whole months since she'd sat and read. In Mark terms she would have been in for some major teasing and spankings. Such defiances, the ones that took away from what he thought she needed, were the most severe. If she forgot his tea or bought the wrong brand of pretzels the consequences were less than if she let her lotion bottle go empty or put off getting her hair cut because she didn't feel she had the time.

"Polly."

How could she forget he was in the house? Because David was quiet as a damn mouse, she thought. Earlier, before the kids went to school, he'd been down in Mark's office. It was also their toy room, so she hadn't been able to face it yet. She looked up at him and wished she hadn't. Whatever he had to tell her had put a displeased look on his face. The instant desire to change his mood swept her nearly to the floor on her knees, but she kept control over herself. They weren't there yet. She didn't even know if that sort of submission was what pleased him. Some Doms weren't pleased unless their sub was naked, chained, masked and gagged.

"Yes?" She swallowed the surprising lust and burst of nerves to hold his gaze.

He stiffened like he knew what she was thinking, and as an astute man, he probably did. That was a sign of a very good Dom, one who noticed the tiny, intricate things about his partner. It was a must in a good relationship. To meet one's limits was one thing, to know when to push them was something time and observation to detail allowed.

"I have time now to teach you the budget system Mark used," he said, holding his place across the room.

She immediately put down her book with a fond smile at the sparrows on the cover. There was something about old and new and allowing time to move forward. She'd read it somewhere, but couldn't put the words together. It seemed true. There was a time to dwell in the past, but there was more to move forward. With David standing across the room, waiting, she knew the time had come to take a step, at least a small one.

"I know it's stereotypical," she said, pushing to her feet. "And somewhere women's libbers are rolling in their graves, but I am not good with numbers. I can do a basic budget, but I have a hard time following investments and that sort of thing."

"No problem," he assured her, stepping aside at the stairs so she could go down. She felt his hand near her shoulder, ready to catch her if she slipped. It was something a few of the other Doms did. Their job of keeping their partners safe was their utmost priority in life. Some Doms preferred to always lead, but for Mark and apparently David as well, they could catch better if they walked behind in some situations. "The program he used is very basic and clear. Most of your investments are through the bank, so you aren't looking at variable interest rates. There are a few IRAs set and several lump savings accounts with good interest."

"He was always good with money."

"He was." David sat in front of the computer, a smaller chair pulled up as well. "Please sit. From what I see, you were in charge of the household budget."

"Mark and I discussed what I needed every month to keep things going smoothly. We reevaluated every six months and adjusted as needed. I sent the household bills out of my budget. The money there was from his paychecks. Anything I made was put into savings and trips."

"I see a separate account marked Italy," he said and brought up a new screen.

Her heart stuttered as she saw the tiny amounts put in every month for the past four years. Two or three dollars at a time, fifty and a hundred once in a while. The total was just over five thousand dollars with the goal of seven thousand at the bottom of the sheet.

"Oh, Mark."

"You didn't know?"

"Faith was born premature. The medical bills took most of the savings we'd set aside for the honeymoon we didn't take. We were both in school and didn't have the time so put it off. After Faith we didn't talk about the vacation anymore, because I knew building a nest egg was more important. I'd actually forgotten about it."

"Well, he didn't and there's a note right here," he said and clicked on it.

She noticed that he pointedly looked away so she could read it.

She placed her hand on his shoulder to show her appreciation and leaned closer.

She laughed out loud.

"What?"

"For Polly. Woman. Use this money after I'm gone to get something you want. Don't put it into an IRA. Don't add it to the girls' college funds. Don't use it for home equity advancement. I couldn't take you to Italy, and I die regretting that we never made the time, but it comforts me to know you'll get something you want and think of me because of it. If there is a way, I will spank the hell out of you from heaven if you don't comply. Love you. Mr. Angelin."

Tears were falling again by the time she finished reading, but she was still able to laugh and that was the best gift Mark could have given her. After so much pain and anger at the unfairness of the world, the little message, probably an afterthought, put a lot in perspective. He was gone, but she was not. He had loved the best he could, and he knew she'd done the same. Not all couples could say that. The only regret she had about their relationship was it didn't last until they were old.

In more than one place now, he'd given her permission, hell encouragement to go on with her life. That had been his goal in their relationship, to make her the best she could be. The more important part, though, had been to make sure she was happy. He was still doing it, but she'd been too stuck in grief to realize to what extent. Her life was always better when she listened to Mark. The little reminder on the computer, blinking in no-nonsense black with the spanking threat in red, helped her understand.

"So?" David asked. "Where does the money go? There is a cash card connected to the account, or I can have it moved to a higher yield CD if you need more time to think."

"Well." She couldn't stop her smile. "Since it was for Italy, I can't think of a better use for it than to go to Macy's and get the insanely priced shoes and purse I've dreamed of for years."

"What about the rest?"

She laughed out loud at his innocent question. "Sweetie, I'll be lucky if I don't have to dip into my mad money to cover exactly what I want."

"No way. A purse and shoes can't cost that much."

"Of course they can. It's why they've always been dreams. They're extravagant and much more than I would ever, ever spend on myself." She smiled at the red words still on the computer screen. "Which is why Mark added the warning. He meant business when he threatened a spanking so…I'll do this and carry the purse and wear the shoes and I'll remember."

His expression was doubtful, but she didn't expect him to understand. If she'd said she was going to spend the money on a motorcycle or new bedroom toys, he might understand, but shoes and purses were women things for the most part. He finished showing her around the financial system, and she admitted it wasn't more difficult to follow than the smaller program she used for online and paper bill paying.

It was good to know she could do it and even if David hadn't been there, Mark had carefully outlined everything for her. She wondered how many other little messages he'd left. The letter was still tucked under her pillow. She wanted to open it, but wasn't ready. If it had been imperative, it would have said so on the envelope. Because it simply said *Polly* she knew she could wait, at least a little longer.

"That's everything."

"Huh, I can do that. Thanks, David. I appreciate you going through everything for me," she said as he turned the screen back to its sample budget page. "I'm glad he had all the tax stuff lined up. I always hate tax season, all the deductions and nonsense."

"I'll take care of that for you."

"Really?"

"Well, I'll need to do it too," he acknowledged. "And I'll probably need a professional since I switched states in the same year and sold my house and all that."

"Have you bought a place here?" she asked, realizing she didn't know a whole lot about his plans other than he wanted a place with her.

"Not yet. I start work the first of November with a cement company doing sales and management, but since things happened pretty fast, I wasn't able to line up a house."

"Good. I mean the job is good," she assured him. "And the house thing. You should stay here."

"For how long?"

She looked around the room instead of answering. The space was Mark's playroom. Before they'd finished soundproofing their bedroom it was the only place they could get loud. He'd loved to make her scream for all the right reasons. There were cuffs tucked inside the book case, rope in the drawer, and in the locked compartment were toys he'd used to make her crazy. Depending how she answered, she would be setting those memories aside to make new ones.

After the past six months of dealing with Mark's illness and grieving his death, was she ready for that? With only days between them and a decade separating the time, did she actually know David enough to build a relationship?

"You don't have to answer that." He interrupted her thoughts. "I've waited ten years for you. I'm willing to wait as long as you need to welcome me into your life. If you choose another Dom, then I'll check him out and make sure he's safe, but I'm not going to make you do anything. Especially not today."

"You would really do that? Interview another Dom for me?"

"To choose the top she wants to be with is part of the rules and rights of a sub," he said through clenched teeth. "I wouldn't like it, but I would never deny you that right."

"For now, David, I would like you to stay. If that changes I'll let you know, but for now," she said, and the pleasure in his eyes assured her she'd given more than what he expected, her favorite kind of pleasure, "I want you to be here."

CHAPTER 4

"Shhh."

Polly smothered a chuckle at Hope and Faith's joint hushing. Movie night. They'd been to the library and picked out a DVD in addition to the big bag of new chapter books and bedtime stories. Popcorn was overflowing, juice boxes had been broken out for the occasion and bedtime was extended an hour in honor of three chipmunks.

They'd put off movie nights because they were always Mark's thing, but Polly was taking them back. The whole family enjoyed the time, and the girls especially were smiling and happy. David was beside her on the couch doing some texting, but he seemed content with the night's plans. Considering his dominant personality, he also managed to be very easygoing. Nothing seemed to bother him, especially not when it came to the kids. What they needed was important, and he did what he could to make their lives easier.

She didn't know what she needed. The thought made her pause, because it wasn't right. She did know what she wanted. She'd always known. God, family, love; those were what she needed to be happy. Adversity hadn't taken her faith. Her family was broken but not demolished, and she was missing the love she knew David could provide.

It was impossible to look at him and not see the boy he'd been. The boy she'd adored.

She lost her brother, Scotty, in a car accident the year she met

David and Mark. He'd been two years her junior, and she'd adored him from the moment he was born. That summer she'd been feeling his absence but with her new friends, she'd let herself get taken away from her sadness. They'd played softball together, gone mini-golfing and done the innocent things that made her feel special. She hadn't even kissed David that summer.

She hadn't kissed him ever.

With the previews over, the movie grabbed the kids' attention and David finally set aside his phone. He stood and headed into the kitchen while she continued to process her new dilemma.

They'd never kissed, yet she was already thinking about forever with him. She'd felt the same way about Mark before their first kiss, too. Something about him, and that same thing in David, drew her in. Like a moth to a flame, she couldn't stop herself from wanting everything they offered. Back in their first summer, it had simply been David's attention she'd desired. Now they could have more, if she was willing to make the right moves.

David plopped down beside her, rocking the popcorn bowl. He righted it before there was a mess and offered her some. She shook her head, so he put it on the coffee table. There was a foot of space between them without the bowl and she hated the distance, yet she was the one who'd demanded it.

The music started and the girls began to sway, enthralled by their show, and Polly felt the same way as she looked at the side of David's face. Suddenly the distance was too much, and she remedied the situation with a little scoot.

He looked at her, his eyebrow cocked in surprise, but when she cuddled to his side he put his arm around her shoulders. The age-old action made her smile, and he grinned down at her.

"How was your day?"

David's question was immediately shushed by Hope and Faith. She nudged them both with her foot.

"Sorry," they muttered.

She wouldn't let them be rude, but she understood the sentiment. She didn't want to talk, either. David sighed and wiggled farther into the soft sofa. The cushions trapped a person in their comfort and more than once he'd fallen asleep on it. She loved that he was comfortable in her home. She nudged his shoulder.

He pulled back some so he could look at her. His waiting expression told her he didn't know what to expect and, really, had she given him a reason to expect anything from her besides friendship?

She pressed her lips to his mouth, catching his bottom lip between hers as she kissed him. His surprise didn't stop him from kissing back, and just as she'd expected he took over, not deepening the contact but jumping right in by gently sucking her top lip. The sweet thrill of the first touch was there and delicious in its own right, but there was something more.

Kissing David felt right.

She sighed and moved closer. He pulled her pajama covered legs over his knees and tugged her in until she was almost sitting in his lap, though her butt still remained on the sofa.

His hands dug into her sides, and she realized he wanted a lot more than he was taking. She gave more, opening her mouth and slipping her tongue along the bottom ridge of his lip. Her willingness spurred him on, and his tongue thrust deep into her mouth, her acceptance all he required to delve deeper.

With his fingers at her waist she used hers in his hair. The kids ever in the back of her mind, she kept the situation PG-thirteen but she pulled him closer, wanting to feel the edge right before he consumed her, right before she lost herself in him.

"Oh, gross."

"Eww."

She broke the kiss, David's tongue still out when she pulled back. He was as deep into the kiss as she, and she was grateful her legs blocked his erection. He was wearing pajama pants, and it was very impressive to her, but probably confusing to the girls.

"So now you two gotta kiss?" Faith asked, wrinkling her nose. "Mommy only kissed Daddy before."

As affective as a bucket of cold water, Faith's words sobered Polly and David's arousal. She had only kissed Mark before. Dating hadn't crossed her mind since his death, so the ramifications of what the girls would see hadn't popped up. Until David came into their lives.

Both girls turned back to the TV. The movie played, and the silence between them that had been so comfortable and hot was now flat and awkward. Hope looked back every few minutes with accusing, narrow eyes, but didn't say anything. It was her eldest's way to let her questions and anger simmer, and Polly didn't want to inflame Hope's uncertainty.

Polly tried to move away, but David had his heavy arm across her feet, like he understood but didn't want her to go. Conflicting emotions warred and even though Mark and her daughters were on her mind, she didn't want to move either.

David turned his attention to the movie. They both needed to think, at least she did, so it was good they couldn't talk for a while. His phone vibrated a message halfway through the movie and he took it. Hope's gaze was on him again, thoughtful instead of angry, and Polly was hopeful that there wouldn't be a massive tantrum about David's presence, at least not yet.

She wished David wouldn't have taken the call, but he didn't quite get family time yet. But it wasn't like they were playing games or doing a craft. Movie time had more leeway. A few minutes later her phone beeped.

She ignored it until he nudged her arm. She looked up, and he gestured with his chin. It was from him, circumventing the 'no talking' rule. Feeling like a naughty teenager, she hopped up and grabbed her phone and cookies for the kids and David while in the kitchen. With Faith completely absorbed in the movie, Polly squatted beside Hope.

"Are you okay?" she whispered.

"I don't know why David is here. We don't need him."

The lack of "uncle" in the title told Polly that Hope wasn't sure about the way things were changing, and Polly couldn't blame her.

"You're right, we don't need him, but David is here because he loves us, Hope," she explained. "And he's going to be here at least for a while."

"At least?" her daughter asked suspiciously, keeping her voice very low.

"Yes, at least. He's got a special place in our family, and we have to be patient with each other until we figure out where that place is."

Hope nodded slowly, but not for a second did Polly think those were the last words on the situation. If David became more than a houseguest, and every second he was near Polly knew that was going to be the case, then all their lives were going to change. Polly kissed Hope's cheek and was relieved when her daughter smiled a little and kissed her back.

She retook her spot and was thankful the awkwardness had eased after she'd spoken with Hope. She threw her feet up on David's lap and brought up her messages, turning the phone to silent.

D: everything okay?

She looked at him and he waited, like waiting for a verbal reply. She wasn't sure how to answer but went with the closest thing to honest that she had.

P: yeah. Hope and I need to have more talks, but I think she just needs time to get used to this new situation.

D: and the other?

She thought a moment and remembered the reason the night had snagged earlier.

P: Oh, that. I love kissing you. Our first kiss.

His fingers flew over the tiny keypad on his phone, much faster than her clunker phone, but the look on his face was what caught her attention. He was happy. It sent thrills through her.

D: I almost kissed you ten years ago. I had big plans for the

Ferris wheel. Woulda been epic.

She smothered her laughter to avoid another reprimand.

P: Epic, huh? I think we should limit your TV time, Sir.

He grinned.

D: I do love being called 'Sir'. Damn Mark, the butt got you first. I was going to kiss your pretty brains out that night.

Her smile softened, and she knew what he was doing with that one simple message. He was letting her keep Mark. He was gone and she couldn't have him physically, but David wasn't going to begrudge her the memories she had and he wanted to share those.

P: He was such a stinker.

He set his phone down and patted his lap and she adjusted to sit there, tucking her head under his chin. They didn't have to talk or even kiss anymore and they didn't as the chipmunks ran amok. It was enough to be together, and that was what Polly missed most. She liked herself, enjoyed her own company and that of her girls. But that special something that had made her so happy with Mark shined bright from David, and when he wrapped his arms around her, she knew she was in a good place.

CHAPTER 5

It amazed Polly that in a group entirely made of submissives, gathered to discuss their feelings and adventures, some still felt the need to submit. There were officially no dominant personalities in her living room, yet Mary and Candice continued to hold themselves in extreme respect and deference. Polly thought part of it was the competition the two felt, but knew part of it was their personalities. They were both very submissive people. She wasn't going to put them down for it, just like they never faulted her for not going further.

The group was a fail-safe for submissives in the Green Bay area. It was relatively new, but was starting strong especially after one of their own who had at one time attended BDSM functions had been abused.

There was both a fine and bold line between the submissive and the abused. It was sometimes a state of mind for the participants but Carey had exhibited the behavior of one who was abused, not thriving under the care and tending of a stronger personality.

It had taken over a month to get Mark to say something when she'd first suspected something was wrong. He was a police detective, but they'd been new to the local lifestyle group. For all his experience, Mark had been easing her into it before they had Hope. He hadn't wanted to push any boundaries, especially if the dungeon Master hadn't done anything yet. Polly insisted, had taken her punishment for her insolence, but in the end Mark said something to Max who in turn said something to Carey.

She'd been on a plane to Florida the same night and Alexi, her Dom, had been kicked out of their group. The details were never broadcasted, but after the incident Max encouraged the submissives to talk with one another, learn from each other and confide if need be.

What had been horrible enough to make the private, extremely open-minded Master so radical was beyond what Polly could fathom, but Mary, who was also very private, came every month and shared, which meant it was important to Max.

"Who has the kids tonight, Polly?" Melody asked. She was a middle-aged woman whose children were nearly graduated from high school. A weekend sub with a taste for the extreme, she planned to move full time into the lifestyle after her kids were out of the house. Polly didn't know how she kept up, but Melody was willingly passed among the three single Doms in the club, Levi, Eddy, and Ellen.

"David took them to a Halloween party with Felix and Max." Polly topped off the wine glass Melody offered.

"David is the new Dom in the house?" Jeremiah asked, sticking to apple juice because he was meeting his wife later. They'd been together since he was barely legal, and he had a lot to say about the sub and slave life. Polly learned a lot from him about stating her rights and maintaining her own person while still adoring her Dom. In Jeremiah's case he was more of a slave and often took on that persona during scene play but as he aged, he was beginning an identity crisis the others were trying to help him through.

"He's an old friend," she explained, topping off her own glass of zinfandel. "Before he died, Mark asked him to watch out for me. David wants to be my Dom, I just wasn't sure if he realized all that entailed for me."

There was silence a moment. None of the others had dealt with the death of their tops before. Some, like Melody were passed often but knew they could choose and go back. Mary and Jeremiah started their lifestyles with the partners they'd married and still had them both healthy and strong. Candice was the newest to the group and didn't say much, but hadn't offered any advice after Mark's death either.

"And what do we think of this?" Candice asked, tilting her head to the side. Somewhere in her thirties or very well-preserved forties, she was the prettiest of the group. When she'd first come to Green Bay two years earlier she'd been with Gregory. They'd put on many scenes, Candice thrived under the eye of others. Gregory moved on a year later, and Darren took his place. With their fetishes for all things painful and medical, the club was still learning many interesting, and for Polly, extremely disturbing things.

"We think..." she said, the question one she'd tossed in her mind a thousand times in the last three weeks. "We think my husband did me a huge favor. The other Doms in the group, no offense intended for any of them, really, wouldn't be a good fit."

"Oh yeah, none would work," Melody agreed instantly. "The guys called Mark a fluffy Dom because he wasn't as into the pomp as they are and of course he didn't live by the code of having the most toys in his bag. They want you—and they definitely do, Polly—because even without that stuff, you always looked at Mark with the highest admiration. I'm a slave. I adore each of my Masters, but with you it was different."

"Because she loved him first," Mary said, her Russian accent very soft as she kept her face pointed to the ground. "Obsession and obedience are easy for those with our appetites. We equate love with dominance sometimes and lead happy lives. But some know love first, and it feeds the soul. For a Dom the desire to protect and guide is that much stronger and more pure. For a sub it means seeing the pleasure in your top's face in response to most miniscule thing is what we yearn for."

"So, she won't be the same with a new Dom?" Jeremiah asked.

Polly wondered the same thing.

"Is there love? Is there the same motivation Mark always had? He dominated not to make himself better, but to make Polly better. He protected her from the need she has to constantly put others first even at the sake of her health. Would this fellow follow the same path or does he like the pain for the pain? Does he need the dominance to put himself above another?" Mary questioned, looking down at the floor. "It is something that only time will tell."

Polly was allowed a reprieve from the intense questions Mary posed when the group's focus turned to Jeremiah. She was happy to concentrate on his desire for children rather than the men, past and present, in her life and how love was the factor that made their relationship work. It was something she knew, had always known, but having it pointed out made the importance of having her next relationship one of love that much more crucial.

She listened as Jeremiah poured his heart out about possible fertility treatments for his wife, who was in the middle of menopause. It was a hard place because he knew she didn't really want children and only went along with the procedure for him.

He was having attack after attack of conscience for what he felt was going against his collar in making his Mistress do something she had little desire for. It went against the grain of any submissive, no matter how deep they were into the life, to force something on their tops. Yet, he couldn't deny himself the chance of being a father.

By the end of the night, Jeremiah switched to wine. His tall, skinny frame absorbed the alcohol and sent it straight to his brain. There would be no play, which meant he would be punished once he was sober. Polly called his wife, Linda, after he fell into a lump of tears on the futon, the other subs looking on with compassion. He was coming to a crossroads. If his Mistress didn't embrace parenthood, he would ask to be released from his contract, and in the process break the only family he had known for a dozen years. None of them envied his place.

Polly opened the door at Linda's knock. Small, but extremely dominant, Linda exuded power and some scorn. She immediately looked away from the Domme's eyes. Next to Max, Linda was the most dominant in their circle and Mark had early on given her permission to look away in Linda's presence, a gift because Polly was uncomfortable around her.

"Where is he?" Linda demanded. Menopause was playing hell on everything, including the timbre of her voice and the look of her skin. Everyone in the group knew she wasn't happy about it. The fertility treatments weren't helping her temperament either.

"He's in my office, Mistress," she said quietly and led her in as the other subs also looked away, Linda preferring the deference.

With Linda's back to her, Polly was able to watch how she dealt with Jeremiah who continued to cry into her pillows. Her hand was gentle in his hair despite her obvious annoyance, and the tone she used was very soft, too soft for any of them to hear. "Help me get him to the car."

Mary immediately moved to help. It was another point Mark had sheltered her from, never giving other Doms permission to give her orders. Linda could have asked and Polly would have happily helped. Mary, on the other hand, lived by a set of rules that had her hurrying to answer any demand a Dom made.

"I should go." Candice placed a gentle hand on Polly's shoulder. "Darren is expecting me tonight. Thank you for your hospitality."

"Of course, Candice. The door is always open," she said, a familiar motto since the meetings first started. No matter the day or situation, the submissivehood they shared allowed for communication and pleas if the need arose.

"And mine, too. Call if you need to talk about this new one. I have contacts around the States if you know his club name. I wouldn't mind looking him up for you," she offered.

Reputations were key in the community, and she had intended to ask Max to look into David's history. He'd given her his names and previous hangouts but because she was still considering her options, she hadn't made the necessary calls.

"Actually, I would appreciate that very much. His name is David Lowe. He has lived the past six years in Arizona, before that in Iowa and New Mexico."

The secretive smile Candice often wore turned to one of real pleasure. "David? He's your friend?"

"Yes, did you know him?"

"Yes, and if you are his woman, the one he's always wanted, then you are in a very special position, Polly. To be loved so intensely by two men in one lifetime is...well, it's enviable." She slipped her coat on and flipped the fur collar to cover her elegant neck. "Don't worry about David's appetites. I would describe him as a gentleman Dom. Much like your Mark in many ways. He is very experienced though, be prepared to be taught."

"Taught? What?" she asked, turning on the porch light.

"He specializes in currents and electricity. Max doesn't understand it well, which is why we're so limited in our play here. Mr. Lowe doesn't have such limitations. It should be very, very fun and should you choose to share..."

"You know I won't, Candice."

"Then it's my loss," the other woman said and winked. "From one sub to another, he is a respectable Dom. My promise on that."

"Thank you." So many worries that hadn't fleshed out were put to rest with Candice's honest assessment. "Have a good night."

"Polly, can you step aside please?" Mary asked softly. Polly followed Candice out and held the door while Mary and Linda propped Jeremiah between them.

"Can I help?" she offered, more for Mary and Jeremiah's sake than Linda's. The female Domme rubbed her the wrong way.

"His tote is in the living room," Mary replied.

The clock read after ten o'clock when the house was cleared of the guests. Polly poured another glass of wine, her third, and set out a bottle of Tylenol to remind herself to take some before bed to avoid a headache. Hope and Faith both had school in the morning so after she got them to the bus she would be able to nap which made taking another sip unproblematic.

Without looking at the calendar, she knew it had been three full months since Mark's death. David had been staying with them, doing the things to winterize the house and helping with the kids for nearly a month. His background check, one Mark had sent for before he died, came through, assuring her he'd never had a state or federal conviction or even an arrest. His college transcripts also arrived with soaring details about his business management degree. Random letters from David's associates offered even more reassurances. Polly couldn't think of anything else she could request.

The funny thing was—it wasn't David doing the pushing. He'd been as surprised as she was when the letter from former instructors came, praising his quick thinking, practical judgments and trustworthiness. When the letter of recommendation came from his boss, he'd called and they'd learned Mark was the one who'd requested that they send the notes after David had been gone a few months.

All Mark's hard work was having the intended effect. Because David wasn't pressing, and she didn't have to be constantly worried about him being a wolf in sheep's clothing, she was seeing him for the man he was. A good man who was like the boy she remembered. How could she forget the summer they'd met.

"Come on, little lady." David pulled a five out of his wallet and handed it to the booth attendant. "I want to see those dart throwing

skills. Since you're a preacher's kid and have probably been to hundreds of church fairs, I expect you to be pretty good at this. Not as good as me, of course, but respectable."

"Are you sure your three balloons will beat me?" She accepted the brightly colored darts. "I mean, I am pretty fantastic. You could be eating some of that pride in a minute."

"Nothing would make me happier than to see you always win."

What an odd thing to say, she thought, as she lined up for her shot. With five darts she knew she would beat him. Out of the corner of her eye she saw him move. The heat that had been between them since the softball tournament returned, and shivers started through her. Why did he look at her like that? He looked like he couldn't look away and wanted to, well, taste her. She felt like an ice cream cone or something equally delicious and lickable.

She lined up her shot and bit back a curse when the dart landed between two deflated balloons.

He tsked. "You have to focus through the distraction, Polly."

"You're not distracting me," she insisted and threw her next dart, popping the blue balloon she'd aimed for before. "The first miss was a fluke."

He moved closer so more than his gaze touched her. His hand was almost innocent on her hip. David was always careful, she'd noticed, to keep a respectful distance and if there wasn't distance there was still respect. It reminded her of how her father treated her mother. Mark also had that discipline, but he didn't hesitate to touch and get close the way David did. She wondered what Mark would think about

David's position when he got back with popcorn.

She threw her next dart and barely popped the orange balloon she aimed for. The fingers curled at her hip, the pressure not enough to bruise but definitely enough to hold her attention with iron claws.

"David..."

"Throw the dart, sweetheart," he whispered.

She did and nailed the balloon with no problem. She lined up and the pressure increased, almost to pain but not necessarily painful. When the pressure was released at the same time as the dart, she knew she would miss, and she did. The instant of distraction taking away her concentration.

"Why did you do that?" she demanded, accepting her little prize. The booth attendant's twisted grin made her feel dirty.

"Just an experiment," he said warmly, and the thought that he couldn't stand to see her win fled at the approval in his eyes. "You did a good job. How about a ride on the Ferris wheel? Maybe we'll get stuck on top."

She'd almost gone but Mark had returned and effectively butted David out. In only three weeks she'd fallen head over heels for the man who would be her husband. Very much her father's daughter, she'd held out until their wedding night for sex and never regretted it.

Her only regret from the whole summer was the disappointment she'd seen on David's face the day of the wedding. He'd served as Mark's best man, eaten and left before the dance started. A part of her had fallen in love with him that summer, and she was reminded why every minute she spent with him now.

He was a sweet man. He was strong and strict but he was good, too. That wasn't something all Doms could boast. The need to dominate sometimes carried them too far and they did things that were dangerous or illegal. When their motivations weren't clear, pride sometimes got in the way of sense. Having their own way became more important than what was right.

Her phone beeped, announcing a text. She didn't get many of those so knew it was David. He was a texter, which surprised her. Mark hated anything text or email related, preferring handwritten notes and verbal messages if they were necessary. There were many similarities in the men, but enough differences that she knew the distinctions and felt them.

D: Kids sleeping, half-hour from home.

She texted him an *okay* and tidied up the kitchen. In a half an hour he would be back and she'd ask him to carry the kids upstairs. He would most likely just do it if she didn't ask, but she liked to see how he responded to her requests. Mark had always said her self-sufficiency was one of the things that made her submissiveness such a gift. She didn't need him to do things but when she asked, it made him feel ten feet tall.

Feeling a little sappy with the wine in her veins she headed to her makeshift bedroom. David wouldn't be back for the full half-hour, always especially careful while driving with the girls. Her pillow was soaked with tears, and her bed smelled like a man, a pretty one, so she stripped the bed and bundled the sheets. Tossing the pillow aside revealed the letter she'd still been considering.

The timing was right, and the wine had been well placed for the occasion. She sat and opened the letter.

PollyAnn,

My wife. My best friend. My piece of perfection. I failed you. I should be there for the rest of your life. It was the promise I made, but I broke it. I'll spend the rest of whatever is next regretting that. Remind our babies I love them every day. Remind yourself that even if I'm not there to keep you in line, to stay in the boundaries I gave. You're an intelligent, wonderful woman who deserves to be loved. Let what I gave be enough until you move on.

When I say move on, I mean it. You don't need to be alone, not for any longer than you need to grieve. I respect any time constraint you put to the situation, but one day, move on and love another with the same intensity you loved me. You're a better woman when you love and are loved.

You told me you dream of David. I hated I wasn't able to give you what you needed in that aspect. It wasn't in my makeup to share you, and it's not in his either. Hell, it's not in yours to love two men at the same time—and no, I will not be putting money in the swear pig for that—so I'm doing what I can to fulfill your desires.

If he's what you want, let him be your man without any worry that I'd disapprove. All I've ever wanted was your happiness. Keep an open mind and an open heart no matter who is next. Trust David if he's not the one, to help you make that decision.

In these last few weeks, I've taken to heart the scripture your father always quotes. I go to a final rest loving the Jesus that gave me you even if it was for a limited time. Live a long, happy life, my love, and I'll have your collar ready when you get here. If I have to share it's something I'll accept, because after that many years apart, I'll be happy to have you any way I can get you.

All my love to you and share it with our girls.

Always yours, Mark.

The sound of David entering the house didn't prompt her from her place, as she continued rereading the letter over and over. She'd never doubted Mark's love. When he'd said she would be his last lover, she'd believed him. When he'd boastingly said he would be her only, she'd prayed that was true too.

Now, he was willing to let her go. So she could be happy. And he'd never lied. He meant he wanted her to live long and happily with whoever she chose with his blessing. It was a big blessing.

"Polly, the girls are in bed. Felix and the party wore them out."

She looked up at the man Mark handpicked for her, the man she'd nearly picked years before. He didn't look any worse for wear from spending the evening with little kids. In fact, the chocolate pudding on his shoulder, probably from Faith, completed everything she looked for in a man. Thanks to Mark's note, she wasn't worried about looking anymore.

"Are you okay, sweetheart?" he asked. "Man, why does it smell like the inside of a Boss bottle in here?"

"Jeremiah had a meltdown." The tears still in her throat made her voice sound raw. "Linda came to get him and, well, he's not going to feel very good once he sobers up."

"Are you worried about him?" He sat beside her and nudged the cologne-soaked pillow further away with his foot.

"Not really. Well, yes, but not why you think. He's going through some big changes, and he and Linda are having problems. I worry how he's going to handle the next few months. His punishment will be fine. Linda's a strict Domme, almost creepy, but she never goes further than he can take."

"Then why are you crying?"

"Oh, just drank too much wine," she said, waving away his concern with the letter.

"And read the letter?"

"Yep, I did that too. You know, he had a very poetic side." She laughed. "I'm okay. Thanks for asking. How was your night?"

"I'll tell you all about it as soon as we're out of this boy brothel." He tugged her to her feet. "How can you stand it? I swear I'll smell it for days. Let's go out to the kitchen."

"Or up to the bedroom."

He froze at the proposition. It was one she hadn't made, so she couldn't blame him for being surprised. It was the right suggestion though. She offered her hand, not in an inviting, follow-me way, but in the please-take-me-with-you sort of way. It was a fine art Mary had taught her, one that some Doms accepted and others forbade. Mark had never refused her, mostly because she'd rarely used it. She didn't know how David would respond but when he took her hand and tucked it to his elbow, she had to believe he wasn't too put out.

"I don't like the hand," he told her, leading her as he turned off the lights on the main floor. "If you have a need, I prefer words. I hear inflection better than I read body language. Not in bed so much, but in the regular conversing I've been told I miss the important things sometimes."

"You haven't so far." She was careful to keep her tone meek, so he would know it was praise, not criticism or putting down a past teacher.

"Good. I feel like I understand you better than anyone I've ever tried to read before, so I'm glad I'm right. I just need to hedge my bets. I don't want you to be another lover or sub. I want you to be forever. That doesn't mean right now, but I...well, I think I'll send Jeremiah flowers for smelling up your room so much you want to join me."

She laughed and leaned into his side as they walked up the stairs. The wine made her a little tipsy, and his scent was pushing her into giddy. It would better if she slept very soon to avoid temptation, but when he got her to her room he immediately started undressing her and avoidance didn't seem so important anymore.

"Uh-oh, I think it's my job to strip you, Sir."

"No, it's your job to please me. Stay still and quiet."

She was always careful to dress well around the other subs whose Doms mandated it so she didn't feel like a bum. David was careful with the thin fabrics, like he knew they were expensive, and carefully laid them across the room's rocking chair. Standing only in her white cotton bra and panties, she let him look at her.

They wouldn't go any further. She wasn't worried about that even though the zipper on his jeans was pressed tight. They wouldn't have sex because they weren't ready yet, and she couldn't picture David indulging her tipsy offers should any trip from her mouth. She still wanted to be near him, though.

"Will the girls look for you in here tonight?" His question warred with his command that she say quiet, so she shook her head in answer.

"Lie on the middle of the bed."

She had to pee but hesitated and thought about her options. It was better, she decided, to break the moment than wet the bed.

"I need the bathroom."

He frowned, like she knew he would, and she felt the immediate sadness of letting him down. She kept her eyes averted enough to still see his face and when he nodded she quickly walked to the bathroom. She didn't dare brush her teeth or any of the other nightly things she usually did, just peed and washed her hands before hurrying back to the room. He stood in the same place, unmoved since she left. Hoping they would pick back up where they'd left off, she went back to her place before him.

"Lie in the middle of the bed."

She knew that. Humiliation waved over her again as she'd once again disappointed him. The comforter was pulled away so she went straight to the bed. She lay on the white top sheet, taking his instructions as literally as possible. She kept her ankles slightly apart and hands at her side. It was an inviting pose, one that said she would be led. She didn't know where he was taking her, but she was willing.

He stepped around the bed and pulled the sheet. It took only a minute before he had one side tucked around her, binding her arms to her body and her legs together. He did the same with the other side, leaving her face uncovered but turning her into a burrito. Could Mark have told him she loved the restricted pose? She felt calm seep into her, warmth and serenity infused as she had nothing to do and no demand to do more.

"You asked to come upstairs with me." David stretched out beside her on the bed, still dressed, with his back against the headboard. "This surprised me. It makes me wonder if it's the wine loosening you up. It also makes me wonder what the letter said for you to change so suddenly."

"David—"

"No. I won't look a gift horse in the mouth, but I'll want answers in the morning. Is this going to be an every-night occurrence? Will you expect sex? We've kept the lifestyle to a minimum, but it's time for you to think of what your demands are for our relationship and what exactly you expect us to be. Dom and Sub? Boyfriend and girlfriend? Husband and wife? I want you to think of those specifications, and we'll discuss it tomorrow."

"I already know—"

"No."

"But—"

She didn't have to wait for his verbal reprimand, because he put his hand over her mouth. It was gentle, but firm and made his message clear. Aggravation tore through her. She hated when people didn't at least listen. She licked his hand. Something flashed in his eyes. She wasn't sure if it was anger or lust but she did recognize the disappointment when he reached to his bedside table and pulled out a ball gag, still in its wrapper.

"You are familiar with these?" he asked. "You may nod."

She nodded; the little red balls were the only thing that kept her quiet during her punishments and play at times. She was grateful when Mark allowed them, otherwise her punishments lasted much longer because she couldn't stop herself from crying out in sweet agony and pleasure.

He pulled his hand away and immediately slipped the ball between her teeth, forcing her mouth open and around the ball. She meekly tilted her head forward for him to strap it in place. He was being merciful, she knew. They may not have a contract yet, but there was an understanding building. He was giving her an out before she made the situation worse with words that didn't need to be said.

"You can breathe?"

She nodded but refused to meet his eyes.

"Think tonight. We'll talk tomorrow."

He closed the door and turned off the main light, but left his clothes on. Rejoining her, he lifted the comforter and placed it over both of them, leaving her wrapped and gagged. He made no move to cuddle or comfort, but stayed on his side of the bed, leaving plenty of space between them. She began to fall asleep, snug and safe as she'd longed for. She felt his hand move through her hair and despite the gag she fell asleep with a smile on her face.

CHAPTER 6

She wasn't looking at him. For the past three weeks, he'd known Polly as an adult. She was the beautiful woman he wanted more than anything to posses and love. Always warm, willing and honest, she'd looked at him and smiled every morning, and he was sure if that was all he ever got, it would be enough. Now, he wondered if he'd gone too far and if he'd ever see her smiles again.

The gag came out with no problem and unwinding her from the sheet had taken little time. He'd rubbed her arms and legs when they'd been lethargic at first and offered her water against the dryness the ball caused long-term. There was no sound from the intercom and still in only her bra and panties she refused to look at him.

"Are you ready to talk now?"

She didn't nod or shake her head, just kept staring into the corner like something there was holding her interest. The main downside of their relationship was time. They hadn't had enough for him to understand what her silences meant. Mark never mentioned their sex life or the rules they lived by, and he appreciated that most of the time.

He didn't want Mark coloring their relationship the rest of their lives, but he wished for some kind of insight. If wrapping and gagging put her off so much, he was going to have to revise his rewards and punishment system. In his mind he'd prevented a situation, not punished her. It was a kindness most Doms didn't give.

She finally shook her head.

"Do you need the bathroom?"

She nodded.

"Then use it. Shower and dress comfortably. I'll take care of breakfast so take your time."

It was another kindness but she still refused to look at him, walking stiffly to the bathroom but leaving the door open. It was a new behavior. He rubbed his hands to his face, wondering what he'd started. They needed a long talk and very quickly before feelings got hurt and things were pushed too far.

The girls were putting on their school shoes when Polly came downstairs in pink sweats. She still didn't look at him but helped them with a smile on her face. He checked the time and saw she'd taken every moment right up until ten minutes before carpool arrived. It shouldn't have bothered him that she adhered to his words with exquisite detail, but it did. Something about it wasn't right.

She was glowing and sweet with her daughters, making them laugh as she got them out the door. She still didn't acknowledge him as she closed the living room curtains and locked the door. He watched from the kitchen as she slowly removed her sweatshirt and pants, naked beneath. She was beautiful, not the girl he remembered in tank tops and jean shorts but fuller and softer. The stretch marks on her stomach were testimonials of her pregnancies, but her thighs and hips were still as strong and supple as ever.

She pulled a blanket from the sofa and stretched her hands high above her head, her breasts lifting before she knelt on the blanket. Her thighs stayed close together and her posture was nearly perfect as she arched back to allow her hair to fall against her shoulders. She placed her hands, palm up, on her thighs. He noticed the paper then, a single sheet propped on a pillow at face height.

Meditating. It was something most subs or slaves did very privately, and he felt like he was invading. He thought back to what he'd commanded and realized he'd done it to himself. He'd said he wanted her to think. She'd fallen asleep right away so hadn't done it and was taking the first opportunity to remedy the situation. Her back stayed straight as she quietly read each line aloud. He recognized some of the basic mantra lines from subs past. Mostly slaves used them, but it wasn't a bad practice for everyone especially in early days of a contracted relationship.

"I am a beautiful submissive. I have value beyond compare. My will is my husband's."

Husband. She stuttered over the word but continued, diligently repeating several lines but he heard that one loudest. Maybe she intended for him to hear the mantra. With her history, he had assumed a relationship meant marriage, but hearing it from her lips made it that much more serious.

"I trust my husband with my body and welfare. I trust my husband with the care of my children. I trust my husband to be guided by fairness."

They were basic, humbling things he could agree to.

"I submit control of my life to my husband, because he loves and protects me. I will leave if he abuses the gift. I will be punished if I abuse his good will."

He nodded again, appreciating the lyrical tone the mantra held. He wondered if she wrote it herself.

"I want to wear his collar. I want to be his bride. I want him to smile because in those things I am part of him. I am the best part of my husband."

He smiled again, recognizing Mark in those words. "Better half" hadn't been his phrase. Polly had been the best part of everything in his world. It humbled David that she would keep that line for him. So much about a dominant relationship hinged on the affection between sub and Dom. Some people went into relationships for the short-term thrill and moved on in a few months. Others were so deeply submerged, they lost parts of themselves to their partners.

He didn't know how far they would go. He'd never loved a submissive before. Of course, he'd cared for everyone in his control. Such intimacy demanded various depths of feelings but love was new and reserved only for Polly. Could he punish her? He'd shown the night before he could. Only in her best interest though. He wasn't a Dom who believed in pain for pain's sake. He'd drawn blood and welts plenty of times, but they fit the situation and agreement. If she didn't like that part... He'd seen the toy wall, whips and flogs; he didn't think it was an issue.

"My body is my husband's, but he's made allowances for me."

He perked up when he heard her begin again. It was the start of negotiations, and because he was willing to give her anything she wanted, he had to find something to haggle on.

"I medicate as necessary for the pain our agreed-upon punishments leaves. My breasts are not means for torture. I am made allowances for waxing to my husband's desires. I am allowed to wear feminine hygiene products when necessary. Blades and needles are not welcome on my skin. Asphyxiation is not safe for my body. My skin is allergic to latex."

David grabbed a notebook and wrote everything down, things he would have to remember because there were some specifics he needed to question. The details were important to avoid confusion later. He also had two toys to toss if latex bothered her.

"My husband lo—will love me."

She stumbled hard over that line, and he hoped she understood him enough soon to say it correctly with confidence.

"He will love me. He will be understanding to change. I will not hide my needs from my husband. I will meet my husband's desires with a grateful and happy heart and beg correction when I fail. As long as I meet my husband's needs and he sees to mine, marriage is forever."

Terms and length of the contract from her side were presented. He snapped closed his pen and watched as she remained in her spot. Her posture began to slacken as fatigue set in. She probably hadn't taken the pose since Mark's illness, maybe longer if it hadn't been part of their routine. He liked it, personally. Her focus was on the paper in front of her rather than him, but in another setting she would be looking at him.

Deciding the moment was now, he strode to the living room.

"Those are your terms?" He sat on the sofa after moving her list. She stared at his chest.

"They are." Her demure and meek answer pleased him greatly, and he had to remind himself of his own list before he immediately agreed.

"I have a few questions and changes."

Her eyes averted even more as she waited in silence.

"Why are your breasts off-limits?"

"I want to have more children."

Her response shocked him. More kids. Not only more kids, but his children. It was a thought he hadn't dared entertain because he didn't know if Polly could have more kids. Mark had shared some of their fertility difficulties. It had taken nearly five years for them to get pregnant with Hope, then when Faith had followed so quickly they'd thought everything was fine, but it wasn't. After two miscarriages and three more years of trying, Mark had confessed to needing to go in for tests. But that had been before the tumor.

"Um…babies." Her confession still had his mind reeling, but he tried to focus on the task at hand. "And your breasts affect that how?"

"I nurse my babies until they are on cow's milk. Usually about a year. Mutilation to the nipple or fleshy parts of the breast can impede milk production, so it's safer to avoid anything harsher than light topical whips that don't affect the fat or muscle around them."

"I see. I use light prickly tools for breasts. I'm content with those and electrical toys," he relented. He'd read about breast cancer and abnormalities associated with caning and the tying of breasts. It made sense not to flirt with those problems when other things were effective. "I also like heat, but will stay short of leaving burns on your breasts or nipples. Or anywhere for that matter."

"Thank you, Sir."

"Good girl. I prefer 'Sir' when you address me in private. In public and around the children 'David' is acceptable. You will answer to pet names we acquire along the way."

"Yes, Sir."

"With waxing, do I do it or pay for it?"

The question startled her. She lost focus for a moment, and it made him smile. "Um, forgive me, Sir. In the past I've used a salon downtown. It is your decision, of course."

"Of course."

Her discomfort showed and he pushed it because it was his job now, or would be when she agreed to his demands. "I will take over your waxing every three weeks. I like bare armpits, legs, mound and ass. Other natural hair is acceptable."

"Yes, Sir. If you let me know what you'll need, I'll add it to my shopping list."

He nodded, pleased with her response. He wanted her to make her demands so he knew what she was comfortable with, but he also wanted to push her past the limits she put on herself. It was a fine edge in new relationships, but waxing was a small thing. It was intimate, slightly painful but small and a good place to start learning boundaries.

He looked down at his list again. "I don't like blades in the bedroom. I've seen too many important parts nicked at inopportune moments. I have no medical fetish so no needles or piercing rods. What do you use for medicating?"

"Tylenol, if needed. I also have lotions to use after being punished."

"Okay, I can allow Tylenol but nothing stronger. Alcohol and drugs have no place in our relationship. Last night was further than I should have gone after you drank, but it was preventative, not punitive. In the future, a single drink for either of us turns sex immediately into vanilla. If my punishments send you reaching for anything stronger than Tylenol, you will tell me and we'll reevaluate our methods. I want to correct and pleasure you, not cripple you."

"Yes, Sir."

"I like electricity. I understand Max doesn't know much about it, so it's been limited. I'm not going to give you a heart attack so we'll use it safely and I'll teach you to use it, too. Max asked me to do a few scenes with it in the next few months to teach others. He offered Mary as my assistant since you don't usually do the scenes."

David left the statement open. The group's Master hadn't known who was behind the preference for not sharing or offering open voyeur scenes. He knew they attended the munch meetings every other month with the Dom and sub players, and often went back to Max's home for open play, but didn't participate.

"Fidelity is important," Polly whispered.

"So does that mean you want to do the scenes or would rather I did not?" he asked after her quiet, hesitant reply.

"I haven't…"

"Does that mean you won't?" He was pushing her again, but he had to.

She rolled her shoulders and sat up straighter, her beautiful neck elongated to almost snapping. He'd touched her pride and questioned her desire to please him. It was a dangerous button to press, but he was willing to because there were parts of the relationship they could build to over time. He felt no desire to rush her into things that could grow if nurtured with time.

"I would be willing to participate in a scene with you exclusively and within our boundaries."

"Good girl. I'll let him know."

She looked relieved and nervous, a strange combination but he thought she looked excited.

"I think that's enough for now. We'll go over more and redefine things later. We'll put it in writing and revise your mantra. Updating and changing the contract won't be a problem. You'll need to think of new safe words for only us, but there's only one other thing I can think of to ask."

He let it hang until she finally looked at him. Her brown eyes were bright with happiness, the best sign he could hope for in their new journey.

"Question, Sir?"

"When's the wedding?"

CHAPTER 7

Polly never imagined it would take a seven-hour car ride to corner her daughter long enough to have the conversation her eldest had been avoiding for weeks. Hope wasn't dumb. In fact, her kindergarten teacher expressed worry over keeping her challenged. It was a predicament Polly dealt with by supplying her daughter with third grade homework and problems. Martial arts also helped along with church school, choir and long walks.

That intelligence sometimes made it difficult to tell Hope things she didn't want to hear. She could avoid subjects like a con artist and the last three weeks had been dodge after dodge when any talk of David was concerned. Polly knew her daughters liked him. She would go so far as to say they loved him like an uncle. He was great with them, always an avid listener and block builder, and Hope preferred him driving her to tae kwon do because he understood the moves and could help her more than Polly ever could.

That didn't mean Hope wanted to talk about David's new place in their lives, which is why they'd decided to have the talk on the way home from Thanksgiving with her parents. Polly asked her mom for help. Maureen had never lost a spouse so hadn't remarried, but she'd consoled those who had. It was a hard thing to ask a child to accept a new adult in their lives, but Polly knew David would be good for all of them. Over steaming green beans and mashing potatoes they'd talked while David and her dad were out playing with the kids.

"I don't know what to do, Mom. She won't stop long enough

when the topic comes up to have a conversation, and I'm not going to just tell her she's going to have a stepfather. That doesn't seem right."

"No, no it doesn't." Her mother wiped her hands on her ruffled apron, a treasured gift from her father, one she got every Christmas. "How does she avoid you?"

"Well, if I try to talk to her in the evenings, she falls asleep. If we're at home she goes to a different room or totally tunes out. She's had punishments for being sassy, but they don't help. All the time-outs in the world won't make that kid listen if she doesn't want to."

"Okay, so get her on the way home tomorrow," Maureen suggested. "Obviously she likes David, and your father does too."

"Has it been too fast, Mom?"

"Hm, time is one of those very relative things, dear. What is fast for one, is decades to another. You just need to trust God."

"That's so easy to say. I try, but how do I know I'm not missing some giant sign?" It was a question she struggled with. She knew she missed things, not often, but it wasn't unheard of for her to forget to buy milk when it was bolded at the top of her grocery list. How could she be sure she wasn't missing something right in front of her face?

"That's not so hard, luckily. Just cover your questions. Who, what, when, where and why."

"Aww, Mom that's what you teach the catechism kids. I'm almost thirty."

"And they still apply. Who do you love, Polly?"

"I love Jesus, my daughters, my parents, my friends."

"Do you love David? I'm not asking you if it's too soon to love him. I'm asking if you love him."

"If not for Mark, I'd have fallen in love with him ten years ago. I met two wonderful men at once, and now that Mark is gone and David is here... That sounds so terrible."

"No, it sounds human," her mother said gently. "Honey, women like us do better with men we love in our lives. I'll go so far as to say that every woman does better with love in her life, just like men do. I don't know why it's so hard for us to admit we need other people. Mark wouldn't have done everything he did, if he didn't want you to move on, darling."

"I know, and you're right. I'm more worried about what others will say, than if I think it's right or not. I love him. The second he walked in the door I started loving him again."

"Good. So what do you want in the relationship?"

"I want a good marriage. I want a husband who loves me and keeps me protected and safe. I want a loving father for my kids."

"Does David fulfill those things?"

"He agreed to all of my demands, and the girls adore him. He took a parenting class, Mom," she said, love overflowing.

"He's a smart man, and I know you agreed to his requests. Why would you want to marry him?"

"Because if I don't I'll be jumping him out of wedlock and having his beautiful babies anyway." They laughed together, her mother was a pastor's wife but also a woman.

"Well, I guess that answers where you want him."

They laughed again and because Polly knew her mother's next

question she let her mother hug her close.

"That leaves when, honey."

"By Christmas. I want to start the New Year with him."

The conversation with her mother put things in perspective. Mark had been gone four full months, but she was ready for love and marriage again as long as it was with David. That meant she had to speak with her daughters and prepare them. Her father knew what they planned and wished them well and counseled patience, especially with Hope.

Faith would take things more in stride. She was younger and had more of her mother's personality than her father's. She already told David she loved him every day before she went to school.

Heading north through the southeastern tip of Minnesota, they were two hours into the drive when Faith fell asleep. The big breakfast and excitement of the days before ensured she would be out until they stopped for lunch in Minneapolis.

"Hope, I need to talk to you." Polly turned off the radio and reached back for the book her daughter was reading. "And this time you aren't going to walk away or tune me out."

"Mom, I don't want to talk."

"Hope—"

"I don't want to talk to you either, David. You aren't my dad."

Polly knew the jab would come. No matter how good David was to them, Hope would always remember he was not her dad. Polly didn't want her daughters to forget their father, but wished for less drama. It wouldn't be easy, her father and mother assured her of that fact. She could wish though.

"You're not going to speak to him like that ever again." Polly knew when her daughter needed the kid gloves and when she needed a reminder of her manners. She refused to raise a child who lashed out in anger simply to hurt others. "Apologize."

"I'm sorry, David. But you aren't my dad. Even if you marry my mom you won't be my dad. You'll be my uncle. You aren't even my uncle, 'cause you aren't Dad's brother. And if you were Mom's brother you couldn't marry her because your kids would have webbed feet."

What was she supposed to say? Polly looked to David helplessly, but his eyes were focused on the road. If he was stressed by the girl's words, it didn't show. His hands were loose on the steering wheel, and his mouth was relaxed. When he looked briefly to her, he smiled. He wasn't expecting easy either.

"We are getting married the weekend before Christmas. You have the week off, so Friday we'll get married, Saturday we'll have a little party, then it'll just be us for Christmas. Nana and Papa will come up New Year's Day for gifts and dinner. David will continue to be Uncle David, if you prefer. I would never ask you to hide your feelings or pretend to be happy when you aren't, but I need you to think of Faith before you get too angry. If you need to talk to us, fine, but don't be ugly in front of your sister."

"I wouldn't do that," Hope muttered and looked out the window. "Can I have my book back?"

"Do you have any questions?" Polly asked gently.

"No, but I'd like my book, please."

Polly passed back the little novel and readjusted in her seat. So much change in only a few months. Was it better to let change hit all at once or to spread it out? She wasn't sure. She knew she'd rather deal with a huge lump of adversity between long stretches of peace. She'd had nearly ten years of peace with Mark. Maybe if they'd dealt with more along the way she wouldn't be so challenged now.

David's hand closed around hers. Polly looked at him, though he concentrated on the road. He loved her. He was offering her the world because of that love. Adversity was something she was dealing with, but not alone. She could be alone and had been for months, but life was so much better with a partner.

They hadn't made love or done anything sexual, but she was curious to her bones. It would be good, she had no doubt, but the mystery of him was enough to keep her awake and watching him during the nights they slept together. Sometimes it was more than he could stand, he told her and she'd sleep on the futon. He'd offered the bed, but she couldn't sleep in it alone.

* * * *

David watched as Polly carried Faith to the house. It was late, and they hadn't said another word about the wedding. Hope had watched him suspiciously all day but hadn't said anything inflammatory in front of her little sister. They'd stopped for meals and ice cream, enjoyed the fall leaves during the drive, and endured dozens of word games to keep them occupied.

He would be their father. Their own was gone and he was the only man their mother was going to have. They would make it work.

He thought Hope was sleeping when he opened the minivan side door.

"You aren't my dad."

"I know, baby. I'm going to help take care of your mom and help take care of you and your sister, but you had a dad, a really great one."

"If you marry her, then he can't come home." Tears welled in her eyes, and the overhead car light reflected off them as they fell.

"What do you mean, sweetie?"

"He told Uncle Max he'd argue with God when he got to heaven to get back to Mommy. If you marry her, then he'll know she doesn't love him anymore and won't come home. I want him back, and he can't come back if you're here."

David didn't think his heart could break. He'd had years of hardening and controlling himself, but tears burned his eyes at the child's admission. Damn Mark for letting his baby overhear what was probably an innocent conversation. Damn him for dying young and putting his family in the position to move on without him.

"Honey…"

"I love you, because you're my uncle. You're fun and I like you around but, but if you stay…"

"You're worried your daddy won't come," he finished and pinched the bridge of his nose to stop the tears. "Honey, he can't come home. If anyone could argue with God it would be your dad, but when someone dies, they don't come back. They might want to more than anything, but that's not how it works."

"He's alone," she whimpered.

"Nope, he's not. Did you know your dad had a little sister? Alice died when they were kids after she got really sick. He missed her. And his parents were waiting for him too." David scrambled to make the story sound right. He'd spent his life controlling every detail of his existence, yet here in one of the most important moments he'd ever experienced he felt control slipping through his fingers. "Hope. Do you really think your dad is coming back or do you just wish he would come back?"

It was just a question, words strung together, yet it wasn't what she wanted to hear. David expected her to shut down like she usually did when she didn't want to hear something. It was a trick Mark used growing up that annoyed the hell out of David. Until he was willing to listen, Mark would not hear. His daughter did the same.

"I miss him. I love him, and he's not coming back to tuck me in. He's not at tae kwon do anymore. We don't read."

"He's going to miss a lot of the best things," David agreed. "And he didn't want to, baby. He wanted to be with you for all the good things, for your mom and Faith too. He'll watch from heaven. You believe like your grandpa says, right?"

"It's kinda hard to believe sometimes," she said hesitantly.

"Your dad didn't believe until he met your mom." The conversation was too advanced for her, but David felt like she would understand better if he gave her the facts. "Then he only believed some."

"He always called Mommy an angel," Hope said.

David smiled. "Yeah, that sounds about right. Your mom is an angel right here on Earth, sweetie. She made him believe that there was something bigger to this world, even if he didn't understand it all. When he got sick, he told me he had no choice but to believe God would watch out for you girls after he was gone. He told me to come help and to be nice or he'd angel smack my as—butt."

Her tears ebbed as she giggled at his swear. Such a simple thing allowed her to be a child, and he'd gladly pay her stupid pig when they got in the house.

Polly stood on the stoop, watching. He waved, but stayed near the van, and Polly waited where she was. His fiancée was a smart woman and a great mother. They would help the kids get through this.

"So, Daddy called you?"

Pulled away from his thoughts by Hope's tiny voice, he nodded. "I was your dad's friend since we were your age. He knew I'd help. I've loved your mom for years, and I loved you girls since before you were born."

"Dad said he loved us before we got here, too."

"You've got people who love you, sweetie. Even with your dad gone so many people are here who care. I'm just one more. I'm going to love you and your mom and Faith. I've never had a family, but I'm going to do everything I can to take care of you and make everyone happy and safe. Is it going to be the same as your dad? Probably not, but that's okay. I'm not here to take his place, and no one is going to forget him. I'm just here to love you until you can be back with him. Then he'll have to share."

"Daddy's not good at sharing," she said with a little sparkle of a grin.

"Neither am I," he whispered conspiratorially "But we'll learn. Are you ready to go talk to your mom now? You've been hurting her feelings a lot these past few weeks."

"I used to get in trouble from Daddy when I did that," she said hesitantly as she unlocked her seatbelt.

"I don't like to see your mother hurting either," he told her. "What was the usual punishment?"

"I had to make Mom a card and play Barbies with Faith so Mom could read her book."

"Sounds fair. How about you do that stuff tomorrow? Tonight though, I think she could really use a hug. And talk to her about what you heard your dad say."

"No." She grabbed his hand. "Don't tell her I said that, please. I wasn't supposed to hear Daddy say it, and I get big time-outs for eavesdropping and sneaking."

"I don't keep secrets from your mother, but I'll let you explain. In this case, I'm pretty sure the punishment will be waived."

"Will you tell her that? She doesn't listen to me."

"Hope." He paused a moment to really think of the best response. His class had addressed playing parents off one another. "Just talk to your mom on this one."

"Fine."

David unloaded the van. The three-day trip had necessitated far more luggage than he'd have thought, but they'd used it all. Who the hell would have thought he'd travel with two kids one day? His club friends from Arizona would laugh their asses off if they knew their badass Dom Master had run to Wal-Mart at nine on a Friday night to buy nighttime pull-ups, the ones that look like underwear, because Polly forgot to pack them for Faith.

Ideally there would be a third car seat before the next Thanksgiving. After seeing Polly as a mother, he wanted to give her another baby. One of her friends with a tiny baby had come over and the look he'd shared with Polly had said loud and clear that she wanted a little one. So he wanted one for her. The girls had started in on adoring the baby too and Faith, innocent and younger than Hope in many ways, had asked for a little brother. Hope had looked at Polly, and David had waited for a barb or disagreement, but even Hope had looked hopeful.

David had held the baby too, and it hadn't been so bad. If the little guy had been his own, David was sure he'd do well. He was hoping for a wedding night pregnancy. He was even cutting back on coffee to give his guys an added boost. At forty, he needed the extra help. The books said so.

Part of his job was giving Polly what she wanted and if kids were it, they had to get cracking while his equipment worked. He knew she'd miscarried twice. Those conversations with Mark had been major downers, so he wanted to throw his A-game hard and fast to avoid enduring that kind of pain again. If it happened again...they'd deal with it, but by taking preventative steps at least he felt like he had a little control over a very uncontrollable situation.

"David?"

He closed the garage door, adding two new snow shovels for the girls to the industrial snow plow. Pastor Ike said shoveling was good for building relationships. David was reminded of the reason he'd chose Arizona when he decided to move away from Minneapolis. Green Bay was even farther north with more cold and snow than his birthplace. It was going to be a long winter.

"I'll be right there, babe."

Polly waited on the porch as he made his way back. In yoga pants and an oversize sweatshirt, she looked more comfortable than she had all weekend with her parents. She'd been pressed and perfect for them, but allowed her daughters to be comfortable in jeans and shirts. He'd seen Maureen try to fuss with the girls' clothes but Polly hadn't listened to her counsel, only making a fuss when their clothes were uncomfortably soiled. It made sense to him. He wanted Faith to be able to eat pudding without worrying and Hope to be able to run without thinking of grass stains.

Just like he wanted his wife to be able to stretch and move, something she couldn't do in her pressed linen slacks and starched blouses. If he couldn't have her naked, he liked her in yoga pants. They did excellent things for her ass. And if he didn't love the silhouette of the sweatshirt, he did like that she often went without a bra or only with an undershirt beneath. The convenience of it was not lost on him, even if he'd yet to take full advantage of it.

"Hope and Faith are both tucked in," she told him as he grabbed a piece of trash that had blown onto the lawn while they were away.

"Good. It was a busy weekend for them. They were great."

"They are really good-natured kids and love Nana and Papa. You and Hope had a good talk." She held open the door, offering to take the litter, but he shook his head. She didn't need to handle garbage, silly woman.

"We did. She's worried about getting punished."

David looked over his shoulder as Polly followed him to the kitchen. She was tired. It had been a long few days, and he'd see she got a nap if she needed one after the kids were in school. She'd gotten in the habit of posing for him for an hour before going on to do her work. He could forgo the posing if it meant the circles under her eyes were gone.

"She got a reprieve this time." Her smile was sad. "I knew something was bothering her. I'm glad she finally told me. I wish we'd have talked sooner, but I thought she understood Mark's not coming home. Faith does. I didn't even think…"

"If she hadn't heard him say he'd argue with God she would've let it go." He tossed the trash and washed his hands, the kitchen immaculate, something Polly didn't take pride in, but saw as a necessary evil. The different edges of his sub were fascinating. She wasn't completely sub in any way, and neither was she vanilla or dom. She was wonderful.

"Yes, sacrilegious, bossy thing." She laughed. "He probably had every intention of doing it, too."

"Hell, he probably already did."

"But I know he's happy. He wanted to meet Jesus, and he hoped to see Alice and his parents and our babies."

Her smile and laughter were gone. Her grief wasn't the tangible thing it once was, but death and love were hard. David didn't expect her to be over Mark, even if she was ready to commit herself to him.

He'd been her husband, Dom and father of her children. The bond there was huge. He couldn't begrudge her the feelings. He could wish he could take away her pain.

The permissive words died on his lips as she wrapped her arms around his waist from behind. He finished drying his hands and turned, taking her in his arms. She didn't need his permission to touch, and he was glad she remembered. With this much pain, he needed her to take the comfort she needed. She wasn't crying, he thought, her breathing steady, but she held him tight.

"Okay?"

"A little okay," she replied. "I miss Mark and I miss the babies we almost had, but I'm okay. I can miss them and still be happy with the wonderful things in my life."

"I'm glad."

Her honesty always touched part of him. She held very little back, and he wanted more. He wanted all; it was his nature and it was hers to give.

"You're tired. Go upstairs, I'll be up in a minute."

She nodded, but held him an extra moment. In the future, the delay would get her spanked. For today, it would be forgiven because she wasn't his under contract and wasn't his to control. Once it was signed, they would redefine the rules and she would learn and he would teach. He wanted her to be her very best. He loved her.

"Sorry," she muttered and turned away.

"You'll learn."

She looked over her shoulder, and he saw the little glint of naughtiness in her expression. Her playfulness made him smile. They were going to have lots of fun.

CHAPTER 8

Polly pressed her cheek into the floor. It was a new feeling. She wasn't one for the full submissions, but it had been in David's contract for her to do different poses. With the girls at school an extra hour for Christmas pageant practice, they had time and she'd used it to stretch out on her new blanket.

It was part of her wedding package from David. They'd been married three days earlier in a small ceremony that made her feel warm just thinking about. Her parents had come, along with Max and Mary. David met her pastor and they got along well. He'd married them, even though her dad would've preferred to do it. He'd married her and Mark, and Polly had wanted differences in her new life.

The fuzzy pink collar around her neck screamed different.

Mark had chosen sapphire dyed leather. He'd preferred her in leather over lace. They did call it the leather lifestyle for a reason. So David's care package came as a surprise with all its frills and softness. There was a new blanket, thick and lined with sheerling, a large pillow for long kneeling and the collar. All in pink. She loved pink.

Music was playing, a metal band she didn't recognize, but had heard before at scene parties. It wasn't something David ever left out when kids were in charge of the music selection. Just like their R-rated DVDs were put on a separate shelf, they kept their intimate life very segregated from the kids. No awkward situation or questions needed to happen, not for many years.

She took a deep breath and lifted David's foot. His sock was bright white, and fresh from the dryer, something she appreciated as she settled it on her neck. He put no pressure down but left it there while she rested into her lavender-scented pillow. It was David time. With a full and busy household, he didn't get the full submission so many Doms demanded. She was grateful that he was willing to be flexible, and with that in mind she tried to focus.

She had to forget the dishes in the sink. She had to stop thinking about the costumes she had to finish sewing. Her deadline had to go out the window. The laundry buzzer went off, and she had to not worry about wrinkles.

Just David. For the next hour it had to be his. Her David. Her husband. The one who'd held her the past three nights instead of making love, because she hadn't signed the contract yet. There were fourteen pages and a few essay questions, and he hadn't given it to her until their wedding night. When she'd been expecting consummation, she'd gotten homework.

She was so horny, her clit was in a constant state of near pain. It had been over six months since her last orgasm. Even though Mark let her out of her contract at death, she'd felt the need to maintain parts of it. She read every day. She closed no doors when her man was in the room, and she didn't touch herself without permission.

She felt David's foot press slightly on her neck and knew she'd stiffened or something to show she wasn't thinking of him. She refocused. David. Her David. Husband. The man she loved. The routine of being in love had returned easily. He was the boy she remembered, yet the man she'd thought he could be in time. She wanted to lick him and feel him inside her. She wanted to be on her knees in front of him and take him deep into her throat until he was hard and hot, dripping all of himself in her. Every drop of him was precious, and she'd suck it eagerly until every morsel was inside her.

"Baby, tell me what you are thinking."

"I'm thinking of pleasing you, Sir."

"You're thinking about doing it, instead of doing it?" She thought there was humor in his voice but there was annoyance for sure, and disappointment overwhelmed her.

"I'm sorry, Sir."

"I like that you think of pleasing me, but you need to focus," he admonished gently. "Think about keeping my foot warm. It'll help you maintain a single thought. After, we'll discuss the contract again."

She directed her body heat to her neck. She knew it didn't happen that way, but like he said, it helped her close out her other thoughts, thinking only of warming and comforting his foot.

When he finally moved aside and pet his hand through her hair, she felt renewed. Her thoughts and everything were toward him, but in his demands, he gave her an amazing gift. The calm helped her see things more clearly and helped her be better to the kids, him, and herself. She never wrote better than in the last few days of posing with him.

She looked at the clock and saw she'd lost an hour in the quiet. It was a good hour though, and she'd get more done in the time the girls were gone than she'd done before David. He offered her robe and though the house was a few degrees warmer than she usually kept it, she gladly accepted. The heat bill was thirty dollars higher than usual.

The hours of nakedness made her notch up the thermostat past what she kept it when they all wore sweatshirts.

David didn't mind. Following Mark's example, he'd reviewed finance changes since he'd taken over the family. Polly knew the details in case of an emergency and still handled the household budget, but with more wiggle room than ever before. David simply made more money than Mark had. She was also making more than ever with her writing, her next book due out in less than a month. Polly poured herself and David their morning cups of tea and couldn't keep the smile off her face.

Her husband sauntered into the kitchen with a look much too serious for the nice morning she'd thought they had. She liked when he smiled because his whole face showed it. His eyes had a nice crinkle to them, and they sparkled. It seemed like a feminine quality, but he did sparkle.

He went to the kitchen junk drawer and pulled out the contract she'd been working on the last few days. It was much more than she'd formally written with Mark. They'd had a more oral agreement, probably since they'd had an oral agreement first in their marriage. David had more experience in the Dom and sub world, so the papers he'd handed her were detailed. There was over two hundred specific questions, plus the essays. The individual questions weren't as easy as she'd expected in 'yes and no' inquiries and the essays were a nightmare. For him though, and for the next step in their relationship, she was more than happy to do her homework.

"You're making good progress," he said and nodded as he flipped pages. "Okay, this is good. You should be able to finish today, so we can start things tonight."

She wanted to ask what he meant about starting tonight but held her tongue. Sometimes surprises were wonderful things, and other times she had to use her own power of deduction. Polly hoped it meant they would start the physical side of their relationship. It had been much too long since she'd known the touch of a man, and she hurt from the nights spent cuddled with David with no relief.

"Do you have any questions about the contract? Anything you don't understand or don't agree with?" he asked, continuing to nod through the questions.

"Why the big contract? I read it all and the last line says we can toss it whenever I choose. Why go to this trouble?"

He nodded again and set the paper aside. The tea he didn't care for was doctored heavily with sugar, but he still winced when he took a drink. He was trying to acquire the taste for green tea for its medicinal uses, but it wasn't easy going.

"You signed the most important contract of my life three days ago, sweetheart. You married me and that means we're bound together in the eyes of God for the rest of our days. That beats the hell out of any earthly contract I offer. I don't pretend to know the future so I leave it alone, but I want you to know I'm serious. This contract is nice because it clears things up right from the start, but it's not the end-all-beat-all of our relationship. I love you, and that comes first."

"I love you too, Sir. It's—it's still a little hard to believe it happened so fast."

"I've loved you for ten years, Polly. Every woman I've spanked these past years, anyone I kissed or fucked, had your face. It was wrong, but it's true. I've wanted you, and when my best friend called and told me he was dying the first thing I thought was 'hell, I'll miss him'. The second thing that crossed my mind was with him out of the picture I could finally have a chance with you. Love for you drives me, just like what you feel for me, drives you. It's what makes this work."

"I'd like to sign the papers, Sir."

"I'd like you to do that as well."

She accepted the pen and packet, and with a smile, she signed the bottom of the last two pages. He pulled off the blank essay parts and tucked the completed sheets in his pocket. He handed her the essays and a pen.

"Your homework. I'll take care of lunch before I go to work, but I want the essays done before tonight. We've got plans that I need to study on first."

CHAPTER 9

The toys and books were put away for the night, and the girls were tucked into their beds. The day had gone well, though she hadn't gotten nearly enough done on anything requiring deep thought. Her mind had been too full of David's plans and what he was studying in his office. He'd sequestered that part of the house for himself, though it wasn't necessarily off-limits to anyone. He had building blocks and Barbies stashed in the corner for the kids, but when he needed quiet, it was his place for it. Not that there was much quiet in the house with a six and five-year-old.

David disappeared after dinner, letting her handle dishes and baths on her own. She usually did, but when he helped it was nice, too. She didn't mind though, not if he was using the time to plan an incredible night.

Would they start as they meant to go forth, with whips and toys or would it be a more vanilla, straightforward first time? She didn't know and honestly didn't care. Vanilla was a beautiful flavor. She didn't need the toys and pain to enjoy making love, but she adored them when they were added to the mix. Her first years with Mark had been mostly vanilla, and she'd loved it. Throughout their marriage, smooth lovemaking had been sprinkled in at least once a week when they were too tired for the rigmarole of leather, yet too horny and enamored to go without sex.

She hoped David liked sex and lovemaking. The toys and whips were wonderful but she loved the intimacy of turning to her lover and just being together. Some of the Doms she knew treated vanilla sex as a punishment. Melody hated when her Doms initiated common bedroom positions and basic lovemaking. She'd had a husband who didn't want the lifestyle and thought her deviant for her desires. When Melody needed punishment it was one of the more effective ones, she'd confessed during a sub meeting.

"Your bath is ready upstairs."

She looked up from her computer screen. She wasn't working but she'd tried. David must have snuck past her office, because his hair was wet from a shower and he wore only pajama pants. His upper body was fantastic from years of working construction. His arms were heavy with thick muscles bulging on his biceps and shoulders. His stomach was well defined, not without some softness but definitely calendar-worthy. Even wet, the curls remained in his darkened hair and she wanted to tangle her fingers in it.

Instead, she immediately shut down her program, turned off her computer and went upstairs. David watched her but she stayed demure, not looking straight at him or provoking anything he didn't want to give. Yet. A bath sounded wonderful and when she stepped into her bathroom, she found it even more than she'd thought. Candles were lit around the edges and bubbles filled the tub in a decadent show of pampering. She rarely did the full bubble bath for herself, and Mark hadn't run her a bath except after she gave birth and had doctor's orders to soak, because he never thought of it and preferred showers.

The comparisons would always be there, she thought as she sunk into the nearly steaming water, just short of being too hot. She didn't hold anyone's traits against them. She wanted David to be David, just as she wouldn't have wanted Mark any other way. If she'd wanted something different she'd have gotten it. She couldn't have Mark, but if she'd wanted a man exactly like him, she would have found one. Instead she had David and she was happy.

Was she happy? The lavender-scented washcloth waiting for her was new and indulgent compared to what she usually bought on sale. The soap was new as well, and she spotted a basket under the sink. Inside, she could see wrappers from the candles and soap, brands from an expensive department store's organic line. She should have known David would go all out. She rubbed the washcloth gently over her arm. Since he'd gone to so much trouble, she could certainly enjoy his efforts.

The water was cooling when Polly finally emerged, pruney, soft, and smelling like lavender. She felt like a flower petal and through the open door of the bathroom, she could see their bedroom was illuminated only by candles. She looked at the candle beside the pink thong David had set out for her. It was a paraffin wax, safe to use for heated massage as well as to light the night. The man thought of everything.

"Only the g-string for now."

She left the matching short robe in its place on the counter and tied her damp hair back in a loose braid out of her face before walking into the bedroom. David had offered to buy a new bed and she'd almost agreed, but she loved her bed. The headboard was tall and elaborately carved with squares and geometric shapes. When she and Mark had found a set they could agree on, they'd left off the footboard in favor of a huge, heavy trunk she kept extra blankets in.

The furniture didn't make the bedroom a welcoming place. What made her want to go to her room was the man waiting for her. It was always the people, not the things, that moved and inspired her so changing the furniture made no sense. Polly didn't see it as her and Mark's bed. She saw it as the place she and her husband stayed, and that man was David.

"Hell."

She turned to find him, still in his pajama pants, in her rocking chair. He was so delicious. It was the first night of their intimate relationship, and she made the decision he was the only one she would think of ever again in this room. Mark could have a place in the other rooms, but not this one.

"You're more beautiful every time I see you." The reverence in his tone was a balm to any insecurity she felt being nearly naked in front of him. She had very little shame of her body left, but it filled her with pride that he found her beautiful.

She wanted to be beautiful for him, and the way the candle flames reflected off his eyes showed exactly what he was thinking. He loved her. She recognized the look, and she tumbled deeper into love with him. The love she had for him kept growing. There was no turning point, no big bang, but everything she felt was magnified and increased with every passing moment.

"You are an incredibly handsome man." She kept her arms at her sides, exposing all she had except for the area hidden by the scrap of silk. "I love that you are my husband."

He stood but kept the distance between them as he continued to look her up and down. She felt caressed with every pass of his eyes.

They were drinking her in, loving her. He'd promised in their vows to love her with every piece of himself. The personal vows had been her idea, something special for the unique relationship they would have. His promise to love her and be her family forever had been the sweetest, most poignant line of the ceremony.

"What do we do now, Sir?"

"Just David tonight," he said, pulling back the comforter and quilts on the bed. "Just you and me with no games, no domination, or rules. Just us and the next step into our forever."

"That's so sweet. You're such a romantic, David. It's one of my favorite parts of you." She smiled when he offered her his hand and tucked her fingers in his palm.

"Only because it's what you like," he told her, slowly drawing her near until she felt his heat radiating toward her. "Your happiness is all I care about. That means I'm going to spoil the hell out of you, so get used to it."

"Is it spoiling if it's expected?"

"As long as you're happy I don't really care."

With his warmth surrounding her, she found herself completely agreeing. As long as they made each other happy, the details didn't matter. They were right together. She'd dreamed the past few months and she felt like each one had the possibility of coming true. Some were raunchy and naughty but others were just like this, with candles and the sweet smells of love. The bath left her feeling loose and emotional, and David left her feeling in love.

"What's that sigh for?" he asked.

"Because I love you. I just...I like the feeling."

"Good."

He brushed his lips to hers. A hello, a welcome, and she fell into them without another thought. She wrapped her arms around his waist, pressing herself to his hard body. Finally. So much teasing and desire was peaking into a beautiful moment he'd made for her. She wanted it to be as perfect for him as he was making it for her.

"What can I do to please you, David?"

He lifted her into his arms, cradling her to his chest. She wrapped her arms around his shoulders, held tight and listened as his words rumbled from his chest. "We're going to please each other tonight, just like we are for the rest of our lives. I hope you're ready for this."

"I'm ready for everything. I want it all with you."

He laid her on the bed and climbed in beside her. They lay together, face-to-face on their sides. Her feet brushed his shins, their height difference was very real, but lying together it no longer mattered. His hand stayed at her waist, caressing the bare skin in short strokes, and ignited in a look feelings some men never mastered.

The touch enflamed her and made her shiver at the same time. A delicious combination of anticipation and excitement burst again as she realized the night was finally theirs.

Polly leaned in first; staring at his lips was not getting her what she wanted, so she took. She wasn't afraid to make the first move, not when he'd said the night was just theirs with no games. David was her husband and she desired him above all else, and the first contact was all she'd hoped it would be. She wasn't tentative, didn't hesitate, and his lips opened under hers in invitation for her to take all she wanted.

Sex wasn't all domination. It was love too, and her love for him made her bold. She nudged his shoulder and he turned to his back, keeping his hands on her waist as she hiked her leg across his waist. His hair was soft under her fingers, a little damp yet, but silky and smooth. She moved his head to the side and deepened her kiss, thrusting her tongue as far as she could, trying to be inside him the way her body would allow. He was her husband, her man, and he was about to become her lover.

David's hands moved higher and lower, one to her breast, one to her ass. With no hesitation, but obvious curiosity, he first took her breast in the hollow of his wide palm. He wasn't hesitant either and began rolling her pebbled nipple between his thumb and forefinger. There was no room for pain in their bed tonight so he kept the pressure light, and she moaned her approval in his mouth. His other hand gripped her hip, holding her in place.

When he moved his hips closer, between her thighs, she sighed. Finally. She wasn't going to rush their night and she didn't have it in her to be very bossy, but she wanted him between her thighs, petting and touching her softest place.

"Baby, what's wrong?"

She tried to keep kissing, but his words broke through to her lust-filled mind. Wrong? What could he possibly mean? His hand brushed the lips of her waxed pussy, her vagina all but cried for him to play deeper, and her tongue was down his throat. What could be wrong?

"You're dry as dust," he said, and she felt his finger gently massage her opening, the immediate contact a shock of pleasure but also a dry reminder.

"Lube, we need it." She reached for her nightstand.

"I'm not making you wet? The kissing and petting isn't doing it for you?"

"Are you kidding? I'm about to explode." She squeezed some lube on her hand and rubbed her too-sensitive lips, her moan matching David's who watched her hand intently. "I just don't make my own lubrication easily. It's something to do with hormone changes from pregnancies and breast feeding. My doctor said it's pretty common."

Slick and ready for more, she started to pull her hand away from herself to use on him but he grabbed her forearm. "No, keep going."

Feeling incredibly wicked with his eyes hot on her bare mound, she slipped her slick finger back inside her. It wasn't enough but it was a start, and his look of approval and desire as he moved his hands to her breasts had a similar effect to a lick of her clit. Another finger, she decided and whimpered as her muscles moved along her fingers, trying to suck them deeper to satisfy. She began to rock against them, six months without an orgasm making her trigger nearly nonexistent, especially as David continued to roll her nipples between his fingers, and stare.

"Finish," he commanded, and though he'd said they weren't dominating or playing tonight, she came instantly at his command, conditioned to just that when the situation warranted. She gasped and rocked harder, her short fingers doing enough for the smallest of orgasms but David remedied the disappointing size when he tugged her hand away and pushed her down on his cock.

Immediately, small exploded into more. She felt her toes shake and threw her head back, knowing it was going to be one of those orgasms that she dreamed of having. The kind that made lights flash and left her shaking for hours.

"Harder," she cried. Release stayed elusive, the building infuriatingly slow when all she wanted was to satisfy the crippling hunger that clenched her pussy.

He jerked her to her back, and she cried out in frustration. He lifted her legs immediately to his shoulders, stretching her hamstrings but wasting no time in plunging deep. She rocked into him as much as the firm bed and his hard body would allow, and when the new sensation rocked her, David made no move to stop her screams.

* * * *

"How was that, dear?"

Polly laughed out loud, and David couldn't stop the smirk that kicked at his lips. Such a mundane question after such an amazing feat. They were going to screw themselves silly before Valentine's Day. He required control in his life, and he made no apologies for it. Giving the reins to anyone sexually wasn't something he'd ever done, but in bed with Polly, sex hadn't been control. It had been pleasure.

He was seeing the purity of the Dom-sub relationship between them. Her pleasure was everything to him, which meant tonight, the night they started their marriage, had to be for her pleasure. She'd exploded around him three times and every one intensified what he felt, not only in love for her but sexual ecstasy for himself.

"Well, dear," she said and giggled, wiping her sweaty brow

against his equally sweaty shoulder. "I'd have to say that was a satisfying way of consummating our marriage, and I'll be delighted to do it again very soon. Dear."

He laughed and lay beside her, tugging her naked body into his arms.

"I'm still thinking on what to call you," he told her, pressing kisses to her hair and willing his cock to reload quickly.

"Dad always called my mom 'Mother,'" she offered.

"Yeah, fucking right, I'm going to call you what your parents use," he said and winced at the thought alone. "By the way, do your parents know the more intimate side of our relationship?"

She sighed and dug her toes into his calves, the little appendages cold so he tossed a blanket over them both. "Well, yes, actually."

"How in God's name did that come up?"

"A drawer was left unlocked when they were here on a visit a few years ago. Mom went looking for a pen and ended up finding a bull whip, my collar with Mark's name engraved on it and a toy with 'clit-blaster' all over it."

"Oh, hell."

"Oh, hell is right," she said. "That was awkward. Mom was sure I was being abused, because there was a whip and collar. What would any mother think?"

"Yeah, I guess. What did you guys do?"

"We talked. I explained to my mother what was happening and even let her see our contract," she admitted. "It wasn't easy. I didn't want to share, but she threatened to call the police. She understood better after looking everything over, but now they just sort of ignore it. For the most part."

"And the other part?"

"Well, sometimes Mom gets it into her head to try to change me. She thinks the relationship makes me a weak, feeble-minded female."

"Bullshit."

"Thank you." She patted his chest. "I agree, and I've told her I would never do a TPE—"

"You know 'total power exchanges'?"

"Of course," she replied. "I researched this lifestyle a lot before I agreed, David. I had the choice, and can stop whenever I want, but I love it. I love knowing I'm the center of your world. I love the feel of leather against my butt. The feeling I get when I please you is more than I can describe and for now, it fits everything I want in life."

"And I'll be the first to know whenever that changes right?" he asked, because he needed her to know she could change. It wouldn't be easy for him but if the day came when she no longer wanted the lifestyle, he would do whatever she needed.

"Yep," she agreed like she didn't see it as the monumental thing he did. And he knew she didn't. In her essay she'd described how natural her life felt with him and how it had felt with Mark. She'd seen aspects of dominance in all the relationships in her life and had no problem with it.

A loving relationship was what she expected, and she allowed for variations. Love took many shapes, and she was happy with the form they embraced.

"I wouldn't worry, though. I'm already thinking of ways to sneak whips and leather into the nursing home with me."

He laughed quietly and nuzzled her hair. His wife. She always had the words to please and ease him, even in the smallest things.

"I like the idea of us playing our games until we both cock up our toes," he admitted.

"And, speaking of cocks, I think we need to repeat our wedding night every six months. A first time that good deserves to be repeated often."

She giggled as he rolled on top of her again. "If you thought the first time was good, my dear, the second is going to rock your world."

CHAPTER 10

"Break into small groups. Jared take the blue belts and higher. Maggie, take the lower belts, please."

The rounds of 'yes sirs' were nice to hear, and David smiled as he watched Hope hurry over to her group with an older teenager. She'd just earned her blue belt before Mark died, and was excelling. She was the youngest of the higher-ranking students, but she'd earned her spot. With every kick she showed how quick and precise she could be, and David knew how much she practiced at home between classes. He hadn't done martial arts in years, but it was coming back as he helped her most nights and watched from the stands.

They were in a Lutheran church which seemed a little odd at first but it fit. The basement was big, empty, and easy to wash up after long, sweaty practices. Plenty of parking was available and while the practice could turn intense, it was controlled violence surrounded by people who knew what they were doing and prevented injury while promoting discipline and skills.

The description made him smile. How much different was it from what he did in his life? Especially in the bedroom. It didn't show, but he shivered in lust at the thought of getting Polly back in bed. Making love had been beyond what he pictured, and he was relieved he'd made the right decision to make love first. They'd both needed the reassurance before moving on. He'd set up the sling in his office before leaving for tae kwon do and had every intention of having Polly in it as soon as the girls were tucked in for the night.

"Hey, you're David, right?"

He looked over from where Hope was practicing footwork and tried to place the short, stocky guy beside him. He'd met a lot of people between the new job, marriage and moving, but the guy didn't look familiar.

"We haven't met," he said and offered a hand. David shook it. "I saw you came in with Hope. I know Polly, so since I've been hearing about David from my sub, I thought you might be him. I'm Levi."

"David Lowe," he replied. "I'm Polly's husband."

"Congrats. She's a great piece of ass. We were all pissed when we found out her husband handpicked her next Dom. I guess it would be in our nature to do something like that, but I didn't expect it from a fluff like Mark."

Not often did David rush to a decision about a person, but he decided he didn't like Levi between the time he called Polly a 'piece' and Mark a 'fluff'. It wasn't a flattering term in the Dom world and even if it fit, if a person was a friend in the lifestyle you didn't say it.

"She's my wife," he said calmly, and Levi lost his smirk.

"Hell, you're like Mark, aren't you?" His good-natured groan made David wonder if he'd overreacted or if Levi didn't understand. "For a fluff, he sure got pissed if anyone touched her or looked at her wrong. I was hoping that would ease back some. I love to look and would dearly love to touch. It's probably because she hasn't scened. If I could just watch her ass turn red once I could get her out of my head."

"We're at a children's event."

David turned back to the class, cutting Levi out. He didn't talk about his lifestyle with kids and their parents around. It wasn't their business and if they didn't talk about their sex lives, neither did he. It wasn't polite. Some guys, and women for that matter, told everyone they ever met about their lifestyle. David figured unless others were curious and respectful and approached the topic, they probably didn't want to know. At a munch where new people were screened and friends gathered for a meal before play, he was much more open. Watching his step-daughter do spin kicks, no.

"Touchy-touchy. Hell, I'm here for the kids too. My nephew is out there right now, even if he's a little patsy."

David had met some immature assholes in his circle, but usually dominant men tended to be intelligent or assholes. Lucky him, Green Bay had both.

Thankfully, class let out a few minutes later and he strode away from the bleachers and from the offensive man. He'd have to ask Polly about him and give her express permission to run like hell if Levi was near when he wasn't. Asshole Doms didn't always take 'no' for an answer, and David couldn't be sure until he met the others that someone would watch out for her.

Max might, but his definition and expectations of a sub were much different than David's. What the dungeon Master allowed and demanded from Mary was much more than he would ever ask of Polly.

"Uncle David, did you see that? Jared said I did really good with my side kicks. I'm going to practice so I can do the flying ones next time. Can you do the flying ones?"

"I haven't done them for many years," he admitted, gathering her equipment.

Beside them, he saw Levi made no move to help his nephew with the huge sack of gear every student carried. He was one of those, David thought, as he hiked Hope's bag to his shoulder. A Dom who was into the lifestyle to be served, instead of the other way around. To an outsider, yeah, it looked like David was the same way. His wife washed his clothes, stayed within a budget he set, followed rules he made and lay with her neck beneath his foot. To outside eyes, it looked questionable and he knew it.

What those outside eyes didn't always see were the doors he held for her. Or the savings account he'd already set up for her use since he'd noticed she only spent on herself if she found something on very deep discount. They wouldn't see his interference as him keeping her from doing too much, but it was what he did. He knew she'd nearly worked herself into ulcers and exhaustion after Hope was born and would do it again in an instant if someone didn't stop her. His ways of guidance weren't like everyone else's but they worked for him, and they worked for Polly. Their system of rewards and punishments were agreed on and done out of love. That was all that mattered.

"David, can we get ice cream?"

"Sure, sweetie."

Levi and his nephew were walking behind them, and he heard the boy ask him the same.

"Why the hell would I buy you ice cream?"

Asshole. David made sure Hope was buckled in and safe before getting into his side. He checked all of his mirrors and controls before pulling out of his parking spot while Levi turned burnouts in his convertible, the little boy in the backseat hugged down against his bag.

"I bet he's cold." Hope never seemed to miss a thing, and she looked sad about her friend. The boy was older, and he hoped Levi was taking him home to a nice mother.

"Does his uncle bring him often?" he asked, pulling out of the parking lot and heading toward one of Green Bay's many creameries. He'd googled a list and tried to pick a new one every time he let Hope think she'd conned him into a treat. The latest one was near Lambough Field.

"His mom works a lot, so sometimes his uncle brings him. Ronny doesn't like it. His uncle teases him all the time and calls him a wimp," she explained. "Ronny's not a wimp really, he just doesn't like tae kwon do very much. He plays violin really good and likes that better, but his mom makes him do tae kwon do and football."

"It's good to learn new things," David said carefully, not seeing anything wrong with exposing kids to lots of things young.

"Yeah, I know, but Ronny just doesn't like it much." She sighed. "I don't like to see him sad."

"That's nice, sweetie. Just keep being a good friend for him. That's the best thing you can do."

"That's what my other dad said too," she said, and he wondered if she heard her words. Other dad. David heard them loud and clear but wasn't going to make a big deal out of a few words. "He said it makes us better to be good to other people. The more we make people smile, the more we smile."

"Exactly. Your dad definitely knew about being a good guy. I'm glad he taught you that lesson. It's a good one. What kind of ice cream should we get for your mom and Faith this time? I don't think the last kind went over well."

"No one likes rum raisin," Hope said as she giggled. "What is rum anyway?"

"A grownup drink that tastes great in ice cream," he informed her. "And you said your mom and sister liked to try different things, so I've just been going with the specials."

"Yeah, but if the special is rum raisin, let's not get it."

* * * *

"Peppermint, yummy. Look, Mommy, it's not the runny raisin kind."

Polly laughed at her youngest daughter's words, as Faith attacked her bright pink ice cream cone. David brought home two cones and two milkshakes. Hope's mouth was full and Faith was trying to make up for lost time.

"No rum raisin," he said, handing her a cold Styrofoam cup. He was an easy mark for treats, but he limited the after-TKD ice cream to every other week, so she didn't mind the indulgence. "I was told it does not count as an ice cream flavor."

"Honestly, anything not containing chocolate or caramel can't be counted as ice cream," she told him, taking a sip of the shake. "Yummy. This is good."

"Peppermint bon bon." He grinned and after peeking over his shoulder, nudged her farther into the kitchen. "What about vanilla?"

She smiled back, knowing his game.

"Hmm, I do enjoy vanilla," she admitted. "Once in a while it's the best stuff around. Other times I love the bells and whistles of rocky road."

"So you enjoy being rocked?"

"I do. And sometimes I like tin roof sundae, it's one of my favorites too."

"Because?" His grin told her his thoughts were running with hers.

"'Cause I like to be banged."

His nostrils flared, like he was breathing in her response, and she smiled. "Nice. Did you have a good day?"

"I did, thank you, Sir."

"Mommy, how come you call David, Sir?" Hope asked, sliding across the kitchen linoleum in her socks.

"Hm, that's a good question." Polly thought for a moment. Hope had never asked why she called Mark 'Mr.' but she was older now, it made sense that she would ask. "Because he's my knight in shining armor, of course."

"Like Prince Charming? 'Cause you know, he's a bad guy," Faith reminded her.

"Since when?" David asked, and she bit back a grin. He had so much to learn.

"Since a movie series came out a few years ago, Sir." She took another drink of her shake. "Prince Charming became the bad guy, and the ogre is the good guy."

"Huh, what will they think of next," he muttered.

"Oh, Mom can we have a movie night tonight? So David can see?" Hope pleaded. "He'll like it, because the princess does karate. *Hiyah.*"

"Soon," Polly promised. "But you have a shower to take, homework to do and bed in an hour."

"School. Okay. Maybe this weekend?"

"Soon," David said before she could okay her daughter's request and Polly nodded, wondering what he had planned. "Go hit the showers, lady."

"I'll get your jammies!" Faith shouted, stopping only momentarily to wipe her pink-covered face on a clean kitchen towel before she went to help her sister.

Polly smiled at her daughters. Not all sisters were best friends. At play groups they'd gone to in the past, she'd seen even very young sisters and brothers treat each other badly. She refused to let her girls be horrible to each other. They were built-in best friends in a world that was often cruel.

"Max called and scheduled a munch for Saturday night. And they're going to have a little reception for us too," David explained, the suction from his straw against air noisily filling the kitchen, so she offered her shake. He took a deep sip. "Mmm, my new favorite. Thanks, sweetie. I was at work, so I didn't have the calendar."

"Oh, um." She hustled to the big family calendar she used to keep their lives straight. "Church choir Saturday morning for the Lowe-Angelin ladies. You have an appointment with...oh, dear. David, why are you seeing a doctor?"

"Crap," he said, looking over her shoulder. "I forgot about that. It's just for some test results. They did a second cholesterol test and…"

His neck turned red, and she wanted to ask what he was holding back but didn't. It wasn't for her to ask if he wasn't willing to tell her outright, but she had a hard time with doctors. She didn't want his health to be an issue she didn't know about. Mark hadn't liked to talk about himself, and by the time she'd realized the headaches were migraines and he had them often, it had been too late to help.

"Is everything all right, Sir?"

He looked sharply at her, and she knew it wasn't what he expected. He thought she would be able to do the proper sub thing and not ask, but she couldn't. If she was going to be punished, it was worth it because not knowing was worse than any discipline he could give.

"I'm fine." He was short, and it scared her.

"Then why are you going to the doctor?"

"Polly," he said and stopped. He grabbed the card he'd tacked to the board and shoved it in his pocket. "You need to not worry about this. Go upstairs and finish with the girls, then go down to the harness."

"But David—"

"Last warning."

"What is wrong?" she snapped. "I lost one husband who didn't tell me when he wasn't well. I'm not going to do it again. I don't care if I don't sit for the next week, but this is important."

He pointed to the stairs. She knew she was being dismissed, but this time she went. David knew now she was serious, and he would definitely punish her but afterward they would talk and she'd learn what was happening. It wasn't that she wanted to be defiant, but some things were important enough and for her David was.

He was still in the kitchen when she walked through after putting the girls in bed and making sure the intercom was working. She passed him without looking and flipped on the sound system for the basement.

Nervous tension snaked up her spine as she sat on the office chair and waited. He'd remodeled the basement, painting and changing things around until it was his own space. Nothing remained as Mark had it in the room, and that was for the best. Pictures of him were still up, family outings and formal portraits displayed proudly throughout the rest of the house, but he wasn't alive. It was best to leave the dead in pictures and in the small things and let the living do the living.

"Take off your clothes and be ready."

David's words made her jump and she immediately stripped, placing her clothes over the chair back. Her collar was in the case she'd grabbed from their bedroom. Once it was on it was the physical sign of her submission to her husband. It was much like her wedding ring, only bigger, stronger and sexier. She pulled it out, caressing the leather with her fingertips. The scent of leather had always been okay for her, but now when she smelled it, her clit began to throb. It was conditioned from years of pleasure association. She tossed her hair back and did the clasp, keeping it snug enough not to move around but not tighter than a choker necklace.

In the corner of the room a black ball of fabric hung from the ceiling. She reached up and tugged it down, unfolding the straps and straightening the harness. It was similar to the one Mark used on occasion, but she hadn't spent much time in one. She knew how it worked. She knew how all toys and equipment worked in theory, just knew everyone had their own preferences. Feeling naughty and a little worried, she lay back against the harness and relaxed. She couldn't know what was happening next, but she relaxed and thought of her mantra.

She deserved to be punished. She wanted him to correct her so they could learn and move past it. David was a sweetheart and would tell her his business when he thought it best. It wasn't her place to push him.

Relaxed and deep in her mantra, she didn't notice him until he was right in front of her. He didn't look pleased. In fact, he looked terribly disappointed. Her heart hurt. She didn't want to hurt him. She only wanted to make him smile.

"I'm sorry, Sir."

"I'm sorry too, Polly." He went to the cupboard and undid the lock. Inside was a TV and movies, innocent enough, but beneath the side covers were dozens of toys hanging neatly in their places. "Turn over."

It was awkward in the harness and she wished she'd gone belly down to start, but she managed until her top half was supported by the leather and her bottom hung for him.

"Move out of the harness. It's not set properly for your height."

Again, disappointment filled her. Nothing was going right. She was supposed to please him and already she was messing up. She pushed out of the straps and fell when her foot got stuck. She cried out in pain as her ankle twisted.

"Hell. Are you all right?"

"I'm fine," she whimpered as in an instant he was to her, releasing her foot from the straps and massaging it gently. "I'm sorry, Sir. I'm fine. I'm ready to please you, Sir."

He moved her foot back and forth and just as she'd thought it was a little sore, but definitely okay. He smiled at her some, agreeing before he helped her up and to the wall. She didn't know what to think until he moved aside the pictures on the wall and found arm and leg straps. They were black but lined with pink satin. David didn't give her a chance to turn and face him, only began locking her arms first above her head and her legs shoulder-width apart.

It was a basically comfortable position, but he turned her face specifically to the wall and that meant she couldn't look at him. She hated not looking, but the excitement of not knowing was huge. She felt her body warming up and clenched herself to keep from beginning to drip too soon. She couldn't guarantee her own lubrication since having the girls, but the excitement of the unknown sometimes sped things faster than she realized.

It had gotten her in trouble before because she just couldn't tell when she was dripping and when she was told not to, she wasn't supposed to. She'd gotten a few extra lashings in the past for the mistake. She'd also gotten amazing fucks after taking her medicine, so to speak.

"I understand that you worry. I understand that you will ask questions, but when I say it's time to let something go, you will listen."

She felt the first slap of leather against her skin and bit back a wince. It was a gentle start with the cat of nine tails; the leather strips had knots at the ends but nothing sharp that she could feel. Yet. Sometimes it took time for the nuances of the toys to come through.

"You will answer 'yes, Sir.'"

"Yes, Sir."

Another lash across her backside had her breathing out long and deep. It was important to breath or she'd get lightheaded and not feel well. Breathing made her feel fine and enjoy the pleasure in the pain. If she didn't, it was just pain.

"Thirty lashes," he announced, the whip stronger on her butt.

"Yes, Sir."

"Count."

She realized the first had been warm-ups as he began. She counted out loud as each smack became progressively harder. David kept the same infuriatingly slow rhythm, and she had to hold her hips against the wall to keep from pulling away. It hurt, but the familiar pain sent her deeper into her pleasure. She felt herself slipping into subspace, where the pain was gone, replaced with pleasure. Only the rhythmic counting kept her from completely losing herself into the fog of her mind.

"Twenty-eight, Sir."

"Louder, Polly."

"Yes, Sir."

He brought the whip down hard on the bottom of her backside, nipping the tops of her thighs.

"Twenty-eight, Sir."

"Better."

"Twenty-nine, Sir."

She winced, the full sensation from the whip on her already warmed bottom more than she could focus through.

"Thirty, Sir."

She sagged against her restraints, the satin keeping them from biting her skin. But she wouldn't be able to give herself a break for too long before her wrists became sore. It was another difficult choice. To arch away, to arch toward. To beg for more. To beg him to stop. It was impossible to know which she wanted to do, and David took the decision away when he tapped both of her ankles to make her stand. She didn't know what was next, but she pushed to her feet and braced.

Cool, wet hands touched her bottom, and she leaned toward them. She didn't look because she wasn't supposed to, but she did let her cheek rest against the wall again, wishing the slight texture on the wall was smoother. He massaged her deeper than she thought he would and it hurt some, but the oil was softening and sweetly scented. The soothing was wonderful. Then he smacked the fleshiest part of her hard.

"Ouch."

"Tsk. Tsk." There was playful amusement in his tone.

"Thank you, Sir." She knew the skin-on-skin had made her sex drip. It always did. Nothing got her as close to orgasm, besides oral sex, like a hard smack to her ass.

"I have to put pulleys on these," he said, tugging the straps from her wrists. "You're too short to fuck standing like this. I want to take you hard against the wall so you're unable to move away, with your beautiful ass bright red from the whip and my hand. On your knees."

Polly followed his command without hesitation. The serviceable Berber beneath her knees was nowhere as nice as her blankets, but it suited the room and the punishment. She looked at the button of his jeans expectantly, but was patient as he undid the clasp.

"Turn."

She refused to pout, but she wanted her mouth on him. A lot. She loved taking him deep in her throat. She'd practiced many hours learning to deep throat a man, and David had a cock that would choke any throat so the time had been well spent. She also needed the love she felt when she made him feel good.

The oil he'd used to sooth her butt was moved deeper between her legs without him checking her. He could probably see how wet she was, she thought and tried to bite back a whimper when his fingers plunged deep with little warning. She was already hot and knew what she hoped he would give. Polly wanted him deep and hard, riding her with his hands tight on her breasts or in her hair, pulling her to each thrust.

He smacked the outside of her thigh as he helped her to her hands and knees and moved between her legs. She shifted her legs apart and welcomed him closer. She wanted him, and she didn't have to wait. David slid deep. Her neck arched back, inviting him to grab wherever he wanted, and he chose her hair first. She wished it was longer, but there was enough length for him to sink his fingers in and hold tight as he pulled her harder against him.

The bite of pain from her scalp was delicious, just like the slaps to her thigh. He was thick and felt too big, but the dueling sensations made it all pleasure. Was there an explanation for the science of sensation? Probably. Did she care? Not a bit.

He freed her hair and she whipped it back again, always offering anything he wanted. With his hands on her hips, he rode her long and loose, hard but with the easy rhythm of marking time instead of building strength. He was either trying to delay his own orgasm or work her to one before increasing intensity. Or was he still punishing her and would stop before she reached climax and make her start again? That one was mean. But she'd take it.

He laid his front against her back, his leg hair rubbed hard against her sore bottom, but she didn't mind because his hands wrapped around her breasts. Not too hard, but his fingers dug in enough to hold tight. His face was pressed close to the side of hers, and he kissed her cheek.

"Kiss me."

She'd never wanted to hear the words more and eagerly turned to him. Kissing meant she was forgiven. Mouth-on-mouth privileges were special and intimate and hers once more. His breath felt hot, like he'd been sweating as whipped her. It was a delicious idea that made her thrust her tongue farther for him. He was in charge—definitely in charge—but she could give him everything he asked for.

David broke the kiss and pushed her head to hang as he straightened and took her torso with him until she was nearly sitting though facing away. He had her breasts and used them to lift her up and down like a puppeteer, and she screamed as orgasm hit. He made no move to stop or reprimand, so she let her pleasure flow and flow while he hammered her down on his shaft. He launched deeper and deeper inside until he lodged in and filled her with the hot proof of his completion.

Her immediate thought was to turn and clean him with her mouth, but he held her still and she remembered they were working on a baby. That meant he wanted every drop of semen inside her so she clenched tight, wanting him to stay inside as long as possible. He groaned at the sensation, and she smiled. She loved when she could affect him and move him to drift a bit in control. She wanted him to be strong enough to leave go of that discipline occasionally.

"Lie down on your stomach," David commanded

She stretched out and relaxed against the floor, wishing for softness now that the sex had passed. Her day had been long and it was after eleven. Her bed was calling. If it wasn't on the agenda yet, well, she could always nap in the morning. She felt his hands on her backside again, this time with a warm cloth. She hadn't noticed the sink running, but apparently she'd missed it. Mark had installed his own half-bathroom during their last remodel. It came in handy not having to run upstairs to clean up, but a tub would have been nice. Maybe a hot tub or Jacuzzi eventually would be a welcome addition.

Lotion was poured on her butt, and the scent of lavender filled the room as he rubbed the cream into the welts. She hated the flaws he was face-to-face with, but couldn't do anything reasonable about them. David didn't mind or he wouldn't touch her. The cellulite wasn't so bad, but she had started wearing swimsuit covers when in public. Not in private though. Public made her remember the munch coming up. She was going to scene.

She'd seen scenes before and knew the women came in all shapes and sizes and no one questioned the preferences or their beauty. It felt nice to have that sort of freedom. She'd heard of intellectuals having naked parties where they discussed philosophy and politics without sexual tension. In a way the dungeon meetings were the same. What showed in the nakedness wasn't so important. It was how that nakedness was treated and used that mattered.

"My appointment is with the fertility specialist I saw concerning my sperm count. He wants to deliver the results of several of my tests in person. I don't know what that means, but I know they get more money if I go to an appointment than if they call. I'll let you know what happens."

"I would be happy to go with you, Sir."

"Thank you for the offer, but it's on Saturday and you have choir practice. I'll tell you about it when I finish. I won't lie, Polly. What I learn, you'll know. I've never had a bad checkup. Most likely, they're going to tell me I'm shooting blanks."

"I doubt it." She snorted. "I can practically feel your guys swimming for my egg."

He laughed and lightly patted her butt. She looked over her shoulder, the heavy play over, and found him inspecting her backside.

"Does it look okay? It hasn't taken a beating for almost a year."

"A year, huh?" he said, smoothing his hand over it again. The contact made her wince, but he didn't stop and she didn't complain. "That's a good girl. I have no doubt this was an isolated incident. You are usually an excellent listener and know when to stop and trust me. We'll work on it. You'll go up and dress in your softest pajama top and get some sleep now."

"I'll clean up, Sir?" she offered.

"No, to bed. Now." He slapped her butt, harder than a pat, and she quickly got moving. The heavy play had ebbed but they lived their lifestyle, not only during sex and that meant it was time to move her butt to bed before the next whip came out.

* * * *

Polly's bright red bottom greeted him when he entered the room. It was beautiful and his hand mark showed brightest. She was a wonderful sub, knew how to take her punishment and find pleasure in it. She made him feel ten feet tall in her ability to please him. It was a sign they were right for each other.

Her eyes were closed and her face relaxed, but she also smiled, telling him she'd enjoyed their time. He was going to buy stock in the lube brand she preferred because he'd never had to use so much. It was a common thing after having kids he'd learned from his research. He'd never been with a mom before and since he planned to have insane amounts of sex with Polly, he needed a well-stocked supply for her comfort.

David shifted his supplies and the electric razor buzzed. Polly opened her eyes, and he smiled when she gave a little wave with her hand.

"You need to turn all the way on your back so I can do this."

"Do what?" she asked sleepily, though she turned without hesitation.

"You said I'm in charge of waxing. I'm here to do pre-shave tonight, then we'll do waxing tomorrow night. Spread 'em."

"Um." She didn't hesitate to open her legs, but her relaxed face took on a nervous edge. "Have you done this before, Sir?"

"Would it matter?" He'd inspected her thoroughly. There wasn't much fuzz, but it was time to wax before too much came and the simple chore became more painful than necessary.

"Um, no, but I could offer help if you wanted."

He patted her mound, soft prickles meeting his hand. "I've done this, sweetheart. To myself and others."

"You've waxed yourself?"

"Not myself, but I do trim things down there." He winked and she giggled. He liked humor and laughter in their bed. It was a welcome guest just like passion, love and pain. "I'm not going to do much, just trim some of the longer stuff so it waxes better. No getting wet or coming on the shaver. It gunks up the razors. If you're a good girl for this I'll take care of you again."

"Yes, Sir."

He started at the top, buffing away the stray hairs below her belly button. Her little belly wasn't taut, the skin stretched from babies, but it was healthy. He didn't mind the differences in her and knew if they were lucky she would have more stretch marks by the time they retired. More babies for the abused tummy.

He kissed the mole on her left hip and kept moving lower, running the shaver in circular motions over her pelvis bone and finally the top of her mound. She was holding herself very still, the relaxation from earlier gone. Vibrations did that to a woman, and he knew she loved vibrators and toys.

She was keeping to his rules though. Nothing was wet when he worked the shaver over her lips though she did moan.

"Uh-uh," he said, tapping his fingers hard against the top of her mound. "No coming yet. Flip so I can do your ass."

She flipped and her cheeks were still red. He smacked the left one and grinned when she moaned again. She wasn't too close. He would be able to finish the shaving, then take her hard and long before they slept. It was only midnight.

Some women he'd groomed were unbelievably hairy. Polly wasn't so bad. Her body hair matched her fair hair and complexion. He took special care between her vagina and anus, removing every long hair he could find. That area always hurt the most for waxing, and he didn't want to leave more than necessary.

She was shaking when he finally turned the shaver off, and he knew if she lubricated naturally she'd be dripping she was so near to orgasm. He patted her butt again and her thighs fell farther open. Reaching in her nightstand he pulled out her lube and squeezed a dollop right into her waiting opening. She jerked at the cold and shivered.

He mounted her backside, loving to watch the sinew of her back and neck as he plunged deep inside her waiting vagina. She grabbed his cock with her inner muscles, tight as a fist from the kegels she did every day, and she started coming from the first thrust.

He grinned and let himself go, riding hard and fast until she got off again, and he finished quickly. They had to wake up at a reasonable time in the morning, but he wanted her to be nice and tired first.

"David?"

He opened his eyes, surprised to hear her talking when he was pretty sure he was done with most thought and discussion for the night.

"Yes?"

"Can I ask you a question?"

Her tone was hesitantly curious, and he made himself wake from his doze. Emotions ran high after punishments, and it was time for him to play the other side of the Dominant's role. It wasn't all bossing and ass smacking, it was nurturing the emotional side when necessary as well.

"Of course, baby."

"Mark chose the lifestyle because of his parents. When his sister died and they fought so much he wished one of them would take control and make the other one feel better. You've never told me what made you chose this life."

He pulled her closer, tucking her head on his shoulder. The room was warm, but he didn't care. They could kick off the blankets, but he wanted her close. The question had been coming and he didn't fault her for asking. It was well within her right to know, but he appreciated that she'd given him time. If he said he didn't want to discuss it, and Lord knew he didn't, he knew she wouldn't push, and that made the sharing easier.

"My parents were a nightmare too," he admitted. "The Angelins eventually got their shit together, but mine never did. Their weakness always bothered me. They had no ambition and no desire to make things better. The only thing they wanted was their next welfare check and case of beer. They wanted to drag me into it, too. Family tradition.

"I played sports instead, got good grades, worked afterschool jobs for my own money. They didn't understand. No one in the Lowe family had held a fulltime job or graduated high school in two generations, but I wasn't going to be a loser. They stole from me, put me down, and because they were my parents they had that right. I moved out when I was seventeen and never looked back."

"And because they took away the control, you now feel the need to control everything you can."

"Something like that. I've actually been to therapists over the years. They agree with you about that. I think it's more than overcompensating though. Even when I was little my mom would get pissed because I was always looking out for the little neighborhood kids, giving them my snacks and toys."

"You're such a good man."

"I'm just a man, sweetheart. A big, hairy man. If there is anything good in me, it's because I have you. Remember that."

"Yes, Sir."

"That's right, I am the 'Sir'. Now it's time to go to sleep."

CHAPTER 11

Polly wondered if Hannah would ever babysit for them again. In the car on the way to dinner, she bit back a laugh remembering the third degree David delivered to the sweet, young woman who'd babysat the girls for years. He'd thought he'd been subtle and sneaky, but she'd seen right through him and so did Hannah. Polly had spent hours with Hannah and knew her very well. The younger woman was home on break from college, and they were lucky to get her. Polly explained that all to her husband, but he'd still grilled Hannah.

She had taken it with her usual good nature, and Polly would add twenty bucks to their fee because of it. She would rather have David be overprotective than uninterested in the kids.

They weren't going to be gone all night, but Hannah would sleep with Hope and Faith. Mark had always asked her to take care of the children through the night and to keep them in their room unless there was an emergency. Polly knew Hannah assumed she got tipsy on their nights out.

Hannah always followed directions to the letter and had only called once in four years when Polly had forgotten to leave Faith's bottle in the refrigerator. She was self-sufficient and had earned Polly's trust over and over again.

David would learn. Besides their grandparents, Polly didn't trust anyone else for overnights, so having Hannah was freeing. Not having to worry was paramount, because there were other things to occupy her mind.

Munches were the BDSM community's way of getting together with each other and new members. It was a way to enjoy one another as friends, and Polly liked the meetings very much. They ate good food, laughed, and at the end of the evening, if people were agreeable, some went back to the Dorkov home. Not everyone went and not everyone was invited, but she and Mark had gone many times to observe and mingle.

Never to show.

Tonight she was in jeans and a new sweater. Pink again. David bought her a lot of pink. Faith and Hope loved it and often told her she looked pretty. She felt pretty. She'd always adored the feminine color. Mark had preferred the actual leather in the lifestyle and she didn't mind, so she'd always gone along with his preferences. He hadn't protested her sweats and yoga pants during the day, so she hadn't complained when he dressed her for outings. This time David had set out her clothes, and the new twists were divine.

Under her clothes she wore silk. David had presented her with her new scene clothes all made of pink leather. The real treat had been the linings. He'd ordered from a specialty shop that made washable leather gear and paid extra to have every inch lined with pink silk. He didn't want anything rough against her skin unless he was the one directly applying it, he'd told her with a grin. The tiny shorts and bustier had leash loops sewn in different places, the optional hook on her ass one he promised she would like.

The bustier had white fuzz on the breast cups, and it was unlike what anyone else wore at the club. No one liked the frills there, preferring chain metal and leather. She was sure to stand out as the indulged sub, but she didn't care. Polly was spoiled, but she was definitely David's sub. If he gave her the things it meant he wanted to see them on her, to hell with what others thought. She couldn't imagine anyone calling David fluffy and she knew he wasn't, he just had different tastes, tastes that pleased her well.

"What does the restaurant serve?"

"Lots of fish," she answered, turning away from the Green Bay highway she'd been watching pass. "Which I always thought was funny."

"Why's that?"

"Well, several of the Doms consider going down on their subs for oral sex to be an insult or mighty huge reward, yet…"

"They eat fish," he laughed.

"Mark almost got us kicked out of the club when Levi said something to that effect. Levi said only two things taste like fish and one is fish."

"What did Mark say?"

"He told him if he took better care of his sub's pussy then it wouldn't smell or taste like anything but woman, and nothing tasted better than a willing woman."

"Nice," David said with a grin. "I, of course, agree but some guys… I don't know what's wrong with them. There's no telling what will turn people's wheels. I can't believe Mark would have been booted for something like that."

"Well, Max also happens to think oral sex is only for the woman to give and didn't like anyone insinuating they didn't take good care of their subs. It was all manly and grunty for a while, but it passed. Oh, and most of the Doms didn't like Mark's no touching rule for me or that he let me decide if I was going to listen to another Dom while in the dungeon."

"Well, that's just too damn bad, because those rules stand. I know a few of the guys and they have no problem telling another sub to hit her knees. I don't care about their behavior, but we have a fidelity clause that will not be broken."

She smiled at the conviction in his voice. It made her feel safe. They might scene and watch others, but their bodies were for each other and that was a boundary she wasn't willing to cross. They pulled into the golf course parking lot, nothing fancy but it had a private room they reserved. There was also a bar none of them used during munches but she loved their kiddie cocktails. She and Jeremiah usually got one if they asked prettily enough.

David opened her door and tugged her into his arms before closing it behind her. It was their first outing alone as husband and wife. Only two weeks had passed since the wedding, five months since they'd been together, but she was learning the timing of things didn't always matter.

His hands were warm when he slipped them under her coat. They were always warm because even though he was adjusting from living in Arizona, he was warm-blooded. He reached around her slacks and tugged on her leash loop. He had a long, black leather leash for the party in his toy bag, and she couldn't wait until he hooked her on. Mark preferred to leash her collar, but she liked the back because it was sneakier. She couldn't always see how much leash she was on and that was thrilling.

"This is going to be fun." David kissed her and pulled her hat over her ears as he made the announcement. "Your word for leaving is *pineapple*. If you need us to leave, say it and we'll go, no questions asked until we're gone."

"Yes, Sir."

"They might have some ceremony for your collar. Max offered to host a big event, but I declined. The wedding mattered more between us than any BDSM party. After dinner, we're going to play. You'll be beautiful, and it will be a great experience for both of us. I want you to watch tonight and think of our goals for the New Year to talk about on the way home."

"Yes, Sir."

"Damn, I love when you say that. Come on sweetheart, let's munch."

* * * *

Jeremiah looked on at the table's laughing occupants and felt his growing desolation swell. This wouldn't be his home for much longer. He couldn't do what Linda wanted anymore, couldn't deny himself the life he needed. She was his everything, the only woman he'd ever loved. She'd looked at him when he was a skinny nobody and seen the man he would become. She'd made him the man he was but that man needed more. He wanted children. It was part of who he was. He didn't care if they adopted, but he did care that she was still against the idea even if she was trying to conceive.

He sat with the other subs. Melody looked in seventh heaven with her hair teased to extreme, makeup heavy, and her steel studded collar with Levi's name embossed on it proudly displayed. She'd cut Levi's meat and sat at his feet most of dinner, and he'd given her leave to sit with the subs for her meal. Linda had dismissed Jeremiah to the subs' area at the same time.

Polly sat the whole time beside her husband, though still beside the subs. She did his napkin and poured his water and all the other things yet sat beside him at his request. In place of a collar, she wore a pretty necklace. At times she would play with it, and more than once, David tugged it as well. They had a different sort of relationship, one Jeremiah was afraid he would have to settle for in the future if he had to leave Linda.

Polly did look happy and from what Linda said, she'd have her first scene in the dungeon later. It was a big step for her and Jeremiah was proud, but he couldn't be too happy for his friend when his life was falling apart.

Linda had cried gallons of tears the night before, because the hormone shots left her crazy. She wasn't the woman he loved because of the changes the medications were causing. She cried all the time. She slept and had hot and cold flashes. Discipline was light because she couldn't focus, and their relationship was suffering.

When he offered adoption so she could stop the damn meds, she screamed that she was woman enough to give him children. If she couldn't, then they wouldn't have them and he would accept it. It was the only edict Linda had ever given that he wasn't sure he could embrace.

"Polly." He whispered the word, not because he didn't have

permission to talk, but because subs were supposed to be very quiet at the table as not to interrupt the others.

She turned to him, her face nearly devoid of makeup in the same way he wished Linda would return to. She'd started adding layers of the stuff as she aged, trying to look younger, though he thought she was most beautiful first thing in the morning before the gunk was in place. Polly smiled and turned back to David, whispering in his ear a moment before the big blond man nodded slightly.

"Yes, Jeremiah? I only have a moment though, tonight is my Sir's."

"Of course. I just wanted to say congratulations on the marriage. We didn't make it to the reception, but I'm happy for you."

"Thank you."

She nodded and returned to resting her head on David's bicep when he patted it. She wasn't a slave like Jeremiah was but she was a good submissive. Her job was to make her Dom feel good and make him happy. David looked like a happy Dom. A look across the table at Linda made Jeremiah's heart sink. His Mistress didn't look pleased. She'd always been more of a smirker with a sarcastic bent, but now she looked genuinely unhappy and it broke him.

If he gave up the quest for children, she would be content again. She would smile and whip him and ride him with the toys she loved until he cried out for more. Or if he was really lucky, she'd whip him into submission until he was too tired and hurt to move. Those were the times he felt her love.

He couldn't ignore himself though, not this time. His heart longed for little ones in their lives. Polly had her girls and made their relationship work. Hell, her relationship with Mark had gotten better after their youngest was born. Jeremiah could see it, everyone could, and at sub meetings when he'd commented on it, Polly had agreed wholeheartedly. It made for adjustments and compromise, but more love was never bad.

Children offered the purest form of love, much like the Master and slave relationship. He wouldn't raise his kids like that, of course. He'd be a loving, generous father, just as Linda would be a wonderful mother. A more disciplined, loving mother he couldn't imagine. He wanted that experience with her. If he couldn't have it, he didn't know what he would do.

"I can't believe you didn't have a collar ceremony, Polly."

Melody's declaration got all the subs' attention. Polly whispered again to David, and he kissed her before nodding and returning to his conversation. She turned to the sub side and smiled. "I didn't want anything big. The wedding was more than enough pomp and circumstance for me."

"I know, but, a collar ceremony, it's so special," Melody insisted.

Jeremiah remembered his own. "I was nineteen at mine," he offered. "It was amazing. My Mistress gave me my promises and purpose that day."

"My husband did the same for me in our wedding vows," Polly said softly, and Jeremiah knew the wedding really was enough for her. They were Christian, really big into church and all that, so he figured they'd been acknowledged by the main Man so they were good.

"I'm having a DJ who's in the lifestyle, so the music won't suck like it normally does," Melody continued, and Jeremiah fought himself not to roll his eyes. She was such a glory whore. If she had a ceremony with Levi, Jeremiah had no doubt the Dom would show his true assholeness in no time at all. They seemed to get along, but everyone except Melody could see the guy had a complex. "We'll serve prime rib, and I found these little tiny whips for party favors. Oh, and one of those really awesome cakes from a fancy bakery, but I think we'll have them paint whips and chains on it instead of flowers and junk."

"How far away is this party?" Polly asked, and Jeremiah bit back a smirk.

"A few years, unfortunately," Melody replied, her sour expression not one of sorrow as he remembered feeling when Linda made him wait two years after meeting before presenting him with his formal collar. He still wore it on occasion, even though after fifteen years it was nearly worn through at spots. "My youngest graduates in two years, and my ex is worthless, so our son needs me until then. But after that, it's mommy's time. I don't know why you guys are all lusting for babies. I mean, Mary, you had a total power exchange. If I'd known about those before I had my kids, I'd have had a doctor rip out all that stuff."

The slave of the dungeon Master was naturally the most submissive of them all. The bitch. If Candice were in the room Mary would have been bowing and scraping, making them all look like hell. Since it was just them and they didn't threaten her place as "super sub," she sat at the table with the rest.

"There is nothing like the love of a child," Mary said softly, her accent exotic and seductive without trying to be either. "And a TPE doesn't negate one's ability to think and make decisions, Melody. It does simplify life to only one's Master, but once one stops counting their lifestyle in months they've lived it and simply lives it, they learn about themselves all they've ever needed to know. Understanding myself made me want my son. Felix taught me I didn't know love until he was born."

Jeremiah was shocked at such candor from the one who was above them all in how below she was. Mary had been a fountain of insightfulness during the past few months, first at their parties and now imparting her thoughts on parenthood. It was the way he felt and wanted to feel. He knew what love was, but knew to his core that it would be more with a family between them. Nearly ten years his senior, Linda would most likely die before him, but part of them and their love would live on forever in their prodigy.

"Well, you say that now." Melody snorted. "Just wait until you catch the little bastard in your bed with his slutty girlfriend."

Jeremiah thought about it. He didn't think he would mind. He'd still love his fictitious son or daughter, no matter what they did. If they got too big for their britches, he had no doubt his Mistress would be the sort of loving mother to put things back to rights.

CHAPTER 12

"David."

"In a moment."

Polly hated that answer but stayed quiet. They were at Max and Mary's house and like always, the thrill of the unknown and the darker side of her nature emerged. She loved the smells and sounds of the dungeon, as they called their full basement. It was finished with three bedrooms, a huge gathering area and two showers. It was perfect for the sort of entertaining the Dorkovs did.

The furniture was leather, and chains and harnesses hung from the ceiling. There was a courtesy toy wall, cleaners and towels on a nearby table. Refreshments were also offered, pretzels and clear soda the only thing they would have until the time was over. Most people ate lightly at the munches, especially subs. She'd only had a grilled cheese sandwich and Sprite, not wanting to lose the contents if something pushed her too far.

The medical scenes always made her nauseous, but Candice and Darren hadn't been at the munch so she hoped they had other plans for the night. She saw she wasn't so lucky when they entered. Candice was in complete slave garb, her leash attached to a Y chain from her nipples and clit. Her voluptuous hair was slicked in a sleek tail, and she was blindfolded. Darren looked thrilled with his prize. He always did when he and Candice were in full play mode.

Polly looked toward Mary who'd been posed with Max's foot on her neck and saw hatred flash in her eyes. She wished she knew the full story there, but Mary was discreet in all things, especially her relationship. Candice might tell, but Polly wasn't sure if she wanted to hear only one side. Impeccably well kept for her years, with her body looking much younger than its age, Mary was in better shape than Candice and looked fabulous in her scraps of black leather, but coming in the Y chain was a statement she was glad David hadn't felt the need to make.

"Yes, baby?"

David's question made her wince.

"Um." She'd forgotten what she was going to ask and it must have shown because David shook his head.

"On your knees."

She didn't bother to nod, only fell to the ground. It had the hard texture of Berber over cement, easily cleaned because it was often soaked with sweat and fluids before the night was through. It hurt her knees, but she didn't care. She had to focus or the night would be much harder than it needed to be. Focus was what she was working on and the focal point was David when he moved in front of her.

Mark had found no sexiness in performing. Being watched had made him shrink. David didn't find it to be a problem. She'd pondered what it would feel like to be one of the subs who gave their Doms head in the dungeon while they spoke and did other things. With David's zipper at eye level, she figured she was about to find out.

"Keep your mouth busy."

"Yes, Sir."

Could she take her husband's zipper down and put her mouth on him while others watched? Since she'd started in the lifestyle, she'd had to ask herself similar questions. Could she bow her head to her husband? Could she let him kiss her places other than her mouth? Could she really let him touch her anywhere he wanted?

She carefully pulled down the zipper on his jeans, slowly so the steel teeth wouldn't catch on anything. Beneath he wore black boxer briefs, but he was warm and semi-erect in her hand. Could she do it? His hand touched her hair, not gripping or demanding, just touching, and when she looked up, his expression was tender. He knew she was thinking and because he wasn't pushing her to her spot, she knew he was willing to give her time to make the decision. She knew her word if it was time to leave, and he would take her home if she used it.

The scent of his soap, warmed by his body heat, met her nose when she leaned in closer and took him in her mouth. Some watched; other subs were doing similar acts for their Dom, but David was the only one in her mind. Her husband, her Dom, her man had asked and she knew he would keep her safe as she complied.

Polly happily did all the moving, methodically sucking and licking his cock. He was thick and long, not uncomfortably so, but more than a single mouthful. Deep throat had been a previous goal, so she was well acquainted with the technique. Drawing David deep in her throat as she continued to suck tickled the back of her throat and inflamed her body. She loved orally pleasing her husband. It made her feel strong.

She sucked the tip hard before she released him, and his cocked jerked. It didn't show in any other part of his body, but the tiny movement was telling to her. She was affecting him, and that was what all subs wanted. They wanted to impress and please their Doms, and the heavy vein running along the bottom of David's cock pulsed erratically, showing his nearness to completion. If she kept going and sucked a little harder, she thought, taking him in her mouth once more and running her tongue along that vein, she would have his essence running down her throat.

Her leash tugged hard and she was pulled away from her prize. Her equilibrium off from balancing, she fell to her butt. Embarrassment burned her cheeks, but she didn't look to David or even attempt to move. Maybe he wanted her to fall. Some Doms liked to see their subs helpless. Some liked that little bit of violence and really he hadn't hurt her. She couldn't make herself think he would deliberately humiliate her, and she was right when he squatted beside her and braced her back.

"Okay?"

She nodded but didn't look at him until he took her chin with his finger and turned her face to him.

"Okay?" he demanded again.

"Yes, Sir. I lost my balance."

"I see that. Your ankle didn't turn again, did it?" He checked her legs and bare feet, paying special attention to the ankle she'd caught in the harness earlier in the week.

"No, Sir. I'm fine. I promise, Sir."

He offered his hand and tugged her to her feet. If she'd been wearing heels she might have had an issue, but he'd forbidden her from wearing shoes in the house. That left her with mixed feelings. She knew what was on the floor and…ick. But in heels she was more likely to hurt herself. Why weren't sneakers sexy?

Across the room, the bathroom door opened and Linda and Jeremiah exited. He was in his full slave mask, even more impressive than Candice, with a penis torture device. It was connected to a butt plug. Polly had seen it in action. If he began to get an erection the monster plug in his anus would be pulled. It wasn't one meant to cause pleasure, much too large to come out with simple tugs so it left him in a very uncomfortable spot. His penis was also encased in metal, though his balls were left hanging loose with weights attached to each.

David gave a low whistle at the sight and if she'd been in a position to comment, she'd have done the same. She'd have to add stretching to their contract of things she'd rather not pursue. Polly liked her labia right where they were.

"We will not be stretching," he said quietly in her ear. "Nothing on you needs to be elongated, as far as I'm concerned."

"Yes, Sir," she agreed and remembered what she'd meant to ask. "Sir?"

"Hm?"

"Will you come with me to the bathroom?"

"You have my permission to go by yourself," he told her. "No one is allowed to touch, and they know it."

"But." She hesitated a moment when annoyance flashed in his eyes but she had to ask. "Master Max has an open bathroom policy. Anyone can come watch unless their Dom is present and asks for privacy."

"I see. What's the problem really?"

She hated saying it, hated that he didn't just believe her and walk her to the bathroom like a nice boy, but it was part of the learning process. She had to be comfortable telling him things. She had to be clear and concise and make her feelings known so he could better understand her.

"Master Eddy, standing by the bathroom," she said very quietly, and David looked toward the innocent-looking older man. He wore a black leather vest and leather pants but no shirt, showing off his little pot belly. He wasn't very tall and really, he looked like a mechanic and was one. "He likes to follow female subs into the bathroom and squat right in front of them while they pee. If they leave enough room he puts his hand in for a shower."

"No way."

She watched Max nudge Mary, who then crawled to the bathroom. Polly had heard her ask to use the bathroom an hour earlier, and her Master was finally granting permission. Eddy lit right up and followed Mary inside, not bothering to shut the door, so everyone could see when he squatted like a catcher.

David turned her from the bathroom and stopped watching himself. Polly didn't judge. She really didn't. If playing with pee was Eddy's thing, then that was fine for him. It didn't mean she wanted to do it though, and she certainly didn't want him to play with hers. Some things she couldn't imagine being a group sport.

"I'll go with you to the bathroom."

"Thank you, Sir."

"Any other crazy fetishes in play here tonight that I should be aware of?" He held her leash snug so she remained tight to his side, and she was grateful. She had no desire to cuddle up to anyone else.

"Candice and Darren are into medical fetish. Linda and Jeremiah look like pain is the flavor tonight, so he might get pierced. The Dorkovs are swappers, and he might offer to give her to us. Eddy is into pee and often volunteers to be the second whip in scenes. Lulu and Lala are also medicals, and I saw they brought their catheter set."

He shuddered a little, and she was glad. She didn't love the medical fetishes. Some were interesting, but once needles and knives came out she was ready to run in the opposite direction. Would she try it if David wanted her to? She was glad she wouldn't be put in that position because of their contract. She hated to say no, but for needles and knives she would bold and italicize it.

With David beside her, the facilities were no longer a danger zone. The bathroom was small with a drain on the floor and open shower. It wasn't meant for privacy, and she accepted that. She could pee with others around, just didn't want them face-to-face with her business. David stood in the doorway, effectively discouraging any spectators from getting closer. Mark had closed the door for her and stood on the outside but she didn't mind David's way.

Air freshener was prevalent, the showers and toilets very popular places for those doing last minute touch-ups. She hadn't done any bowel cleansing, wasn't familiar with it because she'd never done much in the anal department beyond superficial penetration. More exploration was something David expressed interest in. She would have to talk to the other subs during their next meeting about preparation.

She cleaned herself well with the wet wipe and flushed, washing her hands as David looked on. There were peep holes and anyone could be watching from the other rooms, but it didn't bother her. It wasn't her first time in the rooms. The first time had been more difficult, but now it was old hat and part of the lifestyle she embraced and enjoyed. It was her body. It was David's body and in any situation he would keep her safe and protected. That allowed her to let her inhibitions go.

She dried her hands and returned to David who reattached her leash with Max watching in approval. She liked the other Master most days, she really did, but she couldn't understand his and Mary's relationship. It made her sad that fidelity couldn't be part of their world, yet she didn't push her values or beliefs on other people, even if watching Eddy with Mary made her a little ill.

"Your station is the first bedroom. Your equipment is inside whenever you are ready," Max said.

Polly knew the equipment. The tiny electrodes and violet wand were attached to battery packs. They'd tried it in small doses and would keep it in very small doses. David knew what he was doing, so she trusted him. Promoting understanding was his goal, and he'd guided her to several books and websites about using electricity. He'd even shown her on himself the sort of intense charge a person could endure and not be damaged.

"We'll go shortly. We'd like to watch a few scenes first, so Polly can warm up. Her first time, right?" David said and smiled at her indulgently.

Max laughed robustly. "I remember Mary's first scene. I had to mask and gag her to stop the tears. Her ass was red and bloody when we were done, but she's loved it ever since. She is still game for the electricity if Polly refuses."

"She won't," David said, and she wouldn't. She would scene because she wanted to, not because he was making her. Exhibition was fine with her as long as it was with her Dom. He would maintain their rules. That's what mattered.

"Good, good." Max clapped his hands. "Well, there's plenty to see tonight. Darren's got a scene started in the back bedroom. The lesbians also have something going on, and in the front Sam and Becca are starting with some anal."

"Good place to start," David decided and shortened her leash until she was beside him again. He put her hand in the crook of his elbow and nudged her face down. "Close them."

She closed her eyes and let him lead. It was new. David liked the element of surprise and she enjoyed it. She didn't know if they would see Candice, Becca, or the other bedroom when he allowed her to open her eyes. If he even did. She might only listen and imagine then tell him what she saw in her mind's eye. Her satin lined shorts grew warmer.

"Open."

She did and found they were still in the main room. In front of them hanging across the back of a sofa was Becca, her ass high in the air. It was a big one, round and a bit dimpled and bright red even in the dim light. Metal music was playing in the background but not loud enough to drown out the cries of pain and pleasure from the surrounding rooms or the conversation from other Doms in the room. It was party music, only the party games were much more…in depth than simply pinning the tail on anything.

Polly knew Becca and Sam. She was a nurse. He was a car salesman. They were weekend warriors, but always attended munches and were lots of fun to be around. When Polly miscarried she'd ended up in the same hospital where Becca worked and they'd become close. The other couple had been attending parties for over a year. They loved to show off, and it was like watching a progression because they were willing to learn and try new things. The ball in Sam's hand was an expression of that.

The last time she'd visited the dungeon with Mark, Becca and Sam had only begun anal play. They'd started with slim, candy cane style anal toys while Sam delivered some very impressive oral skills. Becca had hung from the ceiling at the time and over the months they'd progressed to bigger toys and more extreme play. Polly had missed a lot if they were on the glass ball.

It was bigger than a baseball, but not as big as a softball, and entirely smooth. The dark plug sticking out of Becca's cheeks was deceptive in size. One could never tell from the outside what exactly was on the inside, but Polly couldn't imagine it being small.

In shiny leather pants and an open white shirt, Sam walked around Becca from where he'd been talking to her on the other side of the couch. Polly loved how they always seemed so in tune with each other. Sam asked the questions others in longer relationships assumed, and Polly respected him even if the guys scoffed a bit because he couldn't read Becca as well as the more experienced Doms could even from a distance. He didn't want to hurt her, and to err on that side made him a better man as far as Polly was concerned.

David tugged her leash down and she hit her knees again, the angle giving her a better view of the show. He placed his hand on her head and when he held it tight so she couldn't look away her curiosity exploded.

"We've been practicing for months now," Sam announced as he smeared lube all over the glass ball. It was still clear and oddly beautiful as it glowed in his hand. "For this. Becca is ready and thanks everyone for their help in getting us to this point."

Some of the Doms and Masters clapped. No matter the goal, whether small or extreme, there was pride in the small accomplishments in sexual things because to do them took more than physical desire. There were emotional and time issues to deal with beyond the physical components. When a goal was met it was a big deal. David clapped lightly too.

Polly watched in fascination as Sam smacked Becca's ass hard on both cheeks, making her jerk a little before he slowly pulled out a large-gauge butt plug. Polly had seen bigger on the web and in the catalogues, but the toy was narrowed toward the front and pop-can-size at its widest part. No small feat.

Then he showed the globe again. Excitement filled Polly as Sam opened Becca's legs, exposing her very pink vaginal lips and red-rimmed ass. It was slightly agape but returning to normal. The human body was amazing. Then Sam put the ball to Becca's pucker.

Polly felt her eyes widen along with Becca's anus. The clear globe turned red in reflection of the tissues as it was slowly pushed inside. Becca whimpered but didn't move as Sam continued his slow and steady process. Fascinated and incredibly turned on, Polly moaned.

David tapped her head lightly to remind her to be quiet, and she bit her lip as the ball went completely inside, Becca's sphincter closing nearly all the way behind it.

Becca did whimper and groan then. Gasps and moans came from the other side of the couch and she was glad she couldn't see Becca's face. There was a fair amount of discomfort in her moan but there was also pleasure linked to the intensity of the moment. Polly wanted a lot to be in Becca's position. David had asked her to find a goal and she'd just seen it.

Logic returned as the ball stayed inside Becca. How did it come out? There was a reason anal toys had handles and flares; to keep from getting stuck. Becca's moans got louder, and Sam smacked the fleshy parts of her thighs hard. Polly watched in fascination as pressure began to press out Becca's anus and the red ball emerged. It looked like it might get stuck for a moment then like a finger in the side of a person's cheek, it made a pop sound and flopped into Sam's waiting hand.

David's hand remained on Polly's head, but she wanted to look up and see his reaction. It was probably why he didn't want her to move. He wanted her to decide what she wanted, not do something merely because he enjoyed it.

Sam thrust his fingers into Becca's pussy, and she jerked back into them. He had three and four fingers in her, dripping wet with her juices that seemed to pour and pour. She climaxed around them, and Sam was grinning in pleasure as he licked his fingers. Some of the Doms groaned good-naturedly but like Mark, Sam was a pussy man who held no qualms about enjoying his woman's flavor.

He lubed the ball again and began the process once more, Becca's hungry ass accepting it much easier though she still cried out. He fingered her with the ball inside her and she came again, thrashing wildly against his fingers. The natural and artificial lubes were combining to make her ass and thighs glow. Sam slapped her again, her cue to expel, and the process continued.

She was forcing it out. Polly was amazed at the work and effort they'd had to do to make the scene work. It must have taken months and she wanted to try it so badly. Becca started to gasp and cry out more, and Sam faltered. He smacked her ass again but while the command was there, nothing happened except Becca crying harder.

"Becca, out."

"I…can't." Her gasp from the other side of the couch was desperate, like she was trying to stay calm but beginning to panic.

"Yes, you can. Now do it."

Polly watched with growing concern as another few minutes passed with no ball. Some of the Doms offered advice and position changes which they did. After they'd turned and shifted, Becca was no longer facing away and Polly could see Becca's face was pale under the red-cheeked exertion. When she went back over the couch for leverage, she looked scared and embarrassed. Polly didn't blame her. If things didn't go well she'd have to take some major laxatives to help expel or go to the emergency room for extraction. Not a fun prospect.

"They're doing it wrong," she heard David mutter from above her.

"Sir?" she asked.

"It's nearly out. If he did the massage it would work." He looked resigned about the fact. "Those balls don't stay stuck. It'll come out with laxatives if she doesn't get it tonight. If we try that, I know how to work it so it never sticks."

"Can you help them?" she asked, Becca's scream of discomfort and pain breaking her heart.

David looked at her and let her head up so she could see him. His expression was not a happy one. "You're asking me to touch another woman."

She hadn't realized it would involve more than instruction and hesitated for a moment until Becca screamed again. It was the pitiful kind that emerged when pain was taking over. The ball was nearly out, but before it breached it submerged and the play that looked so fun earlier, had an ugly edge.

"She's my friend," she whispered more to herself than him. "A few years ago she stayed past her shift at the hospital after I miscarried. She sat with me because Mark was at home with the girls until my parents got to the house. I don't want her in pain."

"I'm not pleased." He shoved her head down with more force than usual and it hurt her feelings, but not physically. She kept her gaze down because whatever he had to do, she didn't want to see. If he asked her to do the same one day, help another person sexually because of pain, she didn't know if she could do it. Especially in front of the group, David going to another woman, even to provide help, could open speculation she didn't want. She hated the idea of his hands on another woman, but she couldn't regret her request. Not for Becca who'd held her hand all night.

"Polly asked," she heard David state. "I'm monogamous, but

you're doing this wrong and your wife will be on laxatives for a week to pass it if you keep this up. Do you want my help or not?"

David didn't sound very helpful or welcoming, and Polly sagged lower to the ground. Her leash was beside her, no Dom to hold it so she prostrated herself on the floor in her lowest position. She'd earned the abandoned state by asking him to touch another woman.

"We're monogamous too, but I don't want her hurt. This is the first time this has happened. What should I do?"

Polly didn't look up but the room did get more quiet, the heavy bass of the metal music replacing the moans and advice from the peanut gallery. Becca groaned again, some pleasure but mostly fatigue and pain and finally the pop came again. It had only taken seconds for David to make the situation okay. Clapping came and she heard Becca sighing her thanks and Sam as well.

Still, Polly didn't move or look up. Shame coursed through her, warring with relief for her friend. If she was in pain and Sam could fix it, she hoped Becca would do the same. In fact, she had no doubt they'd do the same.

David stood beside her again. She recognized his shoes, but he let her leash lie. Not a good sign. It was better to be held and led. To be untied was to be alone and unguided in a setting that required the lead.

She wondered how badly she'd damaged their relationship. In reverse she'd have been devastated and didn't know how long it would take to heal. So she stayed down and hoped he would pick up her leash and forgive her. If that meant they didn't scene, it was fine. If it meant he skipped the electric and whipped her in front of everyone, it was acceptable. Whatever it took for him to forgive her, she would do.

Finally, he leaned down and took the leash. He didn't tug it or otherwise direct her but he had it in hand and the relief she felt brought tears to her eyes. She didn't bother to hide her tears or her sobs. Her whole body shook with them, and she wasn't ashamed. She didn't deserve such immediate forgiveness, yet he'd given it without question.

"We're going to our room now."

He didn't pull on the leash, so she didn't stand. She crawled on her hands and knees, because she felt like it was the best thing to do. When Polly peeked up she saw Candice watching them and the speculation in her expression infuriated Polly, but the whole situation was her own fault. She'd find a way to remedy the slight she'd given David and do something to make sure the other women knew he was only hers.

David tugged her up when they reached a bed. They were elevated, made for males or tall females to stand beside and do what they wished. She saw his equipment laid out and took a deep breath when he physically lifted her to the middle of the mattress and turned her on her back so she faced him. He leaned down face-to-face and she couldn't see anything but him.

"I'm gravely disappointed. You'll be punished here and we'll have a very long talk tonight about what you are not allowed to share."

"Yes, Sir."

"You won't scream or make any noise with the electric or whips. Nothing, or it will be doubled. Do you understand?"

She nodded and bit her lip.

"I'm pissed, but I would never hurt you. If it's too much you'll say your word."

She nodded again and wished he would kiss her. Before their practices he'd kissed her hard first as a reminder of the love in the correction and practice. He didn't this time and it was more devastating than all the blows in the world. He passed up the blindfold she'd helped him pack and moved right to the cuffs. One on each wrist to the bed corners and one to each ankle, spreading her wide.

He removed her shorts with the side snaps so she was naked on bottom and left the shoulder straps on her bra but freed her breasts. The room around them was packed, eyes surrounding her. Shame filled her, though the excitement was too prevalent to deny. The mix of love and hate for the situation tangled together with her love for her husband and made it okay.

"The currents used here are the only ones you want to use." David began, systematically going through the currents and watts and where to buy the proper equipment. He listed the dangers and looked at a few of the men who sported scars over their hearts in particular. Electrical current was not for those with circulation or heart issues, he advised. She'd gone to the doctor for a full physical before they'd been intimate for that very reason.

First he started on himself like he always did, carefully testing the current before he put it on her.

"If you wouldn't shock your arm with it," he warned, "don't put it near your partner's fun parts. Same with wax and heat."

David put the first node on her toe, and she felt a light tingle. It was an amazing feeling she loved and it was relaxing so far away from any stimulating parts.

"Take this time to discuss any questions you might have about electrodes," he said and pulled out a whip from his black toy bag. It was multi-tailed and leather with small knots at each tiny end. He reached and unfastened the catch mechanism on the ankle cuffs and physically lifted her to her stomach. The move crossed her hands and restricted her movement more. Without a word he began whipping her butt, both cheeks.

She bit back the initial cry of distress. It wasn't bad, just surprising. She couldn't cry out. He didn't demand she count, but she did in her head, losing track at number twenty-three. With every stroke, her backside heated and pain exploded. There was no doubt she would not feel great in the morning. She felt herself slipping into subspace, her happy place where the pain was pleasure and it was only them. She was the center of his universe, and he was everything to her.

The whip stopped and she eased back on her bottom lip, wishing she had a ball gag. Her mouth would be sore in the morning. The comfort of her mind was ebbing and her ass burned like fire, but it was worth it. He would forgive her and they would move on.

"Have to be careful with wetness." David's voice was practical and unaffected by the lashings. She felt the electrical probe from the violet wand slip between her thighs and the jolt made her jump but she didn't speak. It wasn't painful. It tickled and warmed, but it didn't hurt. Enough power would be painful but he was keeping it reasonable. That calmed her. If he'd let himself be led by emotions, he could have bumped the amps but chose not to.

"It's like a vibrator, only from the inside out. The sensations are deceptively building. You don't need more amps necessarily. Sometimes all it takes is more time." She felt the truth in his words as the intensity grew with each passing minute. The toy didn't move but it felt progressively deeper inside her, and the pain-pleasure mix came again. It wouldn't take much to send her over the edge, which was why she clenched hard to stop the feelings if she could. No climaxes.

He smacked his hand across her butt. Immediately, she flipped to her back, her arms and legs relaxing from the previous tension. The relaxation was dangerous, though. If she relaxed enough, she wouldn't be able to fight the waves that wanted to break in her system. With all the eyes on her, she didn't want to embarrass David by not being able to control herself.

"Max tells me the group doesn't usually use electricity, but if any do they're required to keep all currents beneath the waist. That's smart if you have a heart issue. My bottom does not."

His bottom. The title struck her worse than if he'd hit her. It was something they called each other, tops and bottoms, subs and Doms but she'd never been only a bottom or only a sub. She'd always been a wife and partner. Something must have shown in her face because when he looked up from wrapping a node around her nipple, he paused and gave her breast a tender stroke. She met his eyes and while he still didn't look happy, he gave her a reassuring smile.

"The nipples are very sensitive. If your partner is worried about cancer and damage, which you both should be, electricity is a smart thing to try. It stimulates deeply, and within the safe range it will not affect the heart. Before you try a voltage on your partner, try it on yourself."

"I don't whip myself on the ass, why would I try that? If it's safe, it's safe," one of the men in the crowd said, to a few snickers.

"And if your bottom accepts, then it's fine. But this is something you want to check your contract for. Electric isn't something most of you will have addressed. Talk about it, learn about it before you use it. You can cause burns, and for some it is genuinely uncomfortable and offers no pleasure. Pulses can be very engaging though, right baby?"

"Yes, Sir." Polly couldn't stop herself from arching off the bed when he began the pulses. They were like fire on her sensitive nipples. The current didn't burn, but they did move the whole way through her. Tactile pressure from prickly toys they used sometimes were only skin deep. Pressure trickled superficially and she felt the sensation move throughout her breasts, sensitizing and overwhelming them.

She'd come in the past with only breast stimulation and bit her lip because it was about to happen again. He switched to long bursts of current, and it helped slow her down. Sometimes the small changes in sensation made her last longer, but this time it made the situation more volatile. She squeezed her eyes shut and fought her traitorous body. She couldn't come yet. Not yet.

"Polly. Now."

At his command she arched high and screamed, her orgasm matching the bursts he continued to pour through her. Every time the current began, another orgasm flew through her. They were infuriatingly small, no vaginal stimulation to give the climaxes depth but with one after another they were exhausting. Sweat poured from her temples as the minutes continued to pass. David stood to her left and watched her carefully but made no move to stop.

Around the bed, people moved closer to witness the new action. Fascination filled their faces but she didn't care, not when the pulses wouldn't stop.

"That's pretty fucking amazing."

She cried out again as the next beat lasted longer, David tapping his controller in quick succession so she too pulsed up and down. Her whole body jerked beyond her control.

"It is," David agreed and set aside the controller, the current finally over. "It is also very intense and doesn't tire. I could keep her in that thrall for hours. It wouldn't be pleasant in the hours following. Remember, it makes her muscles contract, not just in her breasts, but also in her back and legs, you saw the arch. It's impressive, but I don't do more to my wife than Tylenol and a warm bath can comfort. Again, check your contracts and talk to your subs."

"For a fucking fluff, he knows some cool tricks."

Polly heard one of the men mutter the words on his way out, but if David was bothered it didn't show as he slowly took the curled wires from around her nipples. The stroke was back, a gentle comfort to her breast, and he kissed it too. The punishment was over, and she was so relieved she began to cry again.

Apologies tumbled from her lips as he began rubbing her body with a soft towel. Max and Mary's dungeon towels were more utilitarian, so she knew he'd brought some from home. The room was still full of onlookers, though not as many. She'd often thought the aftercare was as interesting as the scene itself. It showed the intensity of the experience between the Dom and sub.

A Dom who beat their partner's ass red and then fucked them until they screamed was interesting. The one who lay beside his or her partner afterward and then rubbed them down with lotion was something else.

David finally freed her hands and legs, leaving her bustier and boy shorts to lie on the bed, tucking her arms inside a sweatshirt instead. The superficial orgasms continued to rock her body despite the scene's finish, and she couldn't make herself stop shaking.

CHAPTER 13

"Easy, baby."

"I'm sorry, Sir. I'm sorry, David. I'm sorry."

He continued to dress her as she tried to calm down. Though the current had stopped she was still deep into her thrall and orgasms. She was inspiring. Polly ran right into the currents with no problem, no fear and even though she'd made him do something he didn't want to do and wouldn't again, she'd faced what he'd given her and done him proud. It went a long way in soothing his nerves and the betrayal he felt. They still had things to discus, and a lot to talk about what she'd asked of him, but at least now he knew she understood the severity of what she'd asked.

"David. Can she have some water now?"

The man he'd helped earlier offered a water bottle. His partner, comfortable in surgical scrubs, stood beside him with towels. David didn't like that he'd had to touch her. His vows said he didn't have to lay a hand on other women ever again. He didn't want to, but for a moment he'd touched her very intimately. He accepted the water and a towel for under Polly's neck. She wasn't responding right yet, still locked in orgasm, but it would fade and exhaustion would set in. He hoped to be on the road home before that happened.

"Thanks for earlier."

"What's your name?" David demanded, holding Polly's head steady as she sipped and tried to stop her sobs and shakes.

"Sam Mueller. This is my wife, Becca. Thank you. Really. I know it wasn't what either of you wanted, Polly and Mark were always very private and monogamous and—"

"We are too," he said harshly. "I didn't want to be anywhere near your wife."

"And I don't want you there," Sam said. "But thank you for doing it. She would have been in a lot of pain otherwise. I wouldn't want Polly to be in pain either."

"You wouldn't need to touch her because I know what the hell I'm doing."

"I— What the fuck? We did it right. We followed the books and did what Master Max showed us. We didn't rush, we were well lubed, and she wasn't tired. It should have worked. I'd never even seen the hand thing you did until you did it." He was getting angry, but David didn't care. The more time David spent in Max's dungeon, the more irritated he became.

"The hand thing should have been the first thing you learned. That stroke is basic, and just because Mighty Max didn't know it doesn't mean shit. Do your fucking research next time so you don't hurt your wife or anyone else. Polly, stop crying. Now."

She immediately bit her lip and shoved her face into his side. Damn, he loved her. She was everything to him and even if the night hadn't gone entirely well, some parts had. When she pressed her ear to his chest, he covered her other with his hand, pulling her as close as they could be.

"You're okay, sweetheart. We'll go home now."

"I'm sorry, Sir. Please forgive me."

"Of course, baby. I'm going to put on your shoes now, then we're going home for a long bath."

"The showers are hot," Becca said softly, drawing Sam away so they had more room. "I'm tired, Master."

"Okay, love," Sam said, and David grudgingly admitted he liked to hear the endearment. At least the guy loved his wife. "Thanks again. It wasn't the best way to meet, but I hope we can work things out eventually. Becca would like your wife to call her when she's able."

David only nodded as he continued to dress Polly. Her legs were wrapped around his waist and she didn't want to free him. He carefully pried her away for a moment to get her shoes in place. Some Doms found the clinging annoying but he knew done right, dominant situations brought out intense emotions. He wasn't going to slam her away, not after her first discipline scene in front of others.

When she was finally dressed, David lifted her in his arms. His toy bag was together and after disconnecting the batteries and nodes he tossed them in with the whip he'd used. Her leather was also tossed in to be washed later. The disinfectant in the room was a nice touch, but he liked his own at home since it was easier on the materials. He also wanted her away from the scene so she could relax and sleep soon.

"Hell of a show, David. Hell of a show."

He looked up and found Max at the door, blocking his exit. With Polly and his bag in his arms he couldn't exactly push around him and he wanted to. The dungeon Master had laughed when Becca cried out in pain the last time. David hated guys who laughed in the face of real pain.

"Thanks. I'm going to take her home now," he said, adjusting the bag before pressing Polly's face, still covered with fresh tears, to his shoulder.

"I will trade you any time. Mary is a hell of a slave. I want her trained in the electrodes. I saw you watching Sam and Becca. I could train yours with the ball for you. I know you guys do the monogamous nonsense, but think about it."

Polly shivered in his arms and made a sound of distress but nothing more. It could have been from her still coming down, but he thought it was from Max's words.

"I'll think about it. Thanks."

"All right then," Max said and stepped aside, the atmosphere even darker and dirtier than when they'd entered the bedroom. The sound of leather on flesh rang loudly as several Masters punished Jeremiah in a corner. Polly had seen enough for one night.

Max walked them to the basement stairs. "We'll see you for the next munch and play. I'll call you."

David nodded and took the stairs without looking back. There was no one he wanted to talk to, no other scene he wanted to see or be a part of. Max's house at the top of the stairs was dark, but they didn't have to go through much of it to exit the garage door. Other than the cars, the house looked empty, no lights above ground were on. David wondered if the neighbors knew what they were doing. The neighborhood was decent, not as nice as his and Polly's home, but still respectable. Max did well enough for himself and kept a clean house, or demanded one.

"David?"

He swore under his breath at the call. He didn't recognize the voice and wanted to get Polly home. He settled her in the car and turned back toward the house. A woman he'd seen inside earlier hurried toward him. At least she'd put a trench coat on in deference to the neighbors who could be watching.

"Can I help you?" he asked.

She smiled. "You really don't remember me, do you?"

David wasn't in the mood to play any games, and it must have showed on his face because she lost her playfulness.

"You don't. That's okay. I'm Candice Charmain. I was a sub in the group you and Mark Angelin were part of when we were all much younger," she said and held out her hand. "Polly mentioned your name, and I was glad I could give a good review. I hope not much has changed in fifteen years."

"A lot has changed," he said, shaking her hand, but not remembering her for the life of him. "But not the important things. Thanks for reassuring her."

"Yeah, my pleasure. She's a really nice woman, and tonight was amazing," Candice continued. "Really amazing. I'm sure you've had all sorts of swapping offers, and I'm certain my Dom, Darren, will try to one day, but I know you won't. I'm glad you two have the kind of relationship she had with Mark. I hope you are very happy."

"Are you happy?" he asked. The words trickled out of his mouth because though he didn't recognize her personally, he did recognize her sincerity. Polly needed friends in the community, and it was part of his responsibility not to alienate the ones she already had.

Candice smiled softly, much softer than he'd have thought possible with her face done in such harsh makeup. "I'm very content here. At least for the time being. Thanks for inquiring."

"David?"

She smiled again when she heard Polly's voice. "I'll let you get home, David. Please feel free to call if you need anything. I know what it's like to be new in this town, and I'd be happy to help in any way I can."

"Thanks." David watched Candice walk away.

There were dozens of 'Candices' in his past, women he didn't remember because they hadn't touched him deep enough. They'd offered fun times, demanded them back and he'd done his part. He knew he should feel bad for not remembering her, but even in the days before Polly, no woman had ever held his attention. Polly was his first and only love. He'd loved her even before he knew her.

He got in his side of the car and pulled away from the curb. Thinking of Candice brought the night's events back into focus. He finally had the woman he loved and would love for the rest of their lives, and she'd betrayed their vows and contract with her demands.

"You asked me to touch another woman tonight."

Polly was belted in with the seat, tilted back for her comfort. He had the heat turned on high and had thrown his jacket over her when she continued to shake. The drive home was mostly highway but would take at least twenty minutes. The timing didn't bother him because he knew it would take at least that long to talk. It was better to do it away from the house. Nothing in their discussion could be explained away if

Hannah were to overhear.

"The wedding vows work both ways. I don't ask you to break them, and you don't ask that of me. Now, tell me why it was so damn important I help her. If a man was in sexual pain I would never, ever ask you to assist him. I can't think of a single reason I'd put you in that place. Why did you put it to me?"

"Last time…"

Her voice was quiet, her throat rough from screaming, so he handed her a bottle of water from his bag. She took it and drank deeply, coughing twice before settling back against the seat.

"The last time I miscarried we couldn't find a babysitter. Our church people had no one. Hannah and her parents were on vacation. Max and Mary were visiting her mother. There was no one to stay with the girls, so Mark had to stay home while I was at the hospital. Becca worked a twelve-hour shift in the ER and saw me come in. She stayed with me all night and held my hand when I had my D and C."

"D and C?" He wasn't familiar with the term, but the woman's compassion during a hard time explained a lot. He was grateful for Becca. Was he thankful enough to ever want to put his hand on her anus again? No.

"Um, it's a scraping thing. Part of the baby was stuck, so the doctor had to scrape it out. Mark had to stay home because Hope had a fever and my parents were still two hours away, and I was getting sick so the doctors wouldn't put it off. Becca stayed with me."

"Fuck. Of course she's a fucking saint."

"I'm sorry, Sir. I hate that I asked. I don't want your hands on anyone but me. I knew what I was asking but I couldn't... She's such a sweet woman, and Sam is great too. He brought breakfast and clothes, and they stayed until Mark got there."

David carefully thought of his next words. These were important people to her and he didn't want to trivialize a relationship that obviously meant a lot to her, but he had limits and they were ones he wasn't going to stretch again. "I'm glad they're your friends. But they're on their own if something like that happens again."

"I agree. I'm so sorry. I shouldn't have asked, and it will never happen again," she swore, tears clouding her voice again. "I'm sorry."

"Enough. It's done now and as long as we agree it won't happen again, I'm content with your punishment and apology." He believed her, but it was part of his job to make sure she never asked him to touch another woman. He was her property, just as she was his. He needed her to not want other women in their life.

"I already hate that I asked. I don't share you. I love you. This is why I need someone like you. You won't let me share."

She took the words out of his brain. He needed her to see it was her nature to give everything she had, which was why he stayed close and corrected when she went too far. Being a servant was a wonderful thing. Meekness and humility were gifts, but there had to be a line. When a person couldn't make that line they either got stepped on beyond belief or found someone to draw it for them.

"I won't let you share," he agreed. "I'm glad you understand. You learn quickly. That pleases me. You'll learn my limits. Tonight just happened to touch several of them at the same time. Eddy the pee player, Sam the ass charmer, and last but not least, Max the prick. It was like a concert that went downhill after the first act."

Polly giggled, and he was glad the seriousness had passed some. He didn't want the punishment to last. For him, once it was done, it was done. If she needed a reminder another time he would change the punishment to fit, but with first offenses it wasn't worth the effort to hold anger or disappointment, not in the woman he loved and wanted to do so much for.

"We didn't see much, but was there anything you want to try?"

The giggles stopped, and at the next stoplight he looked over to her because she was still quiet. He wouldn't be surprised if nothing lit any fires. The ones who'd done more public play had been into the medical side for the night other than Sam and Becca's catastrophe. According to her essay section of the contract, Polly didn't like speculums the one time a year she had to endure them for pap smears, so he didn't anticipate a request for that style of play. He had books though. He'd have her do some studying so he could make some goals.

"I liked the ball."

The light turned green but with the street deserted he looked to her.

"Pardon me?"

"The ball. I mean other than it getting stuck, it was fascinating and beautiful."

His girl, he should have known she would be perfect for him in all ways. He loved ass play in any form, but the more extreme toys were incredibly erotic. Teaching and training her would be pleasure in its purest form.

"And obviously you know what you're doing with it if you were able to help Becca. I wouldn't want anyone who didn't know to have that much say over my body."

"That's a very good philosophy. You don't want some guy who doesn't know the ins and outs to try this sort of thing. It's great to learn together in some situations, and you learn together anyway because every body is different, but this will be no novice trick. Are you ready for hours and days, maybe months of hard work? This will invade your everyday life. I'll order the proper stretchers for you, and you'll have to practice every night, even alone. I'll supervise, of course."

She snorted, and he figured he might have sounded a little smug or excited in his willingness to observe. But he loved to watch. A woman with toys pleasuring herself was a marvelous thing, and it was part of what he wanted for her. He wanted her to take her pleasure in life.

"I want you to talk about it at your next sub meeting. Next week, right?"

"Yes. Jeremiah, Mary, Candice and Melody will be over for sure."

"Invite Becca if you want."

"She won't come. They're weekend warriors, not lifestyle. The whole of it makes her very uncomfortable."

"Then invite her for coffee sometime so you two can talk about it. I want your eyes wide open along with the rest of you. The more comfortable you are with the process, the quicker you'll relax enough to do it. This is going to be fun."

Chapter 14

"So tell me all about David."

Polly smiled at Becca. She'd missed having her friend around. When Mark was sick, she'd cut out any extra people in her life to focus on family and didn't regret it, but had missed her friends. Not that she and Becca were terribly close, but the things that brought them together were some of the most important in Polly's life so she was an important friend.

"He's been in Arizona for the past few years, but before that he was close friends with Mark. When he was sick, Mark called and asked him to come help us," Polly explained.

"And one thing led to another," Becca inferred, giving a coffee cup salute. "Well, he's wonderful in my book. Thanks again for having him help. Sam was mortified, but we're always up for learning new things."

"Yep, gotta learn," Polly agreed, though the fact that David had touched another woman still made her a little sick. And the look from Candice still had to be addressed woman-to-woman. Unless some theoretical woman of the future was in a life-or-death situation and David was the only help available, Polly couldn't imagine ever asking him to do such a thing again.

They caught up on everything, Polly sharing details about their wedding again. Becca told her all about their vacation to New Orleans and a few horror stories from the hospital she worked in. If she had a choice, Polly didn't think she would ever be admitted into another hospital. Becca's insider information always left her feeling queasy and hesitant even for the next appointment at the clinic.

"So, I'm heading to Milwaukee all by my lonesome next month. My favorite author is having a book signing, and I have my whole collection ready for her autograph." Becca grinned. "I thought you might like to come. I know you like her books and after the signing we could have a night on the town. We can make it a girls' weekend, spa and all that good stuff."

It sounded amazing, and she immediately started thinking of their schedule in February. Nothing stood out.

"That would be so much fun. Let me ask David tonight, and I'll let you know."

"Really? You have to ask, like for permission?"

"You know how the lifestyle works, Becca," Polly said, confused at the sudden contempt in her friend's voice.

"But I thought Mark was the one who pushed you into the actual everyday stuff," she replied. "I can't imagine why you would go into another relationship with that sort of controlling man again. You're a smart woman, make your own money and raise your kids. How can you tolerate saying you need permission to do anything?"

Polly tried for patience, but she hadn't expected to be attacked about her lifestyle by Becca of all people. It hurt having someone who she'd thought held mutual respect jump down her throat and insult her. Strangers had done it when they found out in a roundabout way about the choices she made, but she thought Becca understood better.

"Okay, maybe that sounded bitchier than I intended," Becca said before Polly could answer. "And I'm sorry, I didn't mean to sound horrible. It's just, I really don't understand, Polly. The sex and kink part, yes, but living this way with your neck under some man's foot and under his whims, it boggles my mind."

"Thanks for apologizing." She took a moment to think of the right words. "Okay, let me say this first. David and I are adults. We pay our bills, our children are clean, loved and very well-adjusted and we are a consenting couple. There is only one being in this world I need to justify my actions to and that's God. But I will tell you this, I love my husband. I love the life I choose to live and even though we keep our life private, it's not something I'm ashamed of."

"But, how? Tell me something so I can understand. Anything."

Polly thought. In David's questionnaire there had been detailed questions about the reasons behind her desires. They were deeply personal, and she didn't think they would help Becca. She could give a hundred reasons and still Becca and other women would think she was a weak-willed, oppressed female who needed to find a backbone. It wasn't her job to change the minds of other women; her job was to live her life in a way that fulfilled her needs.

"Do you know that feeling when you're in leather and your husband looks at you with such…hard love, I guess you could call it? Not the hearts-and-flowers kind, but the kind that's laced with possession and fire that makes your whole body tingle," Polly said and knew Becca understood from the flash of heat in her eyes. This part Becca would be able to identify with, even if nothing else resonated. "You do. You feel it in the dungeons or when you're in bed being naughty and that gets you hot and makes you feel desirable. I feel it all the time with David. There are moments of hearts-and-flowers love, but even those have that edge that makes every emotion feel heightened and more."

"Really?" Becca sounded doubtful.

"You don't have to understand," Polly said gently. "It's okay that you don't. It's not your place to approve or condemn the relationship I choose to have. I appreciate that you are my friend and worry about me, I really do. That sort of caring is a wonderful gift, but you said it yourself—I'm a smart, capable woman who is able to make her own money and decisions. I raise my kids and live my life and I do it while choosing to defer to my husband in almost all things."

"And since you are all of those things, I should use some common sense and not question this decision," Becca finished and smiled. "I'm sorry, Polly."

She waved her hand in dismissal. "Don't worry about it. Curiosity always abounds in this lifestyle because there are also so many secrets. I don't mind answering questions, but like I said, I refuse to justify the way I live to anyone. If the day comes that I need help, I'll get it because I have great friends like you. Until then, I hope we can still be friends."

"Of course." Becca reached across the table. "Of course we can. You're right, I don't need to understand it all to care. Thanks for reminding me."

"Anytime."

* * * *

Polly felt like crap. They'd spent New Year's at home so there was no latent hangover bogging her down. Christmas had even gone better than she'd expected with Hope and Faith both having their sad moments, but overall they'd made the holiday a festive, joyous time. David had been a big help in that and when Polly had sat down and cried with her daughters, he'd seemed to understand that as well. The girls were sleeping well, her insomnia was gone, David was fine yet she was dragging butt. She had nothing in the works for writing, just interviews with some publicity things online since her latest work was with her agent for editing.

She gingerly sat on the sofa, then turned to lie down. It could be all the ass play lately, but she didn't think so. Before going to work, David inserted her next stretcher from the set he'd purchased. She'd started almost immediately after the munch with tiny dildo plugs and moved up slowly. She loved the feelings of being anally penetrated and stretched and hadn't had any adverse affects. Everything worked well but she still didn't get the enema part which she'd have to do before they went any further. He offered to help and she'd probably take him up on it, though she wanted to do it herself, at least to start.

He had full rights to her body, she willingly and gladly gave him all he wanted, but she honestly didn't want him to help her clean her bowel. Call her old-fashioned, but there were certain things that didn't need to be a team production. But last night at the subs meeting with only Jeremiah present, she hadn't made much progress. Jeremiah had tried to talk her through it, even offered to show her on himself or help, but it seemed too intimate so she'd accepted his advice and still didn't know what she was going to do. It wasn't rocket science; insert hose into ass, add water and repeat as necessary, but it intimidated her.

The doorbell rang as she started to doze, images of rubber hoses and nozzles in her mind. She sat up and winced, the latest stretcher had a little device at the end that wasn't forgiving when sat on, yet she continued to forget. She would have to talk to David about finding something different or only using it at night when she could lie down. Though at night she'd been sleeping before playtime the last few days.

The bell rang again, practically screaming impatience, and when she checked the window, Linda Cramer waited. Jeremiah's wife and Master. Polly could think of no reason for her to be over and surely Jeremiah would have warned her the previous night when he'd spent most of the night talking about the positive pregnancy test Linda had taken.

"Hello, Linda. This is a surprise."

"Yes, well, Jeremiah says you're home every morning for work. I hope I'm not interrupting." Linda was a practical woman in some ways, though in dress she was a bit vain and showy. It was freezing outside, but Linda's breasts were thrust high, cleavage displayed despite the conservative-looking white dress shirt she wore under a tight suit jacket and no winter coat. Petite and pretty, any additional softness was eradicated by hours at the gym. They would have a lot in common, Polly thought if she were fifteen pounds lighter, fifteen years older and had a position where Armani and Vera Wang were expected.

"You're not interrupting at all, come on it."

She made tea since Linda was pregnant and though the other woman scowled at the steaming cup in front of her she didn't comment or make different demands. Polly didn't know what to expect. They hadn't spent much time together in the past five years. Linda was nowhere near a fluffy Domme and truly the Master in her relationship. In fact, Jeremiah was probably at home scrubbing something in his chains. He was a house slave, and Linda kept him naked most of the time.

"You have a pretty home," Linda said grudgingly.

Polly knew what her dining room looked like. The craft shelf needed to be tidied, and she needed to scrub the floor. At least the table was clean with fresh coverings. Faith spilled her milk the night before so they'd done a complete switch of linens and placemats. It was nothing like Linda and Jeremiah's home. They had very modern furniture and dark and light paint on the walls. It was an interesting house, and spotless. Polly's home ran to comfortable and basic, and it suited a house filled with kids.

"Thanks."

"Jeremiah told me he shared our news last night."

"He did, congratulations."

"Yeah, well, I don't know how smart this whole endeavor is. I don't think I can live like..." Linda waved her hand at the crafts and toys in the corner. "This."

"Then set aside a room solely for toys and such, a playroom. We thought about it but decided to make the spare room on this floor an office for me instead."

"But look at you." It was almost insulting the way Linda said it. "You look like a mom. You like being a mom and wiping noses and cutting crust off toast. I don't see myself doing anything like that."

"So maybe Jeremiah will do those things." The reason for Linda's visit was becoming apparent. It was her first pregnancy, and she was freaking out. Jeremiah hadn't seen it, only seen her malcontent. The truth was, Linda was afraid and Jeremiah didn't recognize it because he'd probably never seen the emotion in his wife. "Kids are pretty simple, Linda. Love, food, milk, routine, clothes. The basics make their world a good one."

She snorted, and Polly knew the situation went deeper than Linda not wanting children at her age. The woman had been hurt in the past and like so many things in life, it was affecting the present. Compassion, where before she'd only felt mild disinterest and a little fear toward the woman, surged.

"Did you know if you have to do all the treatments the doctors recommend therapy and counseling? Mine did before they would consider putting me on the drugs because I'm older. My therapist assures me I'll be a fine mother, but what the hell do they know really? Yeah, there was always food in our house growing up, there was also a lot of liquor. Mom worked, Dad drank and when they were together, they fought like raging hell. Those two should never have been together, and they wouldn't have been if not for me.

"If you're going to only do the bare minimum for your kid, flush the damn thing. Sending it to school is great, but give it a damn bath once in a while and feed it more than chips. I was fat and dirty because they didn't care. But oh oh, when the family got together, how proud my aunts and uncles were of my stupid parents for having me and getting married and being responsible. Bull-damn-shit, they were horrible. That's in me."

"I'm sure Jeremiah is relieved they didn't abort you," Polly said softly. She was glad Linda had been to a therapist because she had some major issues, but ones that could be addressed and since she was asking for help, it was her place to try.

"Yeah, in hindsight I agree, but honestly, some people should not have children. Especially with other equally inept people."

"I agree." She smiled when Linda looked surprised. "I do. I despise those mothers who send their kids to school filthy, hungry, and without a decent coat or shoes while they drive a new car or have fresh highlights in their hair. I hate the dads who'll cuff their kid on the way out of the car and drive off without a kiss or hug. The saving grace in it all though, is that no parent is perfect."

"You look pretty fucking perfect."

"Looks are deceiving. The squeaky-clean kid could be the one being molested by their uncle or perfect daddy."

Linda nodded, took a sip of tea and grimaced. Polly drank hers and grimaced too. She'd have to switch flavors. The peppermint wasn't doing it for her anymore.

"Anyway, we aren't our parents, Linda. We grow up in their company, we learn from them, but in the end we have to live with ourselves. There are plenty of parenting classes available, and you should take one if you haven't been around children before. Newborn humans are the most terrifying things in the world. They're fragile and completely dependent, but women have been having them from the start of the humanity. With our partner's help, and sometimes alone, we make it work."

"Do you have classes you'd recommend? There are so many out

there," Linda said and pulled out her Blackberry. "Jeremiah is looking some up, but I'd rather have some from a reliable source."

Polly gave the name of her church that ran first aid and parenting classes. She thought the first aid might be a good way to ease Linda into parenthood by giving her the physical things that required knowledge. The more abstract things like parenting styles could come in later.

It was impossible to forget the fear that accompanied first pregnancies and the mysteries of parenthood. She'd had Mark, though, who'd helped raise his sister, and her own experiences babysitting from the time she was old enough to hold a baby without a pillow. So much had to be learned in the trenches, but as Linda meticulously put details into her planner, Polly was reminded that everyone learned differently just as they loved differently.

"Thank you for the information," Linda said and began to stand but sat back down very quickly. Her fake-tanned face paled under her makeup and she began to pant.

"Lightheaded?"

"This is hell. I don't know how you've done this twice."

Polly hurried to the bathroom, grabbed a washcloth and ran it under cold water a moment before rejoining Linda who'd moved to hanging her head between her knees.

"I've done it four times, actually," she said, sweeping aside Linda's long locks and placing the cool rag over her neck. "Mark and I miscarried a few times after we had our youngest, but the morning sickness was the same for each. With my first pregnancy I threw up for months on end. With Faith I just wanted to sleep."

"Hell, that feels good," Linda moaned, but kept her head down. "I'm sorry for your loss. I didn't realize you'd had troubles."

"Yes, well, we haven't exactly had much in common until you and Jeremiah began making your miracle."

Linda looked up and smiled a little, the color seeping slowly into her cheeks. She was a pretty woman, and Polly hoped as she felt better she would go back to her other look, less makeup and more natural. With a newborn, the makeup would be the first thing to go anyway.

Finally, she sat up and they finished their tea in companionable silence. For a dominant personality, it wasn't difficult to spend time with her. Sitting in the chair long-term, however wasn't working so well with her toy making its presence known. She shifted some and Linda smiled knowingly.

"Jeremiah told me you're working on your ass. Did you figure out the enema yet?"

She was comfortable talking about parenting, but the switch to sex immediately made her vastly uncomfortable. With other subs it was a safe subject but with a Dom without hers present, it was a touchy topic.

"I'm monogamous and don't care for women," Linda said dryly. "Jeremiah is all I want, but he mentioned your situation and your hesitance to let anyone help. Do you honestly not know what to do, or are you being squeamish?"

Humbling herself down, Polly recognized Linda was trying to be companionable, hard for a Dom because she knew in almost every situation, relationship and professionally, Linda gave orders. She didn't ask and didn't care about excuses or reasons. It was what Polly needed though, a woman-to-woman talk with someone who knew.

"I read the box and the directions David gave me, and I'm just...stumped. I don't know how far to go because I can't see. I don't know when I'm supposed to be done. When they say repeat, how many times? How far am I putting water up there? Will it get stuck and make a mess later?"

Linda laughed and set down her purse and phone. "You have the equipment, I presume?"

"I do," she answered hesitantly.

"Do I need to call your husband for permission to help you? It sounds like you need someone to just do it with you once and you'll get it. I don't mind helping with this since you helped me with the other thing."

"Offering parental reassurances and class location doesn't seem on par with assisting in colon cleansing."

"And which do you think I would rather do in the long run?" Linda laughed. "Come on, this will only take a minute."

CHAPTER 15

How could one toy be so devastating, Polly thought as David rode her backside, hard. He was magnificent when he was in full Dom mode. He was all that was male and in command. He could make her hit her knees with a single look and make her beg for whatever he deemed worthy to give her.

The greatest part, she was learning, was his willingness to enhance his maleness and not take it at face value. Mark had been a cock man. When his cock was in play, it was the only tool in play and it had been everything he promised. Hard, long, encompassing. David was all of that, then added toys, and the one vibrating in her vagina while he continued to pump in and out of her lubed ass was brilliant.

"You need to come again, don't you, baby?"

She nodded, the gag in her mouth a little something extra, though they were staying relatively vanilla. Learning about the enema with Linda hadn't been the most glamorous thing she'd ever done, but she'd found another powerful tool in her pleasure arsenal. Linda had gotten her started and left a minute after Polly was full. She'd understood why about thirty seconds later when she'd nearly blacked out in orgasm. The aftermath was a nuisance, but the whole situation lost its ick factor once she knew the pros and cons firsthand. The clear passage made the lube work better and opened her up for the anal sex she'd come to crave.

Adding the vibrator pleased them both. He could feel it against the lower ridge of his cock with every thrust, the thin wall between her vagina and anus barely a barrier in the face of the toy, and he described the sensations for her as he fucked her hard and deep. She felt both him and the vibrator and they made listening to him talk, let alone follow his commands, a trying task.

"Come now."

It was a presumptuous thing to dictate a woman to orgasm, but he knew she'd been holding back for minutes now and the second he gave her consent, the orgasm poured out of her. The gush of fluid freed the vibrator and the sudden lack made her sigh in dismay but David made up for it. He lifted higher on his knees and pressed her down until her chest touched the bed and the change of angle gave him the deepest possible access. All focus was narrowed on him and the pleasure he freely gave, and over and over she came and helplessly bit down on her gag.

It was impossible not to feel him jerk into completion, and relief and pleasure filled her even more. There was always the fear of not pleasing her man, but he never let that happen. They pleased one another and when he eased back and helped her straighten her cramped legs, the tap he gave to her backside with his hand was like a kiss, filled with affection and love.

The shower started in the other room but she wasn't moving. It wasn't happening. She'd barely been awake enough for sex; there was no way she was moving from a perfectly nice, warm bed, even for a shower.

"Polly."

She woke when he shook her shoulder and removed the gag, the water still running in the bathroom.

"You're already asleep?"

"Um, yeah," she answered, eyes already heavy and eager to sleep again.

"You need to shower first. Come on."

The prospect of moving made tears gather in her eyes, and she was horrified when they actually fell as he offered his hand to help her stand.

"Polly?"

"I—um, um."

"Are you crying, sweetheart?" He dropped to his knees so they were eye-to-eye, kneading her belly and back while he checked the sheets, looking for blood or signs of trauma. Why else would she cry but for injury? Yet, here she was nearly bawling because she was tired.

"I—I—"

"Damn it, tell me what's wrong." He was no longer asking. She recognized the tone and knew she was close to being in trouble. She was scaring him which made him more harsh. She was scaring herself.

"Nothing, I'm just tired. I haven't felt well lately. I'm tired."

Relief replaced the concern and he rubbed her bare shoulders gently, his work-roughened hand so gentle that she cried more. She didn't realize how tight and sore she'd been, but with him rubbing them they felt so much better.

"You're pregnant, aren't you?"

David's words jerked her out of her shoulder-rub stupor. Pregnant. Could be, she mused to herself. They certainly had enough physical contact with the only barrier between them a little lube. It wasn't always anal sex, in fact that had only been the last week or two so there was plenty of time for David's army to attack.

"Yep, I think I might be."

* * * *

Great wracking sobs replaced the gentle tears emerging from Polly's body, and David didn't know what the hell he was supposed to do. He loved his wife, she was everything to him, but he'd never dealt with a pregnant woman intimately. In the Dom club he'd belonged with, one of the guys had shared his pregnant slave, but he'd never found that attractive. Polly would be gorgeous pregnant with his baby, but the sudden mood swing didn't seem right and she wasn't drawing closer to him, just sat naked on the bed and sobbed.

A father. It'd been his plan from the day they took their vows to get her pregnant. He wanted to give her the babies she said she wanted. The doctor said his swimmers had the speed and numbers of a twenty-year-old so the chances were good if they were compatible. The uncertainty in the air was an uncomfortable thing. Considering the difficulties Polly and Mark had in the four years after Faith was born, first with miscarriages then with years of unsuccessfully trying for another child, her response was reasonable. It had to be hard to get excited when dreams could be dashed overnight.

That didn't make her tears easier to watch. She stiffened when he touched her, and he wasn't going to cause her more discomfort so he waited. Time he had, the knowledge to comfort Polly out of her tears, not so much.

"Whew." She started laughing, and David figured he needed to buy a book very soon. His calves burned from the squat he continued to hold, but he wasn't about to move when he didn't know if the tears or the laughter would win. "I need to take a test, but I think you're right, Sir."

"I hope I am," he said slowly. She wanted more kids, he knew that but neither of them expected her to get pregnant right away. If his math was right, and it was, seven weeks had passed since her last period. Two weeks before they'd married. The three days they'd waited after the wedding to consummate hadn't affected anything.

"Me too. I love being pregnant. Hell, I'm scared. But excited. I immediately worry, but I also picture our baby. I had a flash of what she'll look like, then she was gone and...I've had them disappear before. It made me incredibly sad for a minute. I'm sorry for crying so hard, Sir."

"I have a feeling it'll be one of those things I need to get used to," he said with a relieved chuckle and instead of offering her a hand up, he lifted her high in his arms. She squealed but relaxed in his hold. "I'm going to take very good care of you, Mrs. Lowe. I'm proud of you, and we'll do our best to keep the little one happy and growing. If something does happen, we're going to the doctor before trying again."

"I don't want to borrow trouble," she protested.

"You want to believe everything will be fine and I want to too. I'm just reminding you, that should the need arise, I'm willing to do anything it takes to make sure your health is not jeopardized. Tonight we'll celebrate. Any cravings? Anything special you want, my love?"

"A shower and warm bed," she requested. "But mostly the bed

with my husband wrapped around me until morning."

"Good requests," he said and checked the hot water with his forearm first before stepping in the big shower tub, Polly still easily held in his arms. He could carry her forever. If it would keep her safe and keep their baby in place, he'd do it for the rest of his life. "And tonight, because you have pleased me so well, you'll receive both."

CHAPTER 16

Parent-teacher conferences, followed by school night at the local fast-food restaurant, two Easter costumes to sew before the next day, and she still had to make cookies for the crew of the Easter play. When David found out about all the things she'd let herself be roped into, he was going to spank her ass raw.

The thought made Polly smile as she pulled into the elementary school's parking lot. Luckily, her husband had been named head of a new project at work so he was in the initial meetings with their client which kept him busy a few nights of the week. He didn't like it and she didn't either, which was probably why she'd taken on more than she usually did. Without him to look after, she needed something more to do; she'd just done too much.

"Mommy, are you going to tell Mrs. Reardon about the baby?" Hope asked.

Hope and Faith were in the backseat and dressed in matching jeans and parkas with coordinating hats and mittens. They liked to dress alike and tell people they were twins. The two-inch height difference and Hope's missing front teeth were inconsequential.

"I think she might figure it out."

Polly's jacket didn't zip any more. Only four months pregnant, but her body was so used to it, it bubbled right out. The doctor said everything looked fine and most of her nerves had subsided after she hit eighteen weeks. She'd never lost a baby after sixteen weeks, so she was finally getting excited. David had been ecstatic from the moment she peed on the pregnancy test. He'd run out the same night they talked about the possibility of pregnancy to buy one, unable to sleep until he had conclusive results. But they'd only told the girls after the sixteen-week mark and now they wanted to tell everyone.

"You mean you're getting chubby because of the baby?" Hope asked. "You told Faith it was because you ate too much ice cream. How long have you known you were having a baby brother?"

"A brother, huh?" she teased, passing over the question. It didn't matter, but Hope wouldn't see it that way, and Polly had no desire to explain. She'd been younger during the first miscarries so Polly hadn't gone into it then and hoped she never would have to. "I guess we'll just have to wait and see. Maybe we need another girl in the house."

"Yeah, but David needs another boy," Faith said. "Then we'd have everything in our house. A mommy, sisters, a brother, and a daddy. Wait, we need a dog. Mommy, can we get a dog?"

Polly looked quickly to Hope to see what her eldest's thoughts on the title were. David did fill the daddy shoes, but they didn't call him that. With the new baby, it opened the door for a natural progression. She didn't know if Hope was ready for that yet. Hope just smiled though, enamored with the idea of a new baby in the house. Polly took her mittened hand, the cold ebbing some in April, but the cold was hanging on late, and smiled at her girls.

"I'm so not changing poopy diapers, Mommy. David can do that," Hope told her.

"Yeah," Polly agreed, holding Faith with her other hand. "I think that would be a great job for Daddy too."

The school was old, but nice because the parents took pride in keeping it in good shape themselves, so taxes stayed reasonable. The community wasn't exactly growing, so they made do with what they had. David had already been tapped to help re-roof the gym over the summer.

Hope and Faith played nicely in the pre-school room as Polly chatted with Faith's teacher. She and David decided on classes three times a week when the education specialist tested Faith and found she had some mild dyslexic tendencies. She saw a specialist and was doing better. The little social butterfly she was, Faith adored school and though Polly hated having her grow too fast, that was the way of kids, especially the second ones who wanted to be like big sis.

After a great report they headed to Hope's class. The kindergarten classroom was nice, fewer toys than the preschoolers, but the teacher had worktables set with color sheets and markers. Faith's eyes lit up, markers a rare treat for the girl who loved how they looked on her hands. Hope tugged her sister toward the corner, but Polly stopped them both with a hand to each shoulder.

"Faith, look at me."

Her eyes were nearly glowing and only made contact briefly before turning back to the markers, the scented kind Polly could see. "Sweetie, we have dinner after this. If you write all over yourself, we won't go."

"But Mommy—"

"If you don't think you can help yourself, then you should use the crayons at the other table. I know you want to go out for dinner, but I won't take you if you're marked up."

"I'll watch her, Mommy," Hope said practically. "I want to go out for milkshakes. She won't put them anywhere but the paper. Right, Faith?"

"Um, maybe we'd better use crayons." She sighed and followed her sister.

Hope's teacher was an older woman, in her fifties, and Polly liked her well enough. Homework was always reasonable and when she'd asked about enrichment opportunities, Mrs. Reardon sent home a packet full of great ideas.

"Hi, Mrs. Reardon."

"Mrs. Lowe. I'm glad you could make it," she said and stood to shake hands before sitting again. "Should I wait for Mr. Lowe?"

David took carpool once in a while and had met the teachers. Polly knew he'd been checking them out but he hadn't said anything so she assumed they passed whatever standards he'd been comparing them to.

"No, I'm afraid he's working. He'll get the full update tonight from me and Hope after the school dinner." Polly pasted on a smile. She was tired and wanted to put her feet up.

"Of course, that's tonight, isn't it? Makes sense though, after a good report lots of parents like to do something special, and I'm happy to say Hope's is very good. Fifteen years ago I'd have told you to send her to second grade next year, but that's just not the way things work anymore."

Polly listened for the next ten minutes about the class goals for the remaining months of kindergarten and what to expect in the next year. Mrs. Reardon already recommended Hope's placement with one of the enrichment teachers, and Polly agreed when she found it was an actual classroom that followed very similar curriculum, just faster paced and in depth. Hope was smart, Polly couldn't deny it, but she didn't want her smart little girl to become antisocial either.

With a file folder full of Hope's best work and activities for the summer, Polly thought they were done but Mrs. Reardon hesitated. The teacher looked over her shoulder to the girls, and then leaned across her desk. Polly couldn't help but do the same.

"I would hate to think I'm overstepping here," she began and Polly fought back a cringe. Nothing good ever started with those words. "But I know you and your family have had a very rough year. The girls are doing so well, both of them from what Faith's teachers say. Your girls really know they are loved by you and by your new husband."

"Oh, thanks. That means a lot," Polly said, recanting her kneejerk horrible feeling.

"Which is why I'm bringing this up. Hope is good friends with Felix Dorkov. I understand that you are friendly with his parents?"

"We are," she said hesitantly. Max and Mary didn't guard their lifestyle like they did but Polly wasn't ashamed of the way they lived. It was a touchy subject but she couldn't see Mrs. Reardon asking inappropriate questions.

"Felix… I don't know if discussing this with you is proper or not, but something isn't right in their home. He's come in exhausted the past few weeks. He's obviously not sleeping well and when his mother came in for conferences… Mrs. Lowe, I'm just hoping you can maybe offer support as a friend. If all I'm seeing is a rough spot for a family, I want to give them a chance to work it out on their own. Felix has been fine in the past, and his other teachers said the same, that he'd always seemed fine so I'm puzzled."

Polly hadn't been expecting such candor about anything, let alone another family. "Okay, I haven't seen Mary and Felix in a few weeks. I've been ill, but I'll make it a priority to see them this week and find out if anything is wrong."

"I'm not asking for a callback or anything like that," Mrs. Reardon said. "I just want to give them the opportunity to ask for help themselves or fix things before I have to consider taking steps to intervene."

"I see." Polly stood and gathered her purse and jackets, her mind full with another detail to compute and worry over. More than anything, she wanted to get in the van and drive to Mary's to see if they were all right, but there was a time and place for things. If Mary and Felix did need help, having the girls along and going without David wasn't the best plan. "I appreciate your thoughtfulness, Mrs. Reardon. Hope has really enjoyed your class, and I wish she could have you again. She's learned so much."

"She's a handful." Mrs. Reardon laughed. "But I look forward to having Faith in class one day, perhaps. And maybe more siblings down the road?"

Polly patted her belly, the sibling in question fluttered wildly beneath her belly button. "That would be wonderful."

Four hours later, Polly was thinking about Mary and Felix as she finished sewing the bottom hem of Hope's shepherdess costume. Of course they needed shepherds and sheep for the Easter scene. New costumes had been needed when the ones sent home from church would have taken more time to fix than starting new.

The girls were both in bed, exhausted from their day off from school, conferences, and a big night out for cheeseburgers. She wanted to be in bed, too. The clock read seven-thirty, and she wasn't that pitiful. Yet. She wanted to be up when David got home. His text assured her he'd be back by eight.

Mary and Max's phone had rung to the answering machine and she wasn't sure what the next thing was. With Carey, she'd fought Mark to get him to say something when she was worried; she hoped she didn't have to fight David. Being an experienced Dom, she thought he might have more familiarity with confronting the narrow but blazing line between abuse and loving correction.

If Mary and Felix were suffering, something had to be done, soon. Polly wouldn't tolerate anything less. If they were having a rough patch, and every family did, then it was also their place as friends to help if they could. She hoped David would feel that way.

"Fuck."

Polly jerked from her project at David's curse as the front door closed harder than usual. He'd had another hard day, she thought in dismay. He needed to have some time off to relax. Work was good and necessary, but she wanted him happy. She hurried from her office and saw him holding his toe. She breathed a sigh of relief. If the curse was about physical pain and not his day, then she'd only charge him five bucks for the piggy.

"Are you okay, Sir?"

"Stubbed my toe the second I took my boot off," he said sheepishly. He pulled off his white sock to reveal his toe was bleeding and already turning black. She felt herself pale. "Hell, might have broken it. Polly?"

Someone was shaking her shoulders and Polly felt the prickling of feeling flow through her body. She realized she was on the living room floor with David kneeling beside her. "I'm okay."

"You passed out," he said grimly and lifted her head to put a pillow beneath it. "That does not make you okay. Did you eat?"

"Yes." She sat up slowly, and he pressed her back down. "David, I'm fine. It was probably just seeing your toe. I get really squeamish when I'm pregnant."

"I remember the needles," he said with a little smile. "I thought it was only needles. I didn't expect to see you go down at the sight of a little blood. I think I should take you to the ER and have them look you over."

"I think you're being overprotective and acting like you've never been around a pregnant woman," she informed him and patted his hand. "I love you for it, but, honey, it's part of pregnancy."

"The books said it could be a part. Have you passed out before?"

"With Hope, I nearly did a few times. Sir, I promise I'm fine. I'm just tired, and your toe is bleeding all over the floor. Can I help you clean it up?"

"I honestly don't think you can, beautiful."

He finally let her up, but Polly didn't make any sudden moves.

She had no aching desire to pass out again and if she did, she knew they'd be on their way to the hospital. David felt the need to take care of her, and after the long few days, she was content to let him. He tucked her on the couch and brought her a glass of water and one of her prenatal vitamins. Too much iron was harmful for the baby, but he brought her one whenever he thought she looked peaked. She'd switched to taking her vitamins at night in case he decided she needed one so she didn't double up.

She smiled at him because he looked frazzled and grim, two things that hurt her heart and she wanted to fix. It wouldn't be long before their days were full of three little people, and the first few months with a newborn were always hard. Polly had no doubt about how great he would be with a new baby, but she didn't want to stress him before they even reached that point.

"How were conferences?"

"Good. Faith's extra classes are helping a lot, and Mrs. Reardon thinks Hope will take first grade by storm next year. In the advanced placement class even," she said, cuddling closer when he sat above her head until her upper body was propped against him instead of the pillow. "It's a good one, so I brought the forms home for you to look at and we can decide on it."

"Good for her. She's so damn smart. I don't doubt she'll be the doctor slash pastor slash architect she says she wants to be. Dinner was good?"

"Yeah, cheeseburgers, fries and milkshakes. I even put extra ketchup on mine."

He grinned and ran his fingers through her hair. "You do need the extra vegetables."

"Exactly. I was just finishing the girls' costumes when you came in cussing and bleeding all over the place."

"You've been doing too much again," he said and tsked gently. "That's why you passed out. I'm going to take a sabbatical from work if you keep it up."

"And spend the time off punishing me?" she asked wickedly.

"And spend the time making sure you're stretched out just like this."

That didn't sound fun and sexy. It sounded, horrible.

"I think we're done with the physical discipline for now, Polly."

"What?" She sat up, ignoring the hand he put on her shoulder. "Why? I'm naughty, you know."

His lips kicked up in a little smile, but she knew he was gearing up to tell her 'no' and state his reasons for it. She didn't want to hear about his hesitancy or newfound fears. She wanted to know them so she could help alleviate his worries, but she didn't want him to act on them.

"You fainted, sweetheart. We don't know what your limits are anymore, so I think we should back off for now. We can run more vanilla with sex and posing so you can concentrate on being pregnant."

"I can focus on both," she countered. "One doesn't mean the other can't happen. I got my butt spanked all the time when I was pregnant with Faith. It was fine. Hell, the night before I went into labor with her I was on my knees."

"Polly…"

"I'm not sick, David." He had to understand and when impatience flashed in his eyes, she was hopeful he'd listen and get to correcting her very soon. "I'm pregnant. I'm going to pass out on occasion. Just like I'm going to have horrible gas occasionally. I'll tell you if you push too far physically. I promise. I won't put our baby or myself in jeopardy, but don't ask me to give up this part of us. I'm already giving up lunch meat and cutting back on caffeine, don't ask me to give this up too."

"I think you need to listen to me. You know I can satisfy you without the other things. We can start that and the anal again after the baby is born."

Polly shot out of his lap, his words unacceptable. He started to say something else but she held up her hand, something she wouldn't have done in normal circumstances, but he was talking crazy.

"I'm going upstairs. I'm going to put on my collar and take out my plug and when you come up, you'd better be ready to fuck me like I'm your woman and not a brood mare. I'm your wife, damn it. I expect you to treat me like the woman you love."

She turned and strode to the stairs, grateful David followed her immediately because the world spun. He caught her before she actually fell and though his touch was rough to start, like he didn't like her walking away as she had, he quickly gentled when she swayed.

"Hell, you're not going to pass out again, are you?"

"No, I just… This doesn't mean anything. I know I get dizzy when I stand too fast. I know I don't do well in the sling or tied down or against the wall for long periods of time, but the other stuff is fine."

"You don't feel like going upstairs and putting your collar on do you?" he asked and lifted her into his arms. She turned her face into his shoulder and breathed him in. He would take a shower before bed, he always did because he sweat throughout his day, but now he smelled like her David under the last traces of his deodorant and aftershave. She liked the post-shower smell too, but the grogginess that already pulled her down was nothing new and she knew she'd be sleeping before he made it to bed.

* * * *

His bride was definitely heavier, David thought as he slowly took the stairs, careful not to bang her head against the wall or hook her toes on the railing. Softer too. She'd started gaining weight right from the start despite the nausea and was ahead of the curve, but her doctor wasn't concerned.

Dr. Sievers had been through two full pregnancies with her and the start of two others, so he knew how Polly carried and assured David she would even out in her middle months, then balloon out in the last month to a reasonable amount of weight and lose most, if not all of it, within six months. Polly told him the same thing, but sexist asshole that he was, it took hearing it from a doctor to not worry about her health.

She was in turns fragile and incredibly strong in pregnancy. She was robust, glowing and breathtaking in the physical aspects. He couldn't get over how much he wanted her sexually. Her breasts were bigger and heavier. The folds of her labia were more sensitive and her clit was engorged from the added blood in her system. He wanted to lie between her legs and eat her all day between playing with her breasts, but so far, he'd had to make do with sex when she wasn't too tired. That's where the fragility came in. She was tired, and her emotions were always on a short string. It was impossible to gauge her moods long-term and more often than not, the only cure for her off times was sleep.

That meant for a few nights a week he was on his own in the sexual release area because she was asleep within minutes of the girls. More than once he'd gone to Hope and Faith's room to collect Polly from her place beside her daughters to put her in their bed.

He was feeling the need for some marital relations, but she was already nearly sleeping in his arms. He'd been neglecting his duties. Business was important and with another kid on the way, he had to think about it, but it wasn't worth leaving Polly to fend for herself so much. She wouldn't be so tired if he was around to carry and feed her. She'd probably forgotten to take her vitamins, and he couldn't remember if he'd ordered her to take a nap or not.

Shameful, he thought, laying her on her side of their bed, toward the middle so he wouldn't have to pull her closer to him when he made it beside her. She slept like the dead lately, which was good the doctor said. If she was able to sleep it was best she do it before the baby kept her awake with kicking and turning. The heavy sleeping didn't mean he wanted to go through the night without her in his arms. She settled in and opened her eyes, her ire and earlier ultimatums a thing of the past.

He'd whip her backside good when she was up to it; he just had to plan better. Evenings were obviously not the time to get her thoughts on lovemaking. She was too tired. He could start his days later and work from home at night, he decided, pulling the blankets over her shoulders. She didn't speak, just lay there looking at him through blinks that lasted longer and longer.

"I'll be back in a few minutes. Do you need anything?" He

stroked her hair from her forehead. She needed a haircut, and he knew she'd been putting it off since she overshot her Christmas budget buying him a coat. It was awesome and he loved it as much as he could a piece of clothing, but she'd put him in front of her own needs and that was unacceptable.

"I want you to come back to bed soon," she muttered, nearly asleep. "Wanna have my way with you."

"Yeah, I just bet you do."

Maybe a spa day, he thought as he checked on the girls, both asleep in their beds. They looked great, clean and happy in their pink pajamas. Missing their conferences hadn't been the highlight of his week, but they would tell him all about it first thing tomorrow. It was Saturday, and they had all morning to catch up on the busy week as well as a tae kwon do tournament. He needed to go to work again after lunch, but he'd be home by dinner. Then there was a Dom meeting Max invited him to. He hadn't planned on attending, and Polly's performance earlier made him want to decline for sure. Life with a family was complicated, but he wouldn't want it any different.

CHAPTER 17

"Ah hell, that kid can't kick to save his life."

David looked over at Levi. The guy was such an ass, but he was at the tournament watching his nephew along with Ronny's mother. That had to mean something. Faith was playing beside the bleachers with some of the other smaller siblings, a whole Barbie drama being played out while the older kids tried their best to earn trophies. David had hoped Levi would understand him better after their last meeting and munch. He'd thought he'd made it clear not to be an ass around him, but apparently the impression hadn't stuck.

"He's learning," Ronny's mother insisted and clapped loudly when he finally scored a point against the boy he was sparring. "Good job, honey."

"Yeah, but look at that chick in the next ring," Levi said, and David felt a burst of pride for Hope who was, indeed, kicking ass. "She's literally a little pussy, and she—"

"You didn't just say that," David broke in.

"Levi!" Ronny's mother gasped. "Sir, I'm very sorry for my brother. Levi, apologize."

"Why would I do that?" Levi laughed at her insistence.

"Because there's a parking lot right out that door, and I'm about to drag your ass to it," David said very quietly but Levi's eyes widened, the intensity not lost on him.

"Oh, hell I was just kidding." He laughed again, though it was nervous. "She's great. I wish Ronny would fight like her. Jeez, don't be so touchy."

"You insulted the man's little girl," the sister said and turned to him. "Hi, I'm Darla. Obviously our mother should have beaten Levi more often. You're Hope's step-dad?"

"Yes, David Lowe." He shook Darla's offered hand. It was manicured perfectly, just like the rest of her. Whatever she did for a living kept her well. She was a striking woman with Levi's dark looks.

"Well, I'm just thrilled Polly found someone so soon," she said. "Such a doll of a woman. She and her husband, two peas in a pod. But I'm sure you two are great, too."

"Hell yeah, they are awesome," Levi said with a smirk David dearly wanted to punch off his face. "I mean, I've seen them at TKD and yeah, they're super nice together."

"Oh, okay." Darla looked at her brother like he was a little off, and David wondered if she knew how off he really was. "So anyway, Ronny's birthday party is coming up and he wants to invite Hope. Would that be okay?"

"I don't see why not," he said.

"Your wife might." Levi sneered at the title. "Darla used to flirt Mark up and Polly got three kinds of pissed."

"That, that," Darla stuttered and smacked her brother's arm. Fire lit in Levi's eyes, and David began to see what drove Levi into his lifestyle. Obviously the women in Levi's family were strong and didn't take his shit. "That's just not true. He didn't wear a ring, so yeah I did flirt with him once, but he set me straight right away. Polly and I never had a problem. I explained what happened, she wasn't thrilled, I mean she was having health issues and the poor thing looked like hell. But we've been fine ever since."

"Mark explained it to her, I'm sure," Levi said. "Put her in her place."

"What is with you and women in their place?" Darla asked, annoyed. "David, tell this bozo where women belong."

"Wherever they want to be," he replied.

"Exactly," Darla said appreciatively, and David was glad she hadn't tried flirting with him. She smacked Levi on the back of the head then and David was surprised to see him take it. "This knucklehead thinks a woman's place is on her knees or in the kitchen. Freaking Neanderthal."

"Did you see that last kick?"

He hadn't because of the two morons beside him, but he smiled and lifted Hope in his arms when she launched up the bleachers. "You did great, sweetheart."

"I did." She beamed as she agreed. "I kicked Bernice in the head three times."

"Atta girl."

"Good job, Hope."

He watched as his little girl's face instantly froze at the sound of Darla's voice. Interesting, he thought, as more and more of the situation unfolded. Every life was its own little drama, he discovered and Polly's world was no different.

"David is married to my mommy."

Darla blinked in surprise, and David readied a reprimand if Hope went too far. He didn't mind her outspokenness, but knew Polly was a stickler for manners.

"I heard. How exciting," Darla said with a bright smile.

"He doesn't wear a ring 'cause of work. He doesn't want to get zapped if he has to do electrical work, but he's married."

"Hope," he said softly.

"Sorry," she mumbled, but gave Darla a look that made the grown woman flinch back. "I'm all done here, David."

* * * *

Polly was on the phone when they got home from the tournament. She had a call with her agent scheduled which was why she'd left him alone with the girls at the tournament. They ran right up the stairs with Hope's three first-place trophies to join the others on her bookshelf.

Polly looked up from her pacing in the kitchen and gave David a smile. He'd have rather she put the phone down and pay attention to him, but she gave him a cute wave and began talking again.

"I understand that, Vanessa, but I think you need to look at the numbers again," she insisted. She grabbed a piece of paper, and he unashamedly looked over her shoulder as she wrote.

Will be with you very soon, Sir. Please forgive the lack of greeting.

He smiled and took the pen.

I'll spank you for it later.

She grinned at him and immediately went back to haggling. David couldn't help but listen in and be impressed by her skills. He knew she was unhappy with her latest contract so he'd recommended they get a lawyer to negotiate. She'd hesitated, and he finally understood why. She could hold her own against her agent. After another ten minutes, she had her percentage where she wanted it. Actually, it was about three points higher than he remembered her saying she felt she deserved.

"Thank you, Vanessa. I'm so glad we could come to an agreement. Of course. Yes. God bless."

He clapped his hands slowly, and when she turned to him her smile was pleased though she blushed prettily. "Wow. That was quite a display by a woman who claims she doesn't know anything about money."

"Oh, that was different. I can do a budget and negotiate a contract and get a loan," she explained. "I just don't follow the heavy investment stuff Mark enjoyed. Multiple compound interest investments never made sense even after he explained it several times."

"Then we'll adjust the savings to accounts you can manage easier." He'd never questioned her intelligence and loved the demonstration of her skills. "That was amazing, by the way. I find women of commerce with your flair to be incredibly sexy."

"I'm not a business woman." Her blush deepened as she laughed. "I'm a mommy who likes to take pictures of birds and write captions. I just like to be paid as much as I can for those captions. How did Hope's tournament end?"

"Your books are much more than that, and we both know it. I don't want to hear you be too modest about them again. The tournament went great. Hope won three first-place trophies and administered at least that many kicks to other people's heads," he said, and Polly groaned. "She's really good at head shots, keeps them soft but fast. A smart fighter."

"That she is."

"She really doesn't like Ronny's mother."

Polly froze at the mention of the woman, and he knew there was more to the story than Darla said. Anger surged at the idea that ran through his mind. If Mark had strayed…it was a bad thought.

"No, I bet she doesn't," she said sadly. "It's my fault. I'd just miscarried, and I got to class late to see Darla cuddled up to Mark. He wasn't smiling or leading her on or anything but I…well, I lost it in the car on the way home."

"He was letting her touch him?"

Fire flashed in her eyes, and he saw exactly what bothered her. Mark hadn't indulged, but he'd let another woman touch him. That level of possessiveness pleased him. The first scene, where she'd asked him to touch another woman, he knew for certain was a fluke.

"Only a minute," she said evenly, biting back anything negative. "I didn't like it. I told him and he told me I was overreacting. Like I said, I wasn't feeling well, I was very emotional—"

"But he'd let her touch him."

"Exactly," she said venomously. "It was the only time we ever really fought, let alone in front of our kids. Hope shouldn't remember, but she does."

"Oh yeah, she does. She told Darla that I was married to her mommy and pretty much stared her to the corner."

"Oh no." She sighed. "I'll have to apologize."

"Nope, you won't."

"But—"

"You won't because she didn't lie and she actually helped me out of a tight spot. The woman's a toucher and I don't want you to ever walk into a situation where you would question me."

"I wouldn't, Sir. I trust you."

"You trusted Mark, but were angered by another woman's actions."

"Well, it was more. He'd questioned me not long before about whom else I would want in bed." She looked past him as she spoke, both looking for the girls in case they'd snuck downstairs and not meeting his eyes. "It was hypothetical I know, but he asked very intently if I'd ever want another woman. I said 'no' but couldn't help but wonder if he'd wanted another woman. We cleared it up, of course. At the time though I thought he might be trying to hurt me because I'd hurt him."

"How?"

She continued to avoid his eyes, and he'd had enough. He stepped in front of her and nudged her chin so she looked at him.

"Look at me, and tell me how you hurt him."

"Sir, I don't want to," she whispered.

"That doesn't matter, sweetheart. We can't make the same mistakes, so tell me."

Tears filled her eyes as he waited for her reply. For a moment, he wondered if she would refuse. She could, it was her right to refuse him anything. There would be consequences if she chose that path, but he hoped she trusted him to share everything. He needed her to trust him.

"He asked." She stopped and closed her eyes. He was about to tell her to open them when she did, a tear escaping the side. "He asked who else I would want in our bed. I had to tell him there was someone else I could see myself with."

"And?"

"And," she said and kept her gaze steady though her lip trembled. "And it was you."

Her reply shook him, and he eased back the pressure on her chin. She stepped away and pushed her hands against her eyes, wiping angrily at her tears but maintaining the eye contact he'd demanded. "He didn't talk to me for three days, and what could I say? It was the truth and he'd asked. I miscarried not long after so we let it go but when I saw him with Darla, I was so angry. I remembered what I'd said and I worried it had pushed him to someone else. We fought and kissed and made up, and we never brought up the option again."

David was stunned his friend would ask such a question. He was shocked at her response. Their first night as husband and wife made so much more sense. The things she'd whispered about her dreams of being together, had been on her mind much longer than he'd thought. How it must have chapped Mark's ass to know she'd wanted him. The thought saddened him, because he'd gone out of his way not to cause problems. It also thrilled him very deeply because he'd always had a place in her heart, even while she loved another. Like she'd always been in his.

"I see."

"Please don't ask me those questions. There is no one I want but you. When I was with Mark there was no one I wanted but him, and once he remembered that we were fine. We had such a good marriage. You and I have something so incredibly special. I don't want there to be any wondering or…or…"

"There's no escape clause and no one I want to be with but you," he told her and closed the distance she'd placed between them. He pulled her close and gently put her head to his chest. "I love you, Polly. I want you to have all you need and in this case, we'll let this die. No deep questions on this topic, no doubts. You're my wife, and you're having my baby. I know I'm in your heart, and that's all that matters."

"You and the girls, David, you are my heart."

"I know it. And you're mine."

CHAPTER 18

"Sir, if I were worried about you leaving me over sex, I wouldn't have crashed last night. I would have been on my knees the second you came home. Instead, I fought with you and fell asleep. How does that not scream confident in our relationship?"

David thought of Polly's words as he drove to the golf course where he was meeting Max and a few other Doms for dinner. It was eight o'clock and after making her announcement, he'd helped her get the girls in bed. Polly followed them to bed and encouraged him to go to the meeting. It was early, after all, and he was used to staying up much later. She understood and wanted him to have fun and meet more people.

He'd have to explain again that she was the only one he wanted to have fun with, even if that meant working on his laptop while she slept beside him. It would be nice to talk to the other Doms, though. He'd missed the last meeting and Polly had been too sick to go to the party so he needed to play catch-up. The others weren't his business, but David did want to be available to help if anyone needed it with the electricity toys. He'd gotten them started; he wanted to help them along the way if he could. It was the best thing to do for the community.

He pulled his truck beside a small Mercedes and headed inside. The sky was already dark in early spring, but the days were getting longer and soon Faith would start Little League, which was something he could do just with her. By fall they'd have a baby to make the days pass faster. The thought put a smile on his face as he entered the room.

"Well, look who decided to join us."

Max's good-natured exclamation jerked David out of his mental musing. He had babies on the brain so decided to keep the meeting short. If Polly slept for a few hours, he might be able to wake her around midnight for some fun. She'd earned a few spankings lately.

"Hello, everyone."

Max, Linda, Sam, Eddy, Levi, Darren and a man David didn't recognize were circled up with various levels of alcohol in front of them. Linda's daiquiri was almost surely nonalcoholic, while Max and his friend had shot glasses stacked neatly between them and several fresh at the ready. Sam drank a beer, as did the other men.

David smiled at the others before turning to the waitress. "I'll have a Coke, please." She nodded and hurried away from their table. The girl looked a little shell-shocked, and he didn't doubt they were being less than discreet.

"Coke, huh? Big plans for pretty Polly tonight?" Max asked, his accent heavy.

"I have to work in the morning," he answered, trying to stay good-natured but Max was drunk. That lack of control was something David didn't usually indulge and if Max had been a quiet drinker it wouldn't have bothered him. Stupidity, whether liquor induced or not, irritated him quite personally.

"Bah, you're going to go work on your trick, yes? The one Sam here fucked up with his chubby sub?"

"David, I had a question about which electrodes I should use," Sam asked, ignoring Max's jab and the laughter shared between only him and his friend. The others at the table looked acutely uncomfortable, Linda going as far as to glare at the dungeon Master.

Happy to have a reason not to talk to the group's Master, David discussed Sam's questions, answering other ones as they came up while Max and the man David had yet to be introduced to had their own laughing conversation. Sam nodded, took notes and after the brief instruction, stood to leave. David couldn't blame him. He fished out a card from his wallet and handed it to Sam as he made his way out.

"Call me if you've got questions."

Sam looked surprised and after their last meeting, David understood why. He could also see how uncomfortable Sam was in a group of very dominant men. It wasn't a comfortable place, especially when a few of them were being insulting and drunk. Sam was smart to leave before anything escalated.

"Thanks. How's Polly doing?"

"Tired a lot, but feeling better, thanks for asking."

Sam nodded. "I'll tell Becca. She's been worried about her being sick like last time."

"I'll tell Polly she should call. Actually, I'll call you too. I need to set up a day out for her, and Becca would probably have an idea about that."

Sam smiled, his youth showing in his braces-straightened teeth. "Yeah, she's a girly one. I'll have her start looking so I have a few ideas for you."

"Thanks."

"So, the bitch needs some pampering? She's pleased you lately?"

Max laughed riotously at his own words, and the rest of the table chuckled awkwardly.

David turned back to the table as Sam strode away, the other man not turning back at Max's calls. David was ready to leave, but there was a certain amount of tolerance in the lifestyle. It allowed more flexibility in conduct than David preferred in his own life. He and Polly were in the minority by being married and monogamous, but that didn't mean he couldn't respect others in committed relationships with different rules.

"My wife's name is Polly," David said quietly. "She's home sleeping right now, and that pleases me very much."

"Ah, Polly is your wife?" The stranger's accent was similar to Max's. "Why didn't you call me? You know I wanted Pretty Polly's pussy, but the fat man never let me near enough to even smell."

"Mark had it all planned out. He died last year, and David was in the wings to sweep her off her feet. She's pregnant again." Max nudged another shot at his friend, and David frowned at how bloodshot both men's eyes were. It was more than alcohol at play.

"Meh, I don't care about the pregnancies. You starve them and run off the extra fat after the baby is born. It makes fisting easy, especially the first day home. How I love those days," the foul man said dreamily, clinking glasses with Max who nodded along with the words. "You should scene while she's still bloody."

"Oh, my fucking God," Linda said, throwing a ten on the table before standing. "I know sick shit. I usually like it, a lot, but that's fucking wrong. Who the hell scenes with a woman who just gave birth? Do you even care about your slaves? Max was right to throw your sick ass out the first time. I don't know what the hell he's thinking letting you back in."

"I'm the boss here, Linda," Max said, rising unsteadily to his feet.

"You're a fucking drunk who's been using whatever that little moron gave you to get high. I'm out until this shit is cleaned up."

David again wanted to follow as she stormed out. Linda was looking better. She wore less makeup, had gained some weight and up until the end, she'd looked pretty happy. It was good to see. She and Polly talked often about baby things, and she was hosting a shower for her and Jeremiah in a few weeks. He looked forward to it. Linda had just proved she was a Master he could respect.

"Finally," Max said. "I fucking hate that one. Cunt with a mouth too big for her pussy, eh?"

Drugs, he remembered Linda saying. It was showing in Max's lack of focus and garbled words. Darren and Eddy were finally looking uncomfortable, Darren was even taking out his phone, probably planning a seamless escape. He was a smooth one. Darren was creepy in scene with catheters and speculums, but his sub seemed content and well cared for. Candice was always smiling and friendly when she arrived at the house for the submissives' meetings. She wasn't inappropriate, but he hadn't made any attempts to restart a friendship either.

"So, David. You will take my slave when Polly has the baby. She is with Alexi right now, learning much. She'll keep you happy while your breeder rests."

"Thanks again for the offer, Max, but I don't want your wife and

Polly won't be going to anyone else. Ever. How is Mary?"

"Bitch." Alexi spat. "She is bound and gagged until I return, maybe until tomorrow. Too special, she thinks she is. I will repair her for you, and she will be a proper slave. One of beauty and humbleness."

"What? You left her?" David demanded.

Max waved his hands. "Bah, she likes it, begs for it and I am giving her what she wants."

"Is someone with her at the house? Who's with Felix?" David wasn't going to judge another person's kink, but there was excitement and then there was danger, and if things were as they seemed in the Dorkov household, David knew they were stepping out of the safe and sane rules.

"Ah, you're an old woman, David. Of course Felix is at home safe with Alexi's girl. She is a good one." Max laughed. "I train her now. Lots of whips and poky things. She hates the needles. I love them! How she shakes when my knife comes out."

"I've got to go," Darren said apologetically, tossing money on the table. "Eddy, did you need a ride?"

"I'd better accept. Can't get caught with alcohol in my blood," the older man said, also standing, his beer mostly untouched. "We'll talk to you soon, Max. David, nice seeing you here. Send your wife our best, and we hope to see you two at the next party."

"Thanks, and we'll see what happens."

Alone with the other two men, David wasn't surprised when his Coke went unfilled. The waitresses were staying far away, and he couldn't blame them. Max and Alexi were loud and drunk, and David hoped they had cab plans. He sure as hell didn't want to give them a ride, but he didn't want them out on the road in their condition.

"We'll see?" Max threw back another shot and slammed the tumbler down. "Of course you'll be there. My slave watches the brats at your house, Polly will be center stage. Alexi will show you how to treat a breeder."

David stood. "All right, boys, I'm out of here."

It was enough. It was more than enough and he'd be talking to Polly about finding a new group or going solo. If a couple couldn't rely on their dungeon Master, they couldn't trust the others in the group, and David sure as hell didn't like Alexi. Worry over their subs came to mind, especially in their current states. If Mary was locked and bound, he hoped Alexi would pass out instead of going to her.

"Already? Hell, short night." Max laughed.

"We should get our cab and go home. Our bitches wait."

"You know the 'sane and sober' rules," David said, tossing yet more money on the table. They'd scared their waitress, but she would be well compensated. "Don't touch your subs until you sober up. You don't want to hurt them."

"Gah," Max said dismissively. "If not for my DWIs I would be perfectly capable of driving my car after a few shots. A slave is worth much less than a vehicle. You worry like a woman."

Ten minutes later as he pulled onto the highway, David was still worrying. He'd seen Max in action, and sober he was as cold as stone. There was no compassion in the dungeon Master. Max knew his limits and pushed the edges of them. Drunk, who knew what he was capable of? There was a reason most people avoided alcohol and drugs if they were in the lifestyle with long-term partners. Loving could turn abusive after a few drinks.

There were codes, spoken and unspoken, that railed in David's head. Forming groups helped them to police their own; it was why couples sought out others, to prevent things from becoming too intense. They were in place to help each other and in the past, he might have gone to Max's house, called him on being drunk and restrained him. Alexi too. But he didn't know them well enough to believe they wouldn't turn their knives on him. Let alone guns. Drugs collided with violence too often, and David wasn't willing to make that sacrifice. Not when a phone call would do the same.

CHAPTER 19

"You son of a bitch!"

When Max tried to launch past David at the front door, Polly grabbed the girls and hustled them to the kitchen. Max didn't look anything like the well-put-together man she knew. His salt and pepper hair was wild, just as his wrinkled face and clothes were grossly out of place. David had awakened her the night before to tell her what happened. He'd made phone calls he'd hoped to never make. Bringing in the police had been a last resort, but it was one she fully supported.

There were so many lines they had to walk in their lifestyle, but common sense said there was danger and Polly was proud of him for making the hard decisions. It was better to ask forgiveness if he'd overstepped than to find a body in the morning and wish he'd said something.

"Polly, I've got this. Take the girls downstairs." David's order was moot as she was already heading down, locking the door behind her. The basement wasn't soundproof but did muffle things, yet Polly could easily hear Max's shouts.

Max was angry about the arrest that had been made after officers visited the house and found him covered in blood. He'd been cutting his slave, and the police had booked him for far more than the drugs in his system. It was why David had hesitated to make the call she knew; a misunderstanding could cost a person their freedom. If the sub was willing, then it was consensual, but a prosecutor and judge wouldn't see it that way.

"You think you know everything?" Max roared and Hope and Faith huddled close. Polly wished she could drown out the noise and held her hands over their ears instead to block the ugliness. "You see, Mary comes home with me this morning. My bitch, she's here."

Polly's blood ran cold. Mary. She could only imagine what the repercussions for her would be. And Felix was somewhere in all of it.

"You try to break my family, you son of a bitch!"

She heard a quiet muttering then a feminine voice that must have been Mary's but it was too quiet for her to hear. She remembered the computer and quickly turned on a movie. It was a Christmas one she'd put in while wrapping gifts months earlier, but it would work. Hope wasn't fooled and neither was Faith, but they sat in David's chair and watched the movie.

"No. *Niet*. You won't go with him. I forbid it."

Polly didn't like the sound of Max's voice and fought herself from rushing upstairs to help. If David needed help, he would call. Until then, her job was to take care of the girls and their baby. Aggression wasn't something she was equipped to deal with, not when it turned violent. David knew what he was doing and had already shown he wasn't afraid to call the police if things got out of hand.

There was more quiet murmuring, and she strained to hear. She wished she could be by David's side.

"If you choose this, the contract is null and void. You will not be welcome with me again. It will be the end. You get nothing from me," Max yelled.

"Except child and spousal support."

David's voice rang through, and Polly finally understood what was happening. Mary was choosing a new Dom. It wouldn't be long-term. Polly wouldn't share, but it wasn't unheard of for a slave to escape a relationship by choosing another Master. It was in most contracts to allow subs and slaves to leave at any time, but it was a daunting thing to go alone, so mostly they found another Dom to take them. She couldn't imagine David not accepting Mary and Felix into their home, even if it was a temporary stop until Mary found her feet.

The house shook when the abovestairs door slammed shut. Faith started crying. Polly lifted her youngest, and Hope, losing her composure with all the shouting, pressed her face against her mother's side.

"Girls, it's okay. David is upstairs and he'll come get us in a little while."

"Uncle Max sounded scary," Faith cried. "I want Daddy to come down here so he's okay."

"Um." Faith had never called David 'Daddy' before and Polly was thrown by it. Hope whimpered at her side.

"Is Felix okay? Daddy won't let Uncle Max take him will he?"

And now Hope had elevated him to 'Daddy' too. The situation was quickly spiraling beyond Polly's scope. It made sense they would cleave to David when they were afraid. Time and again, he'd shown he loved them and would take care of them. In the face of Max, he was their knight in shining armor. He was their daddy. He'd be very pleased when she told him.

"Don't you worry about your daddy," she said, and it felt good to say the word again. Their family had been missing a daddy and Mark obviously understood which was why he'd sent one. "Do you know what he's going to say when he comes down here and finds us overreacting? He's going to say, 'girls, enough being silly'. Then he'll take us upstairs and make us pancakes. How's that sound?"

"I don't wa—want pancakes," Faith sobbed. "I just want him to make Uncle Max go away."

"What's all the crying down here about?"

Polly looked over her shoulder and relief coursed through her at the sight of her husband, unhurt and smiling at them. There was tension around his eyes and his smile was a little forced, but at least he could force it and that meant things would be okay.

"Daddy!" Faith cried and wiggled out of Polly's arms, launching into David's. He looked over Faith's shoulder as she continued to crawl closer, like she was trying to get under his skin. His expression was confused then Faith took his face in her tiny hands. "You didn't come down and there was yelling and it scared me. Why'd he call you ugly names, Daddy?"

"Uh, Uncle Max is gone and he won't be back, sweetie," David promised, and Hope ran to him.

"Did you tell him you'd beat him up, Daddy? He's pretty tough, but I bet you could do it. Then he wouldn't bug Felix anymore."

"Let's go upstairs, girls," he said, hefting Hope as well. They both hugged him, and the look on his face when he looked at Polly between their shoulders was one of pure bliss. He'd been waiting, and he would have kept waiting without comment until they called him 'dad'. If that day hadn't arrived, Polly knew he would have been content being Uncle David. It was better to have that day sooner than later, Polly thought. When the new baby came they would feel more like a family, and David would belong to the girls just like he did to the baby.

"Mary and Felix are here," he said, taking the stairs with no problem, Polly slowly following. "They're going to be staying with us for a while."

"I'll get the basement ready," she said.

"Not yet. For now let's get some breakfast and get dressed. Although you two are as cute as bugs in these jammies."

"Mommy needs to get some with footies too," Faith said. "Maybe we can get some for Felix too. Felix, did you bring your jammies?"

Polly helped David get everything on the island table, the three kids digging into chocolate chip pancakes as the adults milled around. Felix was a little pale and quiet, but he smiled and sat close to Hope. Mary sat near the open window, a cup of coffee in one hand, the other fidgeting fiercely with a pack of cigarettes. Polly would have let her smoke on the back porch, but Mary made no move to do anything but tool them back and forth between her fingers.

Bruised and exhausted, Mary looked like hell. Her eyebrows were covered with bandages and from the dark stains around both eyes she'd almost certainly broken her nose. She wore long sleeves and long pants, but Polly didn't doubt her body was torn up as well. Mary had never been one of the pampered slaves, but she'd always looked healthy. No longer. So much had changed in only a few weeks.

Alexi.

He was a sadistic bastard. She didn't know the ins and outs of what he liked, but it was bad enough to scar Carey and make her leave the state. Max had evicted Alexi from their group then, but unfortunately for Mary, being a Russian 'good old boy' had gotten the monster back in their world.

"I'm going to make up the bed downstairs," Polly said after refilling glasses with milk.

"I can do it, honey," David said, flipping the pancakes again.

"You finish breakfast."

"I—"

"I can help."

They both looked to Mary who now stood. Her head was down, but Polly could see a spark that had been missing almost from the moment she met her.

"That would be great. Thanks, Mary. See, dear, we'll have some girl time and leave you to wrangle the kiddlets."

"She means we're a cross between kids and piglets," Hope explained to Felix.

"I know, she's called me that before," the little boy replied. "Can I have some more pancakes, Mom?"

"Of course, honey. You may have as many as Mr. Lowe will make," Mary assured him, and Polly noticed the slight accent in her voice was no longer Russian. She sounded as Midwestern as she did.

She grabbed blankets and towels from the bathroom closet and let Mary take them from her. Mary's lips kicked up in a little smile. Battered and broken, Mary could still smile and it told Polly she wasn't as broken as she could have been.

When Polly and Mark were first married, the hide-a-bed had been their sole piece of furniture. They'd had so many good memories from it they'd kept it, upgrading the mattress to one that actually covered the bars so it was comfortable. Her parents always used it when they stayed, and she could bring down a sleeping bag for Felix. Mary quickly made up the bed and Polly again thought how rough she looked.

She looked older than her forty years, defeated and abused. It pissed Polly off that it had happened in their club and that Max let his slave down. As subs, they trusted their tops with their lives, it was part of the thrill and closeness between couples. To have it violated so very much broke her heart.

Mary sat on the freshly made bed. "Would you mind if I lay down for a few hours?"

"Go right ahead," she answered. "There is a bathroom and tiny shower through there. I'll watch Felix."

"Thank you."

Mary lay down without another word and Polly quietly left. Mary had probably been up all night. The officer who called David said two had been treated by paramedics, two taken to jail, and one to the hospital. Felix and Mary had stayed in the house. She couldn't picture Mary sleeping much, not after the horrors Polly's mind conjured. Alexi's reasons for expulsion had never become public, but they were ugly. An ugliness Mary had endured.

The kids were putting together puzzles in the living room when she made it to the kitchen. The dishes were in the dishwasher. Her surprise Christmas gift from David had been installed two weeks after the holiday passed. She didn't mind the delay and had hit her knees for him for three weeks straight whenever he walked into a room with only them. He promised her a new one every year if the reception was always the same.

Polly smiled when she walked into the dining room. "Mary is sleeping."

"Good." David looked up from the papers he had strewn over the table. They were police reports and forms for filing charges and orders of protection; all things she never would have expected in their home. "Mary brought all this and handed it off to me. She's going to have a hell of a few weeks coming up. The girl that Alexi had in the house was sixteen. Mary might have some problems because she is an adult in the situation."

"Mary can't be held accountable for what happened," she said with almost certainty. "And she was beaten. I can see it, anyone could."

"But she let things happen to that girl." David's tone was cold and Polly agreed, she really did, but thought he was being harsh.

"I don't think she's been in a position to 'let' anything happen to her the last few years. After she had Felix… A slave is in a rough spot when kids are involved, Sir. She's a victim too and in that way, she might not have been able to function enough to get herself out."

"That is why I hate Doms like Max. Fucking asshole. A woman is willing to give everything, and this is what he does. He turns her into a shadow of a person, unable to think for herself when it counts. You can't do that with kids around." David threw a pen across the table, impotent rage in his posture, but Polly wasn't worried. He wished he'd been able to do more, that was all. And he hated that anyone had been hurt, even if he wasn't in charge of the group.

"David," she said softly and sat down in his lap. He kept his arms to the side, obviously reining in his temper, but she pulled them up around her anyway. "You did everything you could. You've got a family to think about, and the police said they found weapons at Max's house. It was best things were handled like this."

"I know that."

"Then why are you so angry?" She stroked his face, a peek over his shoulder assuring her the kids were still engrossed with their toys and movie.

"Because of him." David jerked his head toward the living room. "He's a baby in all this, and he had to see his mom roughed up and his dad in handcuffs. Kids shouldn't have to deal with crap like that."

"You saw it and you're okay," she said. The nights he'd shared more details about his family life were some of the hardest she'd ever had. The idea of him being alone and abused broke her heart.

"Yeah, I'm a control freak who makes my women do things," he said harshly. "I don't trust people unless they're willing to fully submit. I hated my parents and didn't go to their funeral. I don't want that for Felix. It's a waste."

"I know, and I think we can help Mary," Polly said calmly, stroking his cheek more. "She's into the life so deeply, and in her case, if she had a child with Max, then she loved him. It's why Jeremiah and Linda tried so hard. For a time at least, Mary loved him and thought he was doing the right thing. We all make mistakes, but we helped them get away before anything irreversible happened."

"Like that Alexi bastard going after him," he muttered and laid his head against her chest, finally easing some though tension thrummed through him. "Something is wrong with that guy. He needs to be castrated and have his hands chopped off."

"Alexi is the one who did something so bad we started having sub meetings," she said, wrapping her arms around his neck so they hugged close. "You can't fix or do everything. Isn't that what you always tell me?"

"Yeah, but in this case…" He sighed. "I'd have liked to be able to do a hell of a lot more."

"Hey, Hope's Dad?"

They looked down and found Felix, so quiet on his feet neither had noticed his approach.

"What's up, buddy?" David asked, slipping very easily into the position of Hope's dad.

"Can Aunt Polly check on my mom?" Felix scrubbed his dry hands against his jeans nervously. They were wrinkled but clean like someone had washed and dried them, but left them at the bottom of the laundry basket. "She's been sleeping a while."

"Yeah, you can go down and check on her, Felix," David said, but Polly knew the shy little boy wouldn't have approached David if he didn't need him.

"Should I go do it, Felix?" she asked, squeezing David's shoulder for understanding.

"Please? She's been sleeping a lot lately," he explained, not looking at either of them and rocking himself on his toes. "She's supposed to do stuff and only did some of it, and I haven't got to see her much 'cause Dad said she's tired. I don't know."

"I'll check on her, sweetie. Then you can spend some time with her this afternoon."

"I don't know if she wants to play with me anymore. Can you tell her we don't have to play cars if she doesn't want to? We can play something else," he offered and hurried back to the living room. Immediately, Hope put her arm around him and Felix, only six like Hope, accepted the comfort for what it was, friends loving each other in hard times.

Reluctantly, Polly left David's lap. Before the day was over she hoped to find the comfort of his lap again. After the ugliness he'd put up with, she wanted to make him feel better, and he made her feel good too. It was a grand system she hoped they would work until they cocked up their toes. Mary had shown Polly that everyone was only a bad relationship away from being hurt. Maybe irreparably so. Humans, so fragile.

She grabbed two bottles of water and closed the basement door behind her. If Mary was awake, and she didn't expect her to be after her night, she would offer an ear. She'd never accepted one in the past, but alone wasn't what Mary needed. She had to know they would help her, even if that's all Polly could tell her for now.

"Polly?"

She had tried to be quiet as she walked beside the bed and set the waters on the desk. Mary appeared to be asleep so she'd intended to head upstairs and assure Felix she was fine and let her rest. She looked again and found Mary's eyes still closed.

"Yes, it's me. I was just bringing you some water. Do you need anything else? More blankets?"

"He wasn't a bad man." Mary's eyes still didn't open. "But he wasn't like Mark or David, either. How do you get two amazing men and mine is so very disappointing?"

"Um, Mary I don't know." It was a question she couldn't answer, because she thanked God everyday for the blessing she knew was unbelievably generous.

"I should have waited for love. It came with time, but I was always the slave first. He loved me for a while and was a good Master. For years. Then Felix was born. I wanted my son and needed more between Max and I. We never got to the point you seem to find so naturally."

"What do you mean?"

"You love. They love. Their world revolves around you, and the relationship is about pleasing you. A good Master makes his slave the best person they can be. He puts her on a pedestal and gives her all the guidance she needs to stay there. Master never put me there. His place was on top. The things he did were to make himself feel better, not to make me better."

"I'm so sorry."

"I saw others. Even Linda, the bitch, she loves Jeremiah. She treats him like she loves him every time she smacks him, every punishment and insult is full of love. My Master gave me to Alexi, while they were both high and stupid. How is that love? Max knew what he was doing and left me in the basement for days and made me break promises to our son. How is that love? He broke the contract over and over, but this time…"

"This time he trampled on where you do get your love," Polly finished and Mary finally opened her eyes.

"Yes." Her abused lips cracked when she gave a small, pain-filled smile. "I love my son. Felix loves me, and Max should never have tried to separate us. The other things, I could have tolerated those. Alexi, the drugs even, because he would have stopped eventually. It's a sexual drug, but it impedes his judgment. Alexi is actually a bigger influence than the drugs. But Felix, his clothes were dirty because that woman Master was with didn't wash them. He didn't eat well when I was under Alexi's care. It was unacceptable. I won't have my son harmed by the lifestyle I keep. I'm not a monster."

"No, Mary. You're a very good mother. Felix loves you. That's why I'm here checking on you. He wanted me to make sure you're okay. He's tired. Do you want him to come down here or should I make him a bed in the girls' room?"

"Here, please. He can sleep with me. I'm clean now. I will take care of my son, Polly. I can work. I'm not only his slave, not anymore."

"I can see that. The accent is gone too."

Mary smiled again and blood leaked from her bottom lip. Polly reached around the desk for lip balm and handed it to Mary. "It was part of Max's desire for me to sound and look the part of his Russian slave. I didn't mind. I'm from Ohio."

"Do you still have family there?"

The smile was gone in an instant, and she turned away. "Felix is my only family."

"Okay," Polly said and turned on a side lamp so the overhead light wasn't necessary. "We might not be family, Mary, but we'll help you anyway we can. You're safe here, and you're welcome as long as you need to be. You were good to me when Mark died, and I don't forget my friends. I'll send Felix down to see you."

What else could she do? She'd felt a level of betrayal when Mark died, but it was hard as hell to hold a grudge against a dead man who'd loved her so well in life. Mary had more of a backbone than she'd thought, but Polly wasn't surprised. Mothers had to make the hard decisions. That's why Mary would be fine; she had Felix and she was a woman. There was no other situation than 'okay' that would be acceptable.

CHAPTER 20

Hope sat in David's lap and pouted. He couldn't blame her. Her best friend had just left and probably wouldn't be back for a long time. Unfortunately for his step-daughter, David had found someone for Mary in Arizona. Rick was a good man with two kids coming off of a rough divorce. He was fair, though. Even if they didn't go right into a sexual relationship, they would be able to help each other with the kids. Rick was struggling alone with his kids, and Mary was a good mom. They would help each other make a fresh start.

Hope snuggled into David's shoulder and sighed again. Subtle, his step-daughter was not, but he knew she understood he'd done the best he could for Felix. It was better that they weren't close to Max, who was still hanging around Green Bay, and still pissed. Two weeks had passed, a munch had gone unmunched and David was fielding phone calls from every Dom in the group.

They didn't trust someone who used drugs and had to have the cops break up parties. It wasn't surprising they were looking to him for guidance. He had the most experience and for a bunch of Doms, none of them showed much interest in taking the lead. They all had busy lives and the position held a lot of responsibility, so it didn't surprise him no one was stepping up. Contrary to the group's desires though, he wasn't in the market to be the next dungeon Master. His life was busy too. But there was a group he was looking into in Kaukauna, twenty miles west of Green Bay. There were options, and Sam was keeping him in the loop as he checked out new groups.

"I miss him."

"I know, sweetie." David stroked her hair away from her face, letting go of the thoughts of the disbanded group. "It's for the best though. You know that, right?"

"Why can't all daddies be like you? You're not my real daddy, but you're a good one," she said and like the first time, the title warmed him more than anything else. He loved when Polly called him, 'Sir' but hearing the girls call him 'daddy' was a whole new experience. "Maybe you should give classes."

"Wow, really? That good, huh?" He laughed. "Maybe I can help in TKD class sometime? That might be fun."

"Really? Like family classes? But I don't want Faith to do TKD, she's too little."

"I think she wants to take dance, beautiful," he replied, knowing Hope didn't want to share her limelight but also wanted her sister to have her own, especially with the new baby coming.

"Oh, she'd be good at dance. My friend Tina goes on Tuesday nights, so Faith could go on Tuesday and I could do TKD on Thursday. That way we can still watch each other."

"Good idea. I'll talk to your mom about it."

"I don't think Mommy feels good." She sighed. "She's been working too hard with Felix and Aunt Mary here. I think she needs a vacation."

"We can't go anywhere until after the baby is born, but I like the idea of pampering her a bit. How about we take her out for dinner and all that good stuff? We'll go shopping and get her something nice after."

"Some shoes," Hope said, jumping right into the idea. "To match her fancy purse. When is she going to get back? We could get Mexican food. She likes chimichangas."

He laughed again. His daughters had a way of making any situation better, just by their presence. "They will be back very soon. Faith's appointment was at one."

"Dentist," Hope said solemnly. "She'll need braces."

Forty minutes later they were still waiting, and David looked at his cell. He'd texted Polly twice. It didn't make sense that she wouldn't reply. Unless Faith had to have mouth surgery or something, but he couldn't imagine her not calling him to let him know. Hope was looking out the window. She knew it was long after the time he'd said it would take, and he couldn't wait any longer. He picked up his phone again and called Polly's number. When it rang straight to voicemail he left another message.

He pulled out the phonebook and swore when he saw the number of hospitals in the area. He had no idea where the emergency rooms were or where the ambulances ran from. If Polly had needed medical attention, he didn't know where she would have been taken. As unease crept in, he pulled out his phone again.

"Hello?"

"Candice, it's David Lowe."

"Oh, hi David." She sounded confused and probably was. He hadn't taken her up on her offer of Green Bay advice and hadn't seen her since the night after his first munch. "How can I help you?"

"Which hospital has emergency services? Where would emergency personnel send a pregnant woman and kid?"

"Oh my God, is Polly okay?"

"I don't know, she's late and not answering her phone," he replied. "I need to start making calls, but I'm not sure to where."

"Um, try St. Vincent's and there's a few others, St. Mary's maybe. I don't know, David. I'm not at home to check my directory, but I'd think one of those would be your best bet since they are bigger."

"Okay. Thanks."

"You're welcome. I'm actually on my way out of town now. I don't know if I'll be staying in Green Bay any longer, but please call if I can help you with anything."

"Okay, great. Thanks again."

David hung up and immediately set aside Candice's words and picked up the phone book. He was about the dial the number for St. Vincent's when his phone rang. He saw Polly's name pop up and answered.

"Where the hell are you?"

"Ah, sir, I'm Detective Mason. I'm looking for Mr. Mark Angelin."

It wasn't Polly. "Well, he's dead. I'm Polly Lowe's husband. Where is she? Why do you have her phone?"

"Like I said, I'm Detective Mason with GB police department. What was your name again, sir?"

"David Lowe. Where is my wife?" David tried to hold tight to his temper but fear was raging and answers weren't coming fast enough to ally them.

"She's in the hospital. She and her daughter were attacked on their way out of the mall—"

"What? What hospital are they at? Why wasn't I called?"

"Her information just came in from the clinic. Apparently the hospital's records are behind. She's at St. Mary's. Come down when you can."

"Is she okay? Is Faith okay?"

"They're both stable, a few bruises and Polly is unconscious still—"

"Oh hell, I'll be right down." He hung up. "Hope, get in the truck."

An hour later he was getting the runaround. No one knew anything and if they did, they were sure he didn't have the clearance to know it. Mark's name was still listed on all of her hospital papers as contact. The clinic records had been misplaced somewhere during the ten-minute car ride from home so the nurses weren't letting him any farther than the front desk. The officer who'd called him was no longer answering Polly's phone and while the nurses knew the officer's name and job, they weren't going to any lengths to get them together. Nearly two hours had passed since David had received the call, and he was about to go crazy.

"I want my mommy!"

Hope hit her knees and screamed at the top of her lungs. David had never seen her go so far before. If anyone in the family had control, it was Hope, but she was done waiting. After losing her father, he wasn't surprised she had a limit.

The nurses who'd been evading and putting him off, finally made the proper calls and got things moving. Before David could get Hope calmed down, they were walking to where Polly and Faith were being treated, three floors below where they'd been waiting. The close location and relative ease it had required once the nurses were willing to try, angered him, but with Hope in his arms, still sniffing and upset, he let it go for the time being.

"She's dead, isn't she, Dad? That's why they won't let us see her."

The officer and nurse leading them both faltered in their steps and quickly assured her that her mother was fine.

"Her dad died last year," David said harshly. "The fucking bureaucracy made her cry. If I can sue you for something, I will."

"We had to go through all the proper channels. We followed the rules every hospital has to," the nurse said. "There's absolutely no reason to think about lawsuits."

The officer just shook his head. "You kept them waiting when you had my number and made the man's baby girl cry. There was no reason to keep them waiting. I'd suggest you file a complaint and give administration hell."

David let the discussion drop because they were finally to Polly's room. Faith was in the bed beside her, neither waking when they entered. A waiting nurse smiled reassuringly. "They're both fine. Faith had to have a sedative for the scans we had to do, but she should wake up soon. Polly is just resting from a blow she took to her temple. She had a headache, but she'll be fine."

"Mommy!"

He saw Polly's eyes open and slam shut. Chastising was on his lips, but he let it go when she ran to Polly and began crying again. Hope might act grown-up at times, but in reality, she was still little more than a baby. A baby who'd lost her father and worried about her mother.

"Sir?"

He turned to the police officer who'd walked them up. "Yes?"

"I've got the information you asked for. Would you come out in the hall for a moment?"

Polly was busy with Hope, and Faith continued to sleep, so he stepped out.

"Your wife and step-daughter were leaving the mall when two men approached them. It seemed innocent enough at first but some passersby called the police. When we arrived the men had started pushing her around. She had the child behind her. We ordered them to stop. One of them made another move for her, and Mrs. Lowe punched him in the face. Unfortunately, he pushed her and she hit her head. We tasered both men then."

"What happened to Faith?"

"Nothing, as far as we know," the officer answered. "But she was terrified and honestly, the guys were freaking creepy. Leather and chains, covered in blood."

David's blood ran cold at the announcement. There were millions who could fit the description but it was Max and Alexi. He should have known that when drugs became involved there would be no honor among Doms. Had Max been thinking clearly, even after the cops thing, he wouldn't have gone after Polly.

"We arrested both guys," the officer continued. "They'd been drinking and doing salvia. It's not illegal and in a lot of cases it doesn't do anything to a person, but these guys… It'll be a while before they sleep it off enough to even be charged."

"We have restraining orders against them," David said, and the officer began taking notes. He kept Polly and the girls in sight from the hall as he updated the police on what else had happened in the last few days.

It was a nightmare, something no man wanted in his life. The officer took a cell call and David returned to the room. Polly's eyes were closed and there were tension lines on either side of her mouth, but she looked all right.

"Hi, Sir."

He pulled a chair beside the bed. Hope opened her eyes for a moment but then closed them again. They didn't have much privacy, but they had a little. He put his hand on Hope's back, rubbing the soft fabric of her sweater. He didn't need privacy, not when he had his girls with him. He wouldn't let them out of his sight for a good long while.

"Fighting on the corner again, I see," he teased because he had to. The reality and intensity of the situation made him crazy. She was pregnant and small, and someone who should have watched out for her, had hurt her.

"Yeah." Polly chuckled, but didn't open her eyes. "You would think I'd know better by now than to go looking for brawls. I'm okay. The doctor already said it's a mild concussion and a bruise on my arm and fist. The baby is fine, and Faith is shook up but not hurt. My hand aches."

"I heard you got a punch in."

"Alexi was reaching for Faith."

The grim tone of her words told him she knew exactly what the twisted man could have done. David thanked God that Polly was strong, much too tough to allow anything to happen to her daughters.

"They were looking for Mary, too," she added. "I'm so glad she's on her way to Arizona with Felix. They'll be safe."

"Yes, they will."

Silence stretched with only a few beeping noises for interruption. Her belly had a Velcro strap around the middle and a heartbeat monitor he watched blip to life on the screen beside her bed. Between one hundred thirty and one hundred and fifty times a minute his baby's heart beat. Polly didn't want to know the sex, so he'd agreed to be surprised. The suspense was eating at him, but boy or girl, that was his baby. He or she had been susceptible to attack, and he was going to remedy the situation.

They had to be safe. Polly and the girls were his world. Without them, he was nothing but an insecure man who had to have things his way in order to function. He didn't want anyone else to put up with his fetishes and issues. He just needed Polly.

"Can you talk the doctor into letting me go home today?"

David looked down from the monitor. Faith and Hope were both asleep, but Polly was awake and smiling at him. It wasn't a pain-filled smile either, which told him the meds being dripped through her IV were working. According to the nurse, Polly had been dehydrated. Not assault related, but they'd given her extra fluids to help with her headache. He might have to spank her later for neglecting to drink enough, and he'd get her some of the juice boxes he knew she liked, but saw as indulgent.

"You'll stay as long as the doctors want and you won't complain," he told her and watched her eyes narrow. "Uh-uh, pretty mama. Don't even think of getting sassy with me. I'll take out my big whip at home for that look alone. You scared me today, and that's unacceptable."

"I didn't go out of my way to do it. They came out of nowhere. Who follows a person to the mall to attack them?"

"Why were you at the mall? I thought you were coming back right after your appointments."

"Your birthday is in a week. I went to pick up your gift," she explained.

"Wow, you'd better hope the doctor keeps you here overnight so you can sleep. You'll need it to rest up for your punishment."

"But—"

"And you won't be going out alone while Max and Alexi are still in town. You're with me at all times. You don't answer the door for anyone you don't recognize. You don't go to the grocery store without me as your shadow."

"David, that's ridiculous."

He clenched his hands together, biting back the automatic reply. It wouldn't have been flattering to either of them, and he realized how close he was to losing his temper at the wrong person. She'd done nothing wrong, but circumstances had led her to being hurt. It was a situation he'd caused and hadn't thought to prevent.

"I'll tell you what's ridiculous," he told her. "You thinking you need to get me a gift when you've already given me more than any person ever has. When you married me, you gave me everything. A home, a family, love. I have every damn thing I need and more on the way growing every day inside you. What would I have done if you'd been killed?"

"David—"

"No, I don't want to hear that I'm being irrational. I don't care. You dying is not an option as far as I'm concerned, but it came close today. There are bruises on you from men who would have done worse if they'd gotten you alone. From now on, you don't get me gifts. That's an order. You've already given me more than one man deserves."

She was quiet, and that was good. She probably recognized he was close to losing it. Hell, if anyone knew him, it was her. So instead of trying to talk him down, she lay in bed, quiet and still. The beeps went back to their serenade, and they passed the next hour in silence.

CHAPTER 21

Jeremiah grinned from ear to ear as he introduced the newest addition to their family. Polly couldn't stop smiling either as she looked at baby Donald. Not a name she would have chosen, but he had the sweetest face she'd seen besides her own two angels. Linda lay in bed, her hair perfect, everything in precise place, but Polly hadn't expected anything less. Her eyes were also on Jeremiah and their son. The last eight months had given them time to talk and mend the old hurts.

Polly sat on the chair beside a pile of baby gifts she and David brought, and thought that time was a great healer if the people involved were right and willing. Already things were looking up for all of them, and it was wonderful.

David never let her out of his sight and wouldn't, not until Max and Alexi were deported in three weeks. The assault had been on a list of multiple priors for both men, though Max's were much older. The prosecutors hadn't cared though, not when it came to assaulting a pregnant woman, so both men were being shipped back to Russia.

She didn't delude herself into thinking David would give her much more freedom after they were gone and really, she didn't mind. It was addictive having her husband with her everywhere. She had privacy, yet he was always there and willing to help, support and teach. It was a beautiful thing. If she hadn't loved him so much his behavior would have driven her crazy, but she did love him and wanted even more of his time.

"Would you like to hold him, David? You know, get some

practice before your little one comes?"

"Sure." Smiling, he accepted the baby from Jeremiah's arms. Polly wondered how often he'd put his son down in the past two days. Not often she'd bet, and Linda's indulgent look said she was holding him when her husband wasn't. Polly turned and looked out over the parking lot. The landscape was wonderful, still in bright bloom despite fall approaching. Even the potted plants near the benches looked good.

"Hey, look out here," Jeremiah said, and she stood to look out the hospital window.

"What am I looking for?" she asked, seeing nothing but cars in the bright August sun.

"Linda's push prize." His grin was a cross between pride and love, and Polly adored seeing it back on his face after the misery of last year.

"What's a push prize?" David asked.

"It's what the husband gets for his wife after labor," Jeremiah explained and looked scandalized at his lack of knowledge. "Don't you have one yet?"

"Ah, I didn't know I needed one," he said and looked to Polly in confusion.

"They aren't a big deal and not everyone does them. Mark always went out and got the baby's first outfit, which is a sweet tradition I'd like to keep going but a push prize is unnecessary."

"Unnecessary but awesome," Jeremiah countered.

"So what did you get her?" David moved closer to the window but shielded Donald's tiny eyes with his palm. "Is it flowers? A delivery truck just pulled in."

"No, the Lexus."

Sure enough a gold-colored Lexus SUV sat in the new mother parking spot. Even from the second-story hospital window Polly could see the little window cling that announced *bad ass mama on board.*

"Wow," she said and looked to Linda. "Did that help with the pushing?"

"Hm." The other woman looked thoughtful for a moment. "I don't think so, though I do like it very much. It'll be safer to drive Donald in than my sports car. Meeting him was all the prize I needed. And the look on Jeremiah's face when he held him…"

There were tears in her voice, and Polly knew it was time to go. Linda didn't want to cry in front of anyone, but her system was full of mommy hormones. Polly tapped David's shoulder when he continued to stare between the baby and the new car. He started a little, like he'd been thinking hard, and he probably had. Donald was a big preview for what they would have. He handed Jeremiah his son and they said their goodbyes.

In only a month they would be in a similar room. Mostly great memories came to her as they passed through the maternity ward. She'd never lost a baby far enough along to have the area tainted with sadness. She held David's hand as they walked the generic, sterile halls toward the exit. They passed the nursery and she tugged him to stop.

They didn't keep as many babies in it as they did back when she used to visit parishioners with her mother and father. Most moms kept their newborns in their room with them now, and it was what she did too. There were two tiny ones in little bassinets though, a nurse checking another's weight, and Polly realized they were triplets.

"Oh man, they'll have fun when they get those three home," she said with a little laugh. "Can you imagine three newborns?"

"I'm having a hard time imagining one. Hell, that kid is tiny." He pressed his palms together in an uncomfortable way. "Donald, I mean. Linda was huge, how is he so small?"

"He's almost nine pounds, honey. That's a very good size for a newborn. Thankfully, Hope was nearly eight when she was born. Faith was premature so she was barely five but some get smaller than that."

"Hell," he muttered and tugged her away from the window.

Her parents were in town for the weekend. They were watching the girls and would have a big meal together before they left. With the baby due in a month they would return soon, but it was good to have one last get-together before things changed.

"Sam called me about his new club," David said, buckling her in the front seat. His favorite thing was to touch her during mundane activities, taking an extra moment to rub her belly.

"Is it nice?"

"Yeah, they like it a lot," he answered, moving to his side of the van. "I think I'll head over one night and scope it out and then we can decide what we want to do. I hate starting again, but with Sam and Darren's recommendation it sounds pretty good."

"What about Levi and Melody?"

David shuddered a little in disgust. She knew he didn't care for Levi at all and didn't blame him. Levi was one of the Doms Mark had particularly disliked as well.

"That's another reason I prefer this club. Levi and Melody are going east to Dunn for a group. I hear they are very happy there, so we'll keep our fingers crossed that they remain so. Linda said she and Jeremiah would join the group in Kaukauna after she's recovered."

"I wouldn't be surprised if they're there next week."

"I wouldn't either, especially since you offered babysitting services right off the bat," he told her pointedly. "You need to sleep, not care for a newborn at night."

"That's why I volunteered you, dear. This way we can work together so you can do it alone when our baby comes."

"Alone?"

"Well, the first few nights...it's hell, Sir. I won't lie. They cry and cry and poop and cry and eat and puke...and it hurts to give birth. I know you'll want me to sleep and recover, because I'm going to look awful. This way you'll know how to take care of your daughter or son, and I'll be able to get my baby fix."

"That's nice of you," he said a little sarcastically. "So does this mean you'll stop having me practice diapering on teddy bears?"

"I wouldn't place any bets on that."

* * * *

"What the hell?" David muttered when they pulled into the driveway and found Max sitting on the curb in front of the house. Technically it was legal, the fifty-foot restraining order not broken, but it wasn't good to see him. David saw Pastor Ike on the front porch with the phone in hand and wasn't surprised when his cellphone beeped.

He answered, "I see we have a visitor." He didn't get out of the car, keeping Polly inside for the moment as well. "How long has he been here?"

"Ten minutes, tops. We didn't notice him at first. Hope said she thinks it's Max. He's the guy you've had problems with, correct?"

"Yep. I'll take care of it." He hung up and turned to Polly. "Stay in here until I figure this out."

"Just call the police," she urged, grabbing tight to his wrist.

"He's just sitting there, so I don't think he's here to cause trouble." He gave her his cell. "Call the police immediately if things look rough, otherwise keep the doors locked, got it?"

"Yes, Sir."

He locked the doors behind him and headed for the curb. The weather was plenty warm, hot even in the early days of fall. The yard was still bright green from his fastidious care. He knew how to make a lawn grow in the Arizona desert so the lush ground of Wisconsin was no problem. A new swing set was up in the side yard, new fencing surrounding the whole of it. Mark had kept a project list, and the improvements had all been budgeted for within the next few years. David took the list and expedited the timing, making the changes he needed for the family he loved.

His shadow crossed Max, and since he'd made no secret of his approach, Max barely bothered to acknowledged him. He took a deep puff from his cigarette and crushed it under his scuffed boots. The man looked older than David remembered. He looked like he'd aged fifteen years in only weeks.

"I'm here to apologize. It's been a long time since I've done such a thing so give me a moment."

David continued to stand. The sun at his back shined in Max's eyes when the other man looked up.

Max squinted against the harsh sunlight. "I should have known better. I'm not a stupid man."

"But you're a vain one whose selfish bent cost him his family," David said.

"Yes, my family. Haven't I lost enough? Why send me to a place that is not my home or friendly to my kind? Leave me here to suffer without my slave and son."

"If I had my way, you'd have been tied to a wall and beaten for days."

"Good, then do that and drop these charges," Max said eagerly. "I'll take my punishment like a man. Whip me, cut me, whatever you deem necessary as long as I can stay in the States."

He was begging. Disgust welled at the sight of the man no longer much of a man as far as David was concerned. The castigation Max begged for didn't begin to touch the severity of the crimes he'd committed. As far as David was concerned, being chained, whipped and cut wouldn't even cover what Max had done to Polly, let alone what the bastard had done to his own family.

"No, Max. You'll go back to Russia," he said coldly. "You'll lose your business, your money, your status. You'll be nothing but another drug-using piece of scum. The cops told me you'd left Russia to escape some mob connections. I hope they're still waiting for you, you piece of shit."

Max reached up and grabbed David's wrist. "You don't understand."

David pushed the offending hand away and when Max caught himself on the asphalt, David ground his foot into Max's splayed fingers. "I understand you touched my wife. I understand you scared my daughter. I understand you treated your wife and son like they were nothing. Now you can know how that feels. Get the fuck out of here before I call the cops. I'll be honest, Max. I don't care where you go or what you do as long as you stay away from my family."

Max's eyes narrowed at the announcement.

"But technology is a bitch, old man," David warned. "It's not as easy to hide in the States as it used to be. You're better off going home and facing the music. You're not welcome here."

David ground his heel into Max's fingers before easing back. He wanted to cause the man pain. He could feel his muscles tighten, preparing to fight, but Max only nodded and hurried to his car as if he could sense violence building.

Max didn't look back. Once the car was around the corner David waited, but Max didn't drive past. A phone call needed to be made to the officer in charge of the case about Max's possible plan of running. He wanted the whole situation over with, and the flight risk might be enough to put Max behind bars until deportation. The thought of Max in prison with younger, angrier men with less to lose made the call a pleasure.

The evening sun began to set, but the heat held fast. As he

continued to watch he began to sweat and remembered Polly still in the car. He turned and realized she'd started the engine sometime during his discussion with Max and was in the driver's seat and with the air conditioner blowing. Her concerned face was angled to the glass but she didn't look uncomfortable and that was the important thing. Content Max was gone, at least for the time being, David headed for the car.

He saw that Ike watched from the front window of the house, but the little girls were blessedly absent. The violence and danger had to pass. They needed peace.

He knocked on the car window, and Polly opened it a crack.

"Are you all right, Sir?"

"Fine. Come on out now, he's gone."

"For good?"

"I don't know, honey. I hope so."

CHAPTER 22

Again, David thought as he pulled into the driveway and found Jeremiah and Linda's Lexus at the curb. He didn't mind watching Donald and had learned a lot about babies with him, but three nights in one week seemed a bit much. For wanting a baby so damn badly, they sure didn't seem to mind leaving him.

The first time was understandable. Linda spiked a fever, so Jeremiah took her to the doctor and she was treated for a urinary tract infection, very common after birth he'd learned so he'd made a note of the symptoms in his phone. The second time had been a date night Jeremiah insisted was also crucial for Linda's health, which David could also understand.

He just hoped Jeremiah was ready to watch all three of their kids when Polly needed a night out.

He grabbed a piece of sidewalk chalk the girls had left out and tossed it into the bucket on the porch. Someone was going to have to clean up all the toys tonight without help from him. That was the punishment when they left stuff out Polly could trip on. With only a few weeks until school started again, they were eking out the last days of summer, but they still had to be extra careful to keep Mommy safe.

"Hi, David."

He tried to smile at the greeting but it wasn't easy. Jeremiah was such a pretty boy, but at least he'd eased back on the cologne because it irritated Donald's skin. In tight jeans and an equally tight t-shirt he looked like one of the men's models for the teen shops. Linda liked it and while David knew that was what mattered, he still would rather not see Jeremiah's abs and crotch outlined in cotton every time they were together.

"Hi, Jeremiah. Everyone okay?" He dropped his briefcase on the bench and flicked his boots off, the entry and living room remarkably quiet.

"Yep. Polly and Mistress are upstairs with your wonderful daughters," he answered with a grin David didn't understand.

"Okay, are you guys staying for dinner or is it just little Don tonight?"

"Hm, I think we'll all stay," he answered and the daft grin made David want to go back to work.

"Polly?" he called instead, hoping his wife would come and give him something to smile about.

"Hi, Sir." She waddled down the stairs. The bedroom door must have opened because he could hear the girls' mutters. Polly kissed him on his mouth, a tiny welcome he wanted more of, but she quickly turned away and headed to the kitchen. She was in a pink track suit, her fancy one she called it because it had glittered edges. He, Hope and Faith picked it out for her for Mother's Day, and it was her favorite. Her butt had become more voluptuous in the last month and filled out the cotton to delicious proportions. He hoped it stayed after the baby came.

He breathed deep, expecting to smell food for her to run off so quickly. If his welcomes were brief it usually meant she was worried about burning dinner. Nothing.

"Oh, we're ordering pizza," Jeremiah said.

David considered himself to be a patient man, especially with people of submissive natures, but Jeremiah was being especially irritating and he couldn't figure out why.

He watched as Polly tugged cash from a cookie jar. She always kept household money on hand in case Girl Scouts, Boy Scouts or school kids came around with things to sell. She pulled out three fifties and tucked them in the swear pig and turned to him with a huge smile.

"Time to head to the hospital."

* * * *

A little boy. It had taken more attempts than she'd have liked, but finally her little man had arrived. David Mark Lowe. It was a good name for a good boy who looked just like his father. He was beautiful, though David insisted he was handsome, tough and all things manly. She figured when he weighed more than eight pounds and did more than poop, cry, eat and cuddle they could reevaluate.

"He's so pretty," her mother cooed, and Polly smiled.

"Handsome," David and her father said together.

"Okay, handsome," Maureen said with a laugh.

Hope and Faith sat with David on the rocking chair with new Barbie dolls between them from their baby brother. They'd been wonderful the whole pregnancy and were so excited for the new addition to the family. David looked at his son the same way he did her daughters, confirming what he'd said months before; they were his daughters too. It was a wonderful thing to be surrounded by family.

"Oh, my, look at that." Maureen passed baby David to her

husband and took Polly by the hand to look at her wrist. "What is this pretty bauble?"

"My new mommy gift. It's from my darling son. He has impeccable taste."

"I'd say," she agreed. "Pastor, why didn't we have gifts like this for new babies? I think we might have to talk about it."

"You mean you didn't get your wife a grandson gift, Ike?" David teased.

"On the way home, dear," he promised, and Polly smiled. Her father's eyes twinkled as he held the new life in his hands. "Speaking of home, we'd better get the girls back to the house for dinner and baths. It's already seven o'clock."

"Daddy, are you bringing Mommy home?" Hope asked, and Polly felt her mother take her hand. Her eldest had asked the same thing when Faith was born, but she'd been in Mark's lap that time. So many changes in the last year. Polly squeezed her mother's hand tight.

"She and your brother need another night in the hospital, sunshine," he said and kissed both girls' foreheads. "Which is why Nana and Papa are here. We'll be home by lunch tomorrow, so you'll be able to help them get everything ready for your brother so I can take you to TKD tomorrow night. How's that sound?"

"Sounds good," Faith interrupted. "It'll be better when we're all home. Baby David will like our house, Daddy. We'll make some popcorn so it smells good when he gets there."

Polly bit back a laugh. Her newly middle child was a complete joy. Both big sisters climbed in bed with her for a few minutes before

Hope declared she was hungry and Faith followed suit. It was hard to watch them leave, and her discharge couldn't come fast enough.

"No, I'm not going to ask the doctor if we can go home tonight."

Polly smiled because he knew her so well. She looked up, and her heart ached from how exhausted her husband looked. Labor lasted longer than they'd expected with a third child. The doctor had been sure they'd have him by midnight, but it had been after breakfast when he finally emerged. A lollygagger, David joked when he finally held his son. Patient, she'd corrected, like his father.

The nurse brought in a snack and checked their vitals, basic and non-invasive, though she could tell David didn't like to see her so laid up. He'd be more accepting when they were home, but surrounded by medical equipment, wearing a pink hospital gown, Polly knew she looked frail. She felt weak. Unlike Linda, she did without makeup and tied her hair in a ponytail for comfort.

"Eat." He offered her some cheese and crackers.

"You know, now is when I stop eating for two," she told him, but accepted the snack.

"Nope, none of that crap. You've got milk to produce and an immune system to revamp after birth. I want you healthy and strong." Bossy and tough, he was acting like the man she knew and loved. "I'll let you know if you get too fat."

She laughed so hard she groaned, and the nurse checked in on them again. David stroked her stomach, still swollen and flabby but getting smaller as her uterus went back to normal. He was such a smartass. She loved him for that too. Everything about him was what she needed and it was freeing to love someone so completely, to trust someone so thoroughly.

"I can't wait until we sleep in our bed tomorrow," he said hours later, after their son slept in the bassinet beside the bed. David was tucked in beside her on the bed. She needed him there, and despite the tight squeeze and the side rail poking his butt, he'd climbed in.

"Me, either." She sighed and turned to be closer to him. "I love you so much. I just want to be home with you and our kids. I hate being away from them."

"Uh-uh," he said, grabbing tissues. "No more tears, sweetheart. You need to stay calm and get some rest. Here, how about another present?"

She wiped her suddenly teary eyes on the tissues. The sniffles were nearly uncontrollable, but he had a point. Another crying jag wasn't what she needed. He pulled a square box from his tote beside the bed. David had brought his own bag along with hers and remembered all the things she'd forgotten. The gifts had been stashed there. He'd also had two sets of new clothes, one for either sex. The ones little David would wear home were covered in tools and trucks, the other had flowers to be put away for next time. Because there would be a next time.

"What's this?" she asked. "The afterbirth push prize?"

"Call the gifts whatever you want." He sighed, her contempt for the concept lost on him. "I just wanted to get you something nice. I'm allowed. It's in the contract, so open it and say thank you."

"Yes, Sir. Thank you, Sir."

She pulled the paper off. The heavyweight paper told her he'd had it gift wrapped in the store. It was a little bigger than her hand and surprisingly heavy. It wasn't jewelry, she thought as she pulled tape off the thin, waxy box. Maybe a figurine or something sweet. She pulled away tissue paper inside and her breath caught.

David pounded her back lightly as she choked. The grin on his face told her everything she needed to know about the beautiful gift still nestled in the paper. She coughed and started laughing again.

"Oh, more gifts?" the nurse, quick and quiet on her feet, asked as she gathered the tray. "A mother's figurine?"

Polly looked at the round, Pyrex ball nestled in the wrapping and smiled at the nurse. "I'd say it's more of a wife's figure."

The nurse smiled at David. "That's so thoughtful. All husbands should be like you."

She left and closed the door behind her. Polly lifted the ball from its nest and held it in her hand. It was solid, a little heavy, and reminded her of a paperweight. She inspected it closely and saw a tiny hole drilled all the way through and found a very fine cord at the bottom of the box.

"It's really quite beautiful, isn't it?" she said, rolling the ball back and forth between her fingers.

"It'll be more beautiful in a few months when in proper use," he informed her. "After seeing David come out though, I've decided we're waiting a good six months before it's christened."

"I'll bounce back before you know it, Sir." Even exhausted and sore, the thought of playing his naughty games still excited her. "I'll be ready in a month."

His eyes flashed with desire, but his tone remained firm. "We'll talk about considering it in four months."

She opened her mouth again but he pressed his lips to hers to silence her. Her Dom, a compassionate man, preventing her from going far enough to earn punishment. She slipped her tongue past his lips, and he groaned into her mouth.

She lifted her hand to his cheek, deepening their kiss, but kept one hand tight around the glass ball. His tongue trust deep and he groaned again.

Two months, she thought as she squeezed the ball.

Tops

About Stephanie Beck

Stephanie Beck doesn't like corners. She doesn't paint herself into them when defining her writing, because while stories like Poppy's Passions and David's Angel have more erotic themes, not all of her works will. Steph loves romance and sees the possibility for falling in love in most situations be they steaming hot or innocently sweet and she knows that not every story needs more sex...though sometimes more is so much better.

Steph loves to make lifestyle reading real and nothing does that like adding family and really letting romance build to the 'happily ever after'. Stories of extraordinary love and romance within an everyday life, or even a paranormal or suspenseful life are things Steph is always going to try to find and write. With multiple worlds full of naughty-good fun running amuck in her brain, much more is to come from Stephanie Beck.

Stephanie's Website:

www.stephaniebeck.net